C000021786

"Phillip Telfer is a dear friend and a wi[...]
whose heart for Christ and the gospel is [...]
book is embedded with an important and ti[...]
—STEPHEN KENDRICK, FILM P[...]

"Teens and young adult men and women will enjoy and benefit from this book. It's full of action vividly described. It moves quickly and will engage the reader. This gripping story is full of much truth. In clever and creative ways, Phillip causes readers to think about and evaluate their lives, relationships, goals, purposes, and passions. They may not even realize they're thinking about these things while enjoying the book, but it will be good for them. I expect some readers will make changes in their lives because of Phillip's important story. I don't read much fiction because it doesn't move me, but I could not put this book down."

—KATHY KOCH, PHD, FOUNDER AND PRESIDENT, CELEBRATE KIDS, INC., AND
AUTHOR OF SCREENS AND TEENS: CONNECTING WITH OUR
KIDS IN A WIRELESS WORLD

"Phillip Telfer is a master story-teller, drawing the reader into a tale that is both epic and intimate. This book is an unexpected reading adventure with an irresistible plot line, curious characters, and exotic cinematic backdrops. Why Save Alexander showcases Telfer's rare knack for supplying pithy and profound cultural insight. He blends high stakes drama and winsome fun with a deeply thought-provoking message to produce a delightfully soul-stirring tale."

—ERIC LUDY, BESTSELLING AUTHOR AND PASTOR

"An entertaining story driven by values you can feel good about."

—CRAIG BRIAN LARSON, AUTHOR AND BLOGGER

"There was a time in my life—many moons ago—that I read for fun. Give me a Hardy Boys mystery or Nancy Drew novel (not just for girls!) and I would be transported into a world of adventure and intrigue where the good 'guys' accomplished something daring and noble. That was then. Now? Two of my last books have been about theology and religious criticism. I just don't take the time for mystery and adventure. But I should. Why Save Alexander started out as a read as a favor for a friend, but morphed into a nostalgic throwback—only with a Christian underpinning that came naturally in this story. And left me wanting to read the next book in this series—if one should be written."

—Bob Waliszewski, Former Director of Focus on the Family's Plugged In

"Phillip Teller tells a good story here that is sure to engage the young teen as well as adult reader. Why Save Alexander walks the fine line between the real world and the metaphoric, but leaves the reader with a firmer grasp on reality—God's reality—real reality. The message could not be more powerful and important for the post-modern, thoughtful reader."

—Kevin Swanson, Author, Speaker, and
Host of Generations Radio Broadcast

WHY SAVE ALEXANDER

WHY SAVE ALEXANDER

Phillip Telfer

ELM HILL

A Division of
HarperCollins Christian Publishing

www.elmhillbooks.com

www.philliptelfer.com
www.whysavealexander.com
Facebook @PhillipTelferAuthor

Why Save Alexander

Published in Nashville, Tennessee, by Elm Hill, an imprint of Thomas Nelson. Elm Hill and Thomas Nelson are registered trademarks of HarperCollins Christian Publishing, Inc.

Elm Hill titles may be purchased in bulk for educational, business, fund-raising, or sales promotional use. For information, please e-mail SpecialMarkets@ ThomasNelson.com.

Library of Congress Cataloging-in-Publication Data

Library of Congress Control Number: 2019913444

ISBN 978-1-400328277 (Paperback)
ISBN 978-1-400328284 (Hardbound)
ISBN 978-1-400328291 (eBook)

CHAPTER 1

JUNE 21

"Alex, what are you doing? You are completely ignoring this conversation! What's the distraction?" said Paige. She and two other teens looked in the direction of Alex's diverted glances. The four of them sat in the Los Angeles airport terminal waiting to board their flight.

Attempting to look indifferent, he leaned in closer and whispered, "That girl over there keeps staring at me, I think she must recognize me from the show."

They all zeroed in on the girl in question, a young woman with her face in a book. "She's not staring at you! She's reading a book," said Paige.

"Well, she's not staring now!" said Alex. "She's probably a fan, debating whether or not to come ask me for my autograph."

The others couldn't keep straight faces, and Paige went on the offensive again, "She's not staring at you, she's reading a book. You spend way too much of your life in a fantasy world!"

"She did look my way, I saw it."

"You're sitting under the TV," said Austin. "Everyone is going to look your way eventually. Besides, she doesn't look like the type of person who watches our show or would be interested in a seventeen-year-old high school boy no matter how cute and important he thinks he is. I'm sorry to say it, but I think that girl is at least twenty-five and she's reading a book. I

1

can almost bet she's not watching a reality show about teen gamers trying to go pro."

"You wait and see," said Alex. "When the camera team arrives to film our departure, she'll rush up and ask for my autograph." Alex possessed many faults but a lack of persistence was not one of them.

"You don't even own a pen!" said Paige.

Alex sat paralyzed for a second as he considered the truth of the statement, and then patted his jacket pockets for a nonexistent pen. He quickly broke past the awkward moment, "You're so lame, fans always have their own pens!"

"How would you know? I don't think I've ever seen anyone ask for your autograph," said Paige.

As if it was scripted and on cue, a girl about nine years old pulled away from her mother and ran up to her. "Is your name Paige? From the TV show?"

"Yes, it is! Are you one of our faithful fans?"

"I love your show! Can I get your autograph?" The little girl held out a thin notebook with kittens on the cover and a pen tucked into the spiral binding. Paige signed the notebook and drew a funny face, causing the girl to giggle with delight.

Her mother seemed a bit impatient with the delay but Paige couldn't resist asking her, "Don't you want Alex's autograph?"

The little girl looked sheepishly at Alex with his moppy blond hair, blue eyes, and boyish face with an expression of suspense.

"No, thank you. I've got to go," and she was off.

"You were right, Alex! Fans do have their own pens," said Paige with a smirk.

Alex quickly changed the subject, "Hey, where's the camera crew? They were supposed to be here by now."

Paige rolled her eyes, "I guess the young fawning woman over there has proven to be more distracting than your phone, didn't you see the text?"

Alex felt a twinge of panic as he reached for his phone, "What text...?" and opened his messaging app. Letting out a long groan, he began to rant,

"What? How could they? Stuck on the 101? They know this is LA! They should have known to leave earlier! I can't believe this!"

Her smug look made it clear that she already knew about the delay and Paige took the opportunity to tease Alex again, "And you're not getting your autograph!"

They all watched with amusement as Alex started to make a call.

"Who are you calling? It's not going to make a difference," said Paige.

"He's calling Mommy," Austin jabbed.

At that remark, Alex's eyes filled with fire, and if his imaginations could become reality, the others would have witnessed two lasers annihilating Austin on the spot. Austin stopped smirking when he received an elbow from Chase, indicating that he had crossed the line.

The penetrating stare and the subsequent jolt in the ribs warned Austin to not say another word, not because it offended Alex, but because Alex's mom was a key part of their aspiring lives. Allison was the producer of their fledgling reality show.

Alex finally got through, "Mom, they're late and they don't think they'll get here before the plane leaves!" His words were void of civility much less affection or respect. "Why didn't you schedule them to leave with enough time? It's not like traffic delays are a new phenomenon around here.... You should have scheduled them earlier.... That's not the point, Mom, of course no one was expecting an accident to block two lanes! They don't schedule accidents but you might have scheduled the crew to come earlier. What are we supposed to do? This is our big trip.... What? You're joking! Take the video on my phone? Mom, that's lame! People here will think we're just a bunch of kids fooling around, it won't stir up interest."

In the back of his mind was the passing thought of the girl who wouldn't be inspired to ask for his autograph. "We'll look like a bunch of nobodies!" His voice kept getting louder and more volatile, "Thanks for nothing! At least Dad came through!" After that crescendo he slammed his phone down on the small table next to his seat and everyone within earshot could hear the distinct sound of cracking glass. Alex immediately flopped from his fit of anger to mortification.

His tantrum hardly went unnoticed by those within radius of his rising voice. He unwittingly gained an audience, but not an admiring one. The general disgust that had risen during that short exchange was granted some comic relief at the realization that the shameful boy, who dared to speak to his mother in such a disrespectful way, had just wrecked his own phone. If this were a scene for a sitcom, the writers might have scripted the onlookers to give way to their impulse and burst out in applause at the demise of his phone. Since they were not actors following a script, they only exchanged glances with one another with gloating satisfaction that silently reverberated, *Serves him right!*

Speechless and in disbelief, Alex handled his phone as if it were a childhood pet dying in his arms.

"Man, he really slammed that down hard," said Chase, whispering privately to Austin.

In shock, Alex just stared blankly at his dead phone, holding to a false hope of a miraculous resuscitation. He snapped out of it and realized he had a very short time to try securing a replacement phone before their plane departed for Seoul.

CHAPTER 2

"Chase, hand me your phone, I need to call my dad."

Chase complied without remark. Even though Alex could be a big jerk at times, the loss of his phone was felt deeply by his peers. They knew all too well how their lives were so intricately entwined with their phones.

Handing it to Alex, Chase wondered why he just stared blankly at the screen as if he didn't know what to do.

"What's wrong, Alex? You look like you've never made a call before," said Chase.

"I need to call my dad but I don't know his number. I don't have anyone's number memorized."

"Guess you'll have to call 911 and explain your emergency," said Paige. "You've got that number memorized I hope!"

They all laughed except Alex who just glared.

He opted for a voice search, "What's the phone number for Paradigm Technology Innovations, Inc.?" In a moment, he was calling the main number. "Hi, I would like to speak to my dad. Who? This is Alex, ALEXANDER BROOKS! It's an emergency, just connect me to his extension. PLEASE!"

Alex waited impatiently until he finally got through. "Dad, I need your help.... Why didn't I call your cellphone? That's the problem, I accidentally dropped my phone and it's dead. Is there any way you can get me another one before our flight leaves? We're supposed to start boarding in twenty minutes." There was another pause before, "Are you sure? Can you at least try? Mom? No, she can't help either.... Dad, this is really a bad situation, what am I going to do when I get to Seoul without my phone? I can't live for ten days without it! Are you sure there's nothing you can do? Okay, bye."

"What did he say?" asked Chase.

"He says there's no way he can arrange it with the flight leaving when it is, but he will have one of his business contacts arrange to hook me up with a phone once we land in Seoul. I can't believe this happened to me."

Slipping into a melancholy state of mourning, Alex unconsciously ran his anxious hands through his thick blonde hair heavily coated with gel. Though previously styled forward with a front spiked tuft of bangs, it now resembled a bedhead look. He was oblivious. It amused the others but they cast a unanimous vote among themselves without saying a word to not say a word. It really didn't matter. Anything goes when it comes to hairstyles these days, so they had fun just knowing it would have bothered Alex if he had been aware of his new stressed-out hairdo.

The trip of a lifetime was not starting off on the right foot. What should have been an epic departure for Alex seemed like a false start in an Olympic sprint. Everyone felt the weight of it.

"So, what did your mom say about the camera crew?" said Paige.

"What?" said Alex, off in another world.

"Alex!" Paige was getting irritated. "I said, 'What did your mom say about the camera crew?'"

"Oh. They're not going to make it on time. She says to just use a phone and upload it," said Alex with suppressed angst.

"That's better than nothing, I'll take the video," said Paige. "You had better cheer up, at least long enough for this footage. Look on the bright side, you have first class seats on this long flight, but we're stuck in coach."

A little light returned to his eyes and his countenance seemed to thaw as he smugly replied, "That's executive class, you mean. My dad really came through on this one, so I guess it's forgivable that he didn't get me another phone before departure."

"I thought you were tight with your mom," said Austin. "So why were you so rude to her, and your dad's now a hero?"

"Don't answer that, Alex," said Paige. "I can cover this one. It's like this—when Alex gets what he wants, he's nice, and when he doesn't, he gets ugly!" She flashed a sly smile as she goaded him with this snarky comment.

It didn't faze Alex, "Look, there's nothing wrong with making sure you get what you deserve. They're the ones who messed up my life by divorcing, and if they want to try to smooth it over by trying to do nice things for me on occasion, then so be it. I'll take what I can get."

Paige tried to keep things on track, "So, are you composed enough to let me record a video? Remember, this is a reality show, so try to act like someone less jaded than you is getting to go on this amazing trip in three… two…one…"

With her phone in selfie mode, Paige started recording. "We're chilling out here at LAX getting ready to board our flight. Say hi, Alex!"

"Hi!" Alex had his game face on.

Paige continued, "This is the trip of a lifetime for all of us, we've only dreamed of attending the International e-Sports Championship. So Alex, what are you looking forward to the most?"

"Getting a chance to see my competition in action!"

Paige interrupted, "But we're not competing, we're just attending."

"Duh, of course. I know that, I'm talking about next year. With my new sponsor, and the fact that I'll be graduating from high school, there's nothing to keep me from training and being the best in the country by next year."

Paige rolled her eyes and shook her head. *Could he really be that arrogant and disillusioned? Or was this just part of his show persona? He's either a really good actor or just a conceited, selfish jerk.* Yet he was undeniably the favorite in their show, chronicling the lives of four hopeful e-athletes.

Paige stopped recording while pretending to continue the short inter-view, "One last question, Alex. Tell us about the inspiration behind your new hairdo?" Alex gave a confused look upwards as if he might catch a view of his own hair when the others burst out laughing.

Casting for the show did not depend on gaming achievements. The auditions identified four unique personalities to serve the purpose of entertaining the audience with individual quirks and antics, regardless of loving or hating them.

Paige represented the rarer demographic of hardcore female gamers. It proved to be a difficult task for the producers to find a cute girl with a likeable onscreen presence. Paige almost fit the bill—a petite Asian girl with an infectious smile, a quick wit, and smart looking glasses. She probably possessed a higher IQ than the three boys combined. The casting director discovered one minor problem—she was not a gamer, she was an aspiring actress who did a great job acting enthusiastic about video games.

Austin was Filipino. He almost didn't get the role because the producers had scripted a young African-American for his part to make the show as culturally diverse as possible. Austin wanted the role so bad that he kept insisting he was black and should be given the opportunity to audition during the casting call. Despite being a nuisance, he won them over.

Chase portrayed a timid Hispanic with baggy pants and a cross on a gold chain around his neck. His quiet voice and camera shy personality made him appear awkward. The actor simply acted his part, but in this case, his genuine enthusiasm for games equaled most teen boys.

Then there was Alex, the shoo-in. The concept for the show was his idea and his mom gladly pitched it to the network. He was the epitome of cool. He exuded confidence with his good looks and inflated self-importance. His mom thought this might be a stepping-stone into a real acting career, but Alex couldn't care less about acting. He considered himself the only purist in the group, driven to become a pro gamer.

In his parent's opinion, gaming was a dead end and wouldn't really come to any financial security, despite the handful of pros making over a million dollars a year through contest earnings and sponsorships.

His mom and dad went their own ways, lived their own lives, and rarely agreed on anything. Alex's aspirations for gaming proved to be the exception. They just disagreed on how to handle it. His dad placed his own version of a carrot in front of him. He promised to help Alex by financing a new video game software company if he would go to college and get a degree. While tempting, the thought of continuing education after high school and sacrificing the needed hours for gameplay was too much. Dad's idea lost. Mom's reality show won. The strain between father and son, and between former husband and ex-wife only increased.

The limited custody came to an end when Alex turned sixteen and chose to stay with his mom except for occasional visits. This arrangement seemed to suit everyone. For Alex's generation, this was the new normal—a home divided like two halves of a ping-pong table, with children being tossed and trajected against their will. Back and forth, back and forth, back and forth, until a ball shoots off the table altogether. Divorced parents, like experienced table tennis players, skillfully applying backspin or leveraging the small field of play by using a child to ace their opponent. Rarely do the parents consider the deep impact in the lives of the children.

Alex outwardly milked these circumstances to his advantage, but inwardly, he suppressed the gnawing brokenness in his own life. This dark and lonely place resounded in the cavernous souls of his generation, longing to be filled with something mysterious and elusive.

CHAPTER 3

The entire Silicon Valley high-rise was buzzing like the anticipation of a colossal beehive in early spring. In a workspace outside the boardroom, Brandon craned his neck and caught a glimpse of the door shutting. He shifted his gaze towards Monica who worked across the aisle. She strained to get a view of the glass-walled room. Brandon, having the vantage point, gave her an update. "Mr. Brooks just stepped in."

"Do you think this is it?" asked Monica.

Brandon just pursed his lips and raised his eyebrows, conveying optimism.

Monica continued, "I'm dying to know if we will all be rich soon."

"Well, we all have a stake in the company and if this technology launches successfully, Mr. Brooks will join the sun, moon, and stars of the tech universe, and we will be orbiting somewhere close enough to bask in his glory—all the way to the bank. This is history in the making." Brandon, glowing with admiration, spoke as if his words were being recorded for posterity and archived into the annals of world history. "His life has been wrapped up in this project for the last fifteen years. If he can't accomplish it, no one can. He's a tenacious machine. This is going to happen! I feel it!"

"And we will all be rich—really, really rich," said Monica.

"Yeah, but once you're rich, do you think you'll stay on?" said Brandon.

"Well, it's too soon to say or to celebrate. The success of this launch has been hanging by a thread."

"But imagine that it does, what will it be like to be part of such a breakthrough?"

They both knew it all rested on Mr. Brooks' efforts to collaborate successfully with numerous international partnerships needed to accomplish such a historic technological feat.

Countless employees wished to be a fly on the wall in today's boardroom meeting including Brandon. He contemplated Monica's ominous words that the company's hopeful future was "hanging by a thread."

CHAPTER 4

"I'm very sorry to delay the meeting. I received an urgent call and thought for a brief moment that someone had died, but it was just my son with a broken phone," said Mr. Brooks.

The assembled board members laughed. He closed the boardroom door and turned his attention to the small group sitting around the table. He made eye contact with his personal secretary.

"Della, call Jeff and have him arrange for a new phone to be ready for my son when he arrives in Seoul. There's no need to ship one, we have plenty of contacts over there." Thinking aloud, he muttered, "Of all the weeks for Alex to travel overseas, it had to be this one!" Taking his seat and a deep breath, he looked at the others with a gleam in his eyes and enthusiasm brimming over, "This is it! Are you ready to make history?"

CHAPTER 5

"Allison! What's wrong?"

Maggie took a seat next to her coworker at the little coffee shop across the street from the studio office complex. Her closest arm instinctively wrapped around Allison's shoulder.

"Thank you for coming so quickly, I'm such a wreck," said Allison. Her voice cracked in a high pitch. An overly soaked Kleenex failed to dry her eyes, but did a sufficient job blotting the eroding makeup from the downpour of tears.

"Did someone—is it a family member?"

"No, Maggie, no one has died." Allison tried to catch her breath and eke out a few words in the midst of her blubbering. "Alex is angry with me."

Maggie looked shocked and incensed.

"Alex? He's been angry with you for years, I thought you were over that."

"No, not that Alex. I don't use that name for my ex, it's too confusing, I just call him Mr. Brooks. I'm talking about the other Alex," the tears flowing again.

Maggie looked more confused, "Alex Jr.?"

"Yes, my son."

"You two usually get along great, I would expect this with his dad, but not you."

Allison's voice continued breaking up and at a much higher pitch than usual. She determined to gain some self-control so she could be understood.

"That's usually the case. He never gets angry with me, but he is really upset and I feel so awful…"

"Allison—Allison, calm yourself; it can't be that bad, it's not like him. I know he's a handful, but you two have a close bond."

"That's just it, he's never turned on me like he did today and now he's on a fifteen-hour flight to South Korea. I tried calling him but he doesn't answer, I messaged him but he doesn't reply. What if something happens to him? I couldn't bear it." The torrent of tears resumed.

"Allison, listen. Alex is going to be alright. He's not in any danger."

"You don't understand, Maggie, you're not a mother. I have this terrible feeling that something bad is going to happen, and I may never hear his voice again." She couldn't hold herself together and broke down.

Maggie grabbed Allison's shoulders and made her look squarely in her face.

"Allison, take a deep breath and try to calm yourself. Maybe it would help if you tell me what happened. Start from the beginning."

"Okay, I'll try."

With a pathetic face and wavering voice, she began telling Maggie all about her terrible morning. Maggie's skinny mocha was almost gone by the time Allison finished her story and they both needed to get back to work for a production meeting. Maggie gave her one last hug and made a quick exit as she glanced at the time on her watch and made an anxious wince.

Allison dreaded going back to the office to deal with another snafu. The network had not approved her request to send a cinematographer to film some in-flight footage of the team. Instead, they planned to have a small team ready for Alex and the others as they arrived in Seoul. Unfortunately, that film crew encountered a major flight delay and would not arrive to film the team of gamers as they deplaned.

Allison typed "having a really bad day" with a tearful emoji on her social media app as she walked across the street.

CHAPTER 6

"Flight 2593 to Seoul now boarding all active military personnel, those travelling with small children, anyone with disabilities, and executive class passengers."

Alex jumped up, slung his backpack over one shoulder, and sneered at his peers who were travelling coach. He budged into the forming line ahead of an elderly woman leaning on a cane. He pretended to not notice her presence while truly ignorant of the few bystanders who glared at him. The old women remained unperturbed.

The unfolding scene between these two strangers might have been easy to overlook in another era, but not this one. Hardly anyone emerges from their bubble of personal space, self-interest, and nearly nonstop attention to their smartphone. This was not the case for the woman raised in a former time. At this rare moment, a young jerk and a gentle woman converged. Unruffled, she acknowledged Alex's presence in her quiet, quavering voice.

"You were smart to get in front of me. I walk so slow and you look so excited to start your journey."

Alex was slightly abashed by this unexpected interaction. He hoped to keep his back to her and act as if she didn't exist, intending to not be encumbered by the little old lady.

She had a blue reusable grocery sack suspended from her fragile left forearm, filled with an assortment of items. This seemed to help add ballast to her weak body leaning against the cane. Alex gave a sheepish glance behind him.

"Oh, I—" He was on the verge of lying and making an excuse for himself, but something about her eyes penetrated his. "I—I am excited…how about you?" He had poised his question haphazardly, not knowing what else to say, but before she could respond, he realized that he had reached the attendant checking the passports and boarding passes. This was a convenient excuse to jettison the conversation and put some distance between himself and the old woman, but he felt compelled for some strange reason to be polite and wait in order to bring their conversation to a close. This was shockingly out of character for Alex.

He hesitated for a moment and her eyes caught his again, acknowledging that their conversation had yet to come to an appropriate close. He felt awkward and realized his friends were gawking with acute interest. It wouldn't have been so bad if the woman had quickly gotten past the ticket attendant, but she had neglected to have her passport in her hand and was now fumbling slowly through her grocery bag in search of it. This maneuver was about as precarious as a sailor managing a catamaran in choppy seas. This touched off a fit of impatience in Alex who teetered on the verge of an inappropriate outburst. She gave him another glance that conveyed, *Hold on just a moment and we can finish our conversation.*

For Alex, this was cruel torture. By now, his friends were keen to the fact that he was waiting for the old woman and they didn't know whether they should laugh at him or admire him. Neither seemed appropriate so they just stood and looked with perplexed expressions. Alex was livid when he noticed Paige taking a video with her phone. He was just about to grab the lady's bag and help her locate her passport when she finally found it, simultaneously making her apologies to the attendant.

An uncomfortable feeling came over Alex at the realization that he felt a deep sense of respect for this old woman. She had mysteriously endeared herself to him in a span of mere seconds. Maybe this is what a grandchild naturally feels for a grandma, but how would he know that? He didn't have a relationship with his grandparents on either side of his family.

Hey, snap out of it, Alex! He thought to himself, *What's getting to you? One random old woman says something kind and you start letting your guard down. Don't be getting sentimental now.* He didn't want to give any ground to the emotions that might reveal the genuine struggle he was working hard to suppress. He had never been on a trip this far away from home on his own. He was almost wishing he was flying main cabin with his friends, but that would put too much of a drain on his full tank of pride.

He found himself walking slowly with the woman as if he belonged to her and any casual observer might think this was a grandmother with her grandson.

"That looks like a heavy backpack," she remarked.

"Yeah, it's got the essentials. A couple of energy drinks, my laptop, my good headphones, a tablet, some snacks, and a couple of magazines."

"They will feed you on the plane," she said.

"I know," said Alex, "but I'm certain they don't have my favorite energy drink. You seem to be travelling light."

"Yes, I don't think energy drinks would help much at my age, so I'll just drink what they serve."

Alex looked concerned, "I hope they'll have some good entertainment for you to pass the time. This is a long flight and it doesn't look like you came equipped."

"I have a book to read."

"As I was saying, let's hope they have a good movie or two."

They were looking at their boarding passes as they stepped into the plane. Alex was strangely disappointed when his new surrogate grandma was not going to be sitting anywhere near him. She was in business class. She must have been thinking along similar lines, "I'm disappointed that our seats are not closer. I don't feel like we've had enough time to get to know each other. And beg your pardon, I don't even know your name yet— how could I have been so thoughtless, rambling on like that without asking your name?"

"It's Alex. Well, actually it's Alexander but nobody really calls me that, it's just Alex."

"Well, Alexander, it's nice to make your acquaintance. I'm Agnes, and if you get lonesome up in first class, be sure to stop by my aisle—who knows maybe there will be an empty seat available after everyone boards."

"Lonesome? What gave you that idea? It's not likely, but if you get bored, I can lend you my tablet and teach you a few ridiculous games that are really addicting."

"That sounds adventurous! Maybe I'll take you up on that offer."

"Really?" said Alex.

"It's a fifteen-hour flight and I do get weary."

"Okay," said Alex. "Well, I better find my seat." He continued to first class.

Alex had been so preoccupied with other things leading up to the trip that he really hadn't done any research about the plane he was travelling on or his seat in executive class. He suddenly became giddy at the accommodations in business class and he still had ten rows to go before reaching first class. He was blown away by what he found. There were individual cubicles with a seat that could lie flat to sleep in. He was impressed with the personal seventeen-inch touch screen monitor, giving him access to hundreds of movies, TV programs, and music stations. *What? Bose noise cancelling head-phones! No way!*

A friendly flight attendant with bright eyes and a genuine smile approached him.

"You look a little young for wine tasting or champagne, but how about an energy drink?"

"You're kidding!" said Alex.

"No, I'm not. You may not have any alcoholic drinks, but I can let you get amped up on caffeine."

"In that case, sure!"

"I'll be right back."

Alex was stunned as he took it all in. He felt big and important. He played with the recliner buttons, turned on the touch screen, counted the outlets and USB ports, tried on the Bose headphones, and was rifling through the complimentary toiletries when the stewardess arrived with his drink. She was very nice but seemed a little old to Alex. He thought flight attendants were always young, and she must have been thinking he was a little young to be a business executive.

"Here's your beverage and am I to assume you've started some new website that's been bought for billions and I have the privilege of meeting you before it's yesterday's old news?"

Alex actually blushed a little with this misdirected flattery. He contemplated lying about his identity and pretending to be a young web mogul. He defaulted to telling the truth, not because it was a virtue in him but because he thought the real story would be impressive enough.

"No, I'm a TV star."

It's strange that such a semi-bogus claim can carry weight with the average person who's been fed a steady diet of American fame factory entertainment. His words, like a haphazard arrow shot into the air, hit the target nonetheless. Alex noticed her intrigued look to his inflated identity. His seat in first class was just enough validation to convince her that this handsome teen was in fact a young TV star, which was certainly more interesting than a famous website developer.

"So, what show are you on?" Her interest was piqued and Alex read it in her eager expression.

"It's a reality show called *Gamers*, you probably haven't seen it because it appeals to the younger generation."

"Are you saying I'm old?" she said playfully.

"Well…" Alex didn't know what to say.

"Relax, I'm older and I haven't even heard of your show, but it must be doing alright if you're flying first class to South Korea."

A flood of thoughts rushed through his mind. If truth be told, the "reality" part of the show was that it was not doing well. It continued to get bad reviews and only appealed to a limited audience. His mom had been reluctant to tell Alex that it might not make it to a second season. Alex had youthful optimism that the show was on the verge of widespread acclaim as soon as a critical mass had discovered it. The network wasn't pushing it hard enough was his fallback excuse. They weren't investing in enough advertising. How could the masses not fall in love with him once they were finally introduced?

No time to explain all of that now, he tried to change the subject and let her think what she wanted to think. "I just thought stewardesses were usually younger?"

"Well, thanks for the flattering compliment!" smiling wryly as she said it. "Actually, you're almost correct in your assessment but you must not have been on many international flights. Those of us who have been in the business longer have seniority and many of us prefer these long flights. Fifteen to sixteen hours on duty—a couple days off in a foreign city then another flight back and I'm done working for the month. It's a sweet deal."

Her attention turned to another beckoning passenger. "I'll keep stopping by. I won't be far, but if you need something, just push that button. My name badge says Allison but you can call me Ali if that sounds a little younger."

If she had lingered for a moment longer, she might have been confused to witness Alex's facial expression change drastically at the mention of her name. It made his conscious sting a little.

CHAPTER 7

All of the excitement of the trip, the gloating over friends, the special treatment from the stewardess came to a halt as Alex remembered his behavior and attitude towards his mom. He stared at his broken phone as he toyed with it, turning it round and round aimlessly while pondering his harsh words to her. He made a practice of ignoring the majority of his faults yet his jaded conscience couldn't dismiss the tinge of guilt, which needled him after hearing the flight attendant's name—Allison, the same as his mom's. It was not his habit to be so mean to his mom, or in the habit of knowing how to remedy a situation like this one. His filial bond was not virtuous but natural and instinctive. It had nothing to do with a deliberate effort on his part to be a loving and kind son.

The broken phone proved to be a continuing dilemma. He didn't know his mom's mobile number; all of his contacts were on his phone. He instinctively knew she must be troubled about the ordeal, but he wrongly assumed she would be upset about disappointing him. He prided himself in finding forgiveness in his heart towards her for messing up the departure. It still bothered him that the camera crew wasn't present to capture the moment for his show. He was proficient at holding grudges and his mom knew how determined he could be. He really wanted her remorse to be set at ease but he didn't know how to get in touch with her. He finally decided to attempt an internet call from his tablet to the studio office using the airline's Wi-Fi. He didn't have the studio number either, but a quick internet search did the job.

He dialed the main number but found it impossible to get past the gatekeepers. The more obnoxious and belligerent he became, the less helpful they were inclined to be. It took a rare act of self-control on Alex's part to keep from slamming his tablet down in anger and frustration. His conscience was now pacified. He attempted a call. His warped sense of indignation from this well-meaning attempt rekindled his bad attitude of laying blame on his mom.

CHAPTER 8

The pattern of three short beeps on Mr. Brooks' office phone indicated his personal secretary from the outer office. She was a deft gatekeeper and he had implicit trust that she would not bother him unless absolutely necessary. He didn't hesitate to pick up the receiver, "Yes Della?"

"Mr. Brooks, there are two men here to see you from the FBI. Our security team has authenticated their badges."

"Send them in."

Della's office was just on the other side of his door, so there was very little time for his imagination to formulate any possible reason for this unexpected visit. He wasn't alarmed, just momentarily perplexed. The door opened and the two men stepped in, neither of them looking like Hollywood's version of agents. No dark suits or sunglasses, just business casual and the two men didn't match. He thought they should have a different wardrobe and be identical in height and weight, but it didn't occur to him that his prejudice originated from movies and television caricatures. He just sat there somewhat stunned by the new experience. Gathering his senses, he quickly snapped out of it and stood to greet them with a handshake.

"This is quite a surprise, I'm sure you are used to people being a bit flustered at unexpected visits from your corner of the world." He said this as collected and friendly as possible, but anyone who knew Mr. Brooks well would easily pick up the subtle indications of anxiety. "Please have a seat."

Their expression was not cold or stoic but cordial and businesslike. "Mr. Brooks, I'm special agent Bill Hutchins and this is my partner, Brent Davidson. We are sorry to disrupt your day without notice, but you will certainly agree that it was necessary once we explain why we are here."

CHAPTER 9

B ored. It's hard to believe with all of the entertainment options Alex would find himself discontent and fidgety so soon. He watched a couple reruns of his favorite TV show, played a couple of games, ate his snacks, and drank more energy drinks. He searched the list of movies only to find that he had already seen most of them. He looked at the onscreen flight map and trip information—less than two hours into his fifteen-hour flight. *I'm going to go stir crazy.* If there was such a thing as a media saturation threshold, Alex was certainly a candidate. His present dilemma seemed to stem from being surrounded with first class passengers who were aloof, combined with the absence of peers to experience the moment with. The knowledge that three of his friends were actually on the plane and probably having a great time together in their cramped row made him more uneasy.

It's astounding that the fear of missing out could be experienced with such a short distance of separation. He knew he could go and visit them but that would cost too much from his ego account. *No, that's not an option, but why does it bug me so much?* He thought to himself, *I'm the one in first class, how could I be missing out?*

He didn't have a philosophical mind that could grasp that electronics, mega leg room, endless energy drinks, and selfish pride were poor substitutes for personal interaction with others. Loneliness was a haunting phantom in Alex's life, his nemesis. He continually tried to hide by exploring a thousand different exit ramps off the highway of reality. Loneliness seemed to never stop pursuing him and Alex's skill at performing evasive maneuvers would impress a fighter pilot in a dogfight.

What about Agnes? Alex thought. *She might be really bored and I might cheer her up.* Alex often thought of ways to hide his own selfish plots under the guise of thinking about others. In fact, he had so much practice with this tactic that he believed in his own selfless virtue even now.

He convinced himself that he needed to stretch his legs a little. He hoped that Agnes would see him walking by and invite him to talk. *What if she didn't?* He entered the business class section and quickly surveyed the seats as nonchalantly as possible but didn't spot her. He had no idea which side of the plane she was sitting and he began to wonder if she was in that section after all. He almost reached coach when he finally saw her. She was in the second to last row and so short that her head rested well below the tops of the seats. Alex noticed she was sleeping in her reclined seat.

Why did his heart sink a little at that moment? Why should he be disappointed that an old lady was asleep on the plane? What kind of ridiculous notion would foster such a strange response in a seventeen-year-old who was aspiring to be a pro gamer? These questions remained under lock and key in Alex's heart, but if they were set free and given voice to respond, an ominous chorus would echo, "Loneliness, loneliness, loneliness!"

Chapter 10

"Alexander?"

A sympathetic voice came from behind him as he started walking back to his seat. He turned to look for Agnes. If someone would have taken a picture of his countenance, you could have slipped the image into a wall calendar between the sad puppy picture in February and the cuddly kittens in April. The month of March would be an image of a pathetic boy who looked lost and unsure of himself.

He wondered if she awoke because of his unspoken plea for company. Alex was not sure how his inner thoughts were mysteriously broadcast and tuned in by the old woman's internal receiver. This all transpired in a moment but Agnes's finely tuned perception could calculate these kind of equations faster than the latest computer processor. It's not just technology that advances to new bench marks, so does a person's keenness in reading others when they have been in the practice of observing the subtle nuances of nonverbal communication.

"I am so glad you came by just now, I was dozing off due to terrible boredom and I was wishing I had someone to talk to." Her tired, frail voice seemed to require more energy to produce than what was available in her natural resources. "Would you humor an old lady and sit down for a few minutes and listen to me prattle away?"

In actuality, Agnes didn't know why she had awakened at that moment. Had Alex wished it into being or was there some other explanation or will at work? Whatever the reason, she was awake; Alex looked like he could use a friend and Agnes happened to be sitting next to one of the few empty seats on this flight. This social meeting was such an odd mix and Alex knew it, but he was drawn to this old woman by some invisible pull.

"Please don't think I'm nosy if I start asking you a hundred questions. Women in general want to know details and I'm no exception. Plus, I've got a sneaking suspicion that you don't have much conversational experience with old ladies."

Alex didn't know how to respond. *She's right*, he thought.

"In fact, I don't think young people these days have very good conversation skills regardless of the generation gap. So I won't discriminate against you and assume I'm correct. I'm going to tell you about a conversation tool I've learned and you can give it a try on me when I'm done."

"Okay," said Alex.

"You see, the help is found in an acronym." She paused and asked in a perplexed but not condescending way, "Do you know what an acronym is?"

Alex shook his head no.

"Oh dear, I'm making this more confusing. An acronym is when you use each letter of a word to represent other words. In this case the word is 'FROM.'"

"From?" said Alex.

"Yes, 'FROM'—F-R-O-M, and you can use it to find a little about where a person is coming from when starting a conversation. Let's start with 'F' which stands for family. Tell me about your family?"

Alex groaned, "Can we skip that and do 'ROM'? That's more appropriate for a computer guy anyway."

He was delighted with his subtle pun but Agnes was in the dark and didn't understand his rare attempt at wit. He felt a tinge of frustration and colored a little as she looked confounded. This was partly from his vehement avoidance of the subject of his family and partly from her ignorance of his clever remark.

"Well, it looks like we can each learn something from the other; you didn't know acronym and I don't know what you meant by ROM, though I do believe I know what you implied by avoiding the 'F' for family."

"ROM—like DVD-ROM? Never mind. So can we skip 'F'?" asked Alex.

"I suppose we can make an exception, then tell me about your favorite recreation—that's the 'R.' What are your hobbies?"

"That's easy! Video games. I'm going to be a pro!"

"You mean, there are people who make their living from playing video games?"

"Not many, but I'm going to be one of them!" His voice became very animated and excited.

"You don't mean you invent games but you play them?" said Agnes.

"Yep."

"Do you mean, you play these games to test them for the game companies?"

"No, I play them to compete against others. In fact, I'm on my way to one the biggest gaming events of the year!"

"This is such a new idea to me; I never knew anyone like you existed."

"Well, I'm not a pro yet, but I'm off to a good start."

"So how do you become a pro?"

"Like any athlete, you compete and win and get to the top of your field, then hopefully get sponsorships."

"An athlete? And will you make lots of money?"

"Probably not as much as a game developer, at least that's what my dad keeps harping about, but we're going to avoid that touchy subject right now."

Alex's voice had gone from giddy to grumpy and his tone became tinged with angst. He diverted quickly back to subject and the dark shadow suddenly passed.

"It's not about the money anyway, it's about doing something you love and the notoriety among gamers and fans. It's not easy to get famous, but everyone has to find their own niche and I've found mine."

"What does your mother think about it?" asked Agnes.

His expression suddenly changed again but this time it was a different shade. He seemed troubled but replied as confidently as possible. "Oh Mom? She's cool about it. Sort of. She doesn't think there's a long-term future in it for me, but that doesn't stop her from being supportive. She has her own agenda, but right now, we're working together."

"How so?"

"Well, my mom works in Hollywood. She's a television producer and one of her shows is about me!"

"About you?"

"Not just about me, there are three others on the show. They're on the plane right now—in coach, but between you and me, the others are just props for the show."

"What do you mean?" said Agnes with genuine interest.

"They're not true hardcore gamers, they're just aspiring actors that were cast for the show."

"Oh, so your show is about video game playing?"

"Video game playing?" He emphasized "playing" with disdain. "Sounds babyish, we just call it gaming. But let's get back to the point—they are not gamers and this is supposed to be a reality show! They're just posers, I'm the only core gamer."

"Reality show?"

"You mean you don't know what a reality show is? Are you from another planet or have you been living in a convent without TV? TV's have been around for hundreds of years."

"Actually, Alexander, they haven't been around that long. I think they were introduced at a world's fair in the '30s, and no, I wasn't there." She said with a chuckle, "I'm not that old! But I was around when TVs started becoming more common in homes in the '50s and triumphed over the radio."

"Are you some sort of historian?" asked Alex.

"No, I've just lived through this history with all of the changes and it makes my head spin just thinking about it. So much has changed…" her sentence tapered off while looking sympathetically at Alex, distracted for a moment in deep thought.

"Anyway, there was no way for an old fogey like me to keep up with all of the face tweets, or email posts, or blog texts, or fake reality shows. I became so frustrated with the garbage on TV that I stopped watching it. I wasn't alone in my disappointment, in fact, the FCC commissioner back in the 1960s gave a haranguing speech and called television a 'vast wasteland.' And I certainly agreed."

Alex replied, "Well, you should have held on a little longer because things have gotten so much better: widescreen, HD, realistic graphics, better editing, special effects, more channels, and so many options! I can't believe I have to explain reality TV. Anyway, they are programs which are made so that the audience believes they are watching something unfold in real life and it's just being documented."

"But it's not?" asked Agnes.

"Of course not. People behave differently in front of a camera, especially if they are being paid, and especially if the show is being broadcast. Plus, there are casting agents to get the right type of people that will interest the viewers and you add producers, editors, coaches, scripts, makeup, the whole works. People eat it up. It's like they are living it themselves. They've got this down to a science. And talk about casting! The other three on my show were picked because of their camera presence and personas." Alex went on for a while, describing them and why they were selected.

"So why were you selected?" Agnes asked.

"That's simple enough, my mom started the show because she hoped it might launch me into an acting career, but I'm the only one not acting and I don't have any interest in acting. I'm serious about going pro, so this is just a stepping stone for me and is getting me good exposure in the gaming biz."

It didn't take long for Agnes to learn that Alex was most comfortable talking about himself and video games, but she had her own agenda and she wouldn't be diverted. She was sincerely empathetic towards Alex and aware of his own blindness to the superficial facade that defined his identity.

CHAPTER 11

"Mr. Brooks, the bottom line is that we believe there's an international plot to disrupt the release of your proprietary technology. In light of the government's vested interest since the early stages of development, we are keenly aware of the need to protect your patents and ensure a successful launch of this breakthrough of yours. To get to the point, we believe there has been a breach in security in your company and someone is planning on leveraging it for their own agenda," said Agent Hutchins, the spokesman between the two agents.

Mr. Brooks sat stunned. His company had been diligent to guard their secrets to the fullest extent feasible and the federal government willingly partnered with them these many years to protect his interests and theirs.

He could hardly breathe, this was something he had feared and spent years fretting over and working out security measures, then fretting some more to keep his project secure. He believed this technology would be impossible to reverse engineer and impossible to recreate without knowledge of the entire system. He wasn't working with existing building blocks, he was about to introduce a new block to build with what would likely make existing competitors obsolete. This was a logical reason for any competitor to get their hands on the same technology or to keep his from seeing the light of day.

"So what can you tell me? What do you know?"

"We don't know as much as wish we did but the good news is that we don't think the perpetrators know as much as they wish," said Hutchins.

"That doesn't help me, what do you know?" Alex's voice was clearly full of anxiety.

"We have some disconcerting intelligence that your company is in someone's crosshairs and they are planning to disrupt, delay, or try to steal your project in this eleventh hour."

"Who?" Mr. Brooks was having difficulty not letting his anxiety morph into panic.

"Mr. Brooks," said Hutchins, "the intelligence world is often full of vague and shadowy bits of information that we endeavor to make sense of. The difficulty is that we presently don't have that answer and we are not one hundred percent certain there is a real threat. We have only enough information to cause concern and prompt our department to initiate this meeting to gather some information that might help."

"You still haven't told me what information you have and how you got it."

"We're getting to that. I know this must be extremely stressful to you but we need to be meticulous about this if we are going to be of any help. So please be patient…"

"I'm sorry but I don't have time to be patient; we are going to launch in two weeks! So what do you know?"

"Well, many groups seeking anonymity like terrorists or drug cartels and others that need to communicate internationally have not only been using the Dark Web but are also using massive multiplayer online gaming platforms to create avatars and cryptic messages to conduct meetings, formulate plans, and exchange encrypted information. We have operatives embedded in these virtual worlds just like the tangible world. It was one of these agents who has been methodically infiltrating a suspicious group that was flagged as a possible terrorist cell. In one of these exchanges, a cryptic message was intercepted and a team of decoders have been working around the clock. What we thought was a potential threat to national security was discovered to be a potential plot against your company. The information is not entirely understandable but we believe it is pointed at you, that they are international players, and that your new technology is the target. That is all we know and this limited information is so vague that we might be mistaken. We're taking precautions and have ordered clandestine security, which is already in place for your offices and key personnel. We obviously can't cover everyone in your company. We are also hoping to gather any helpful information from you today."

"Men, before this goes any further, I need to make a call to our government liaison, our legal team, and our security team. No offense, but how do I know for certain that you are not the plot?"

"Do what you need to do, we can wait."

CHAPTER 12

"'M' is for memory. What is one of your favorite memories?" asked Agnes.

"What? I thought we were supposed to talk about 'O'?"

"Oh, you're right! I did skip 'O' because it stands for occupation. It's an easy topic for conversation and even though young people don't usually have a career, they at least have aspirations, and you've already talked about yours."

"Oh, I guess you're right," said Alex.

"But I'm glad you brought it up because I meant for you to have this tool for your conversational toolbox."

"My what?"

"Your conversational toolbox. You might be an exception but it seems that most young people today don't have adequate conversation skills."

Alex went on the defense, "Maybe you don't understand our new ways of communicating. The world is changing and we're gaining new skills."

"Well, I'm not so sure about that, but let's forgo your modern ideologies for a moment and get back to 'M.'"

"What was 'M' again?"

"Memories. What is a favorite memory of yours?"

"Oh yeah, 'M'...hmmmmm, I'm not sure, I guess I haven't thought about it much. I'm not a sentimental person."

"Do you remember a favorite trip or holiday or experience that's left an indelible mark on your timeline?"

"No, I don't think so…other than the Christmas when I got my first PlayStation—it's a gaming console in case you don't know." He paused and looked crossways at her for a moment, trying to read her expression then continued, "No, I'm sure you don't know."

"You're right about that."

"Okay, I'm done. Am I good to go? Is it my turn to ask you the questions?"

"I still wish I knew a little more about your family." Agnes said this with such grandmotherly grace. She anticipated the possibility of Alex opening up a little more. His guard did come down a little.

"There's not much to tell, and we couldn't really be called a family. I don't think we meet the minimum requirements if there were any."

"Why do you say that?" asked Agnes.

Alex relaxed his former stance against talking about the subject, "Dad and Mom divorced when I was eight years old. Dad was hardly ever at home anyway, and when he was home, he wasn't really home. He was building his career and chasing after his own tech empire."

Alex paused and seemed to ponder whether he should continue, but there was something so inviting and safe with Agnes that he didn't hesitate for very long. "Dad is cold and Mom is artsy. Dad is driven and Mom drove him crazy with her passion for Hollywood culture, health food, yoga, her strange religious beliefs, and her overall unique flair."

"She sounds like an interesting person."

"Most people like her, except Dad. And I really like her except for the health food, the yoga, and her spiritual weirdness."

"So your mother is religious? What religion?"

"Well, she wouldn't call it religion but her 'spiritual journey.' She's not devoted to a particular community but she spends a lot of time with a group called Baha'i."

"Oh, Baha'i, I know a little about them."

"You seem to know a little about a lot of things!"

"But what about you?" said Agnes.

"Nothing, I don't believe in God"

"Really?"

"Really!"

"What about your father?"

"Oh, his religion is his work, and he's the most devoted worshipper. And even though we don't get along, to his credit, I don't think he's just chasing money. He thinks he's going to make the world a better place with his company and innovations." Alex paused and made a jab under his breath, "I just wish he could have made our home a better place."

"I'm sorry, my hearing is not as good as it used to be, I missed what you just said."

Alex brought his volume back up to normal again, "If he does help the world I'll be surprised, he sure made a mess of our family."

"That's so sad. But changing the subject a little, did either of them remarry?" asked Agnes.

"No. That's what is weird about this. Most of my friends have step parents or just new people living in the home, but I'm glad that's not us. It's hardly a silver lining, but I'll take what I can get."

"So I guess you live with your mom?"

"Mom, for sure. Dad and I couldn't deal with being around each other for more than a weekend on occasion."

"That's too bad."

"Not really. We don't mind the arrangement."

"I'm a little old fashioned and I just think that boys need their dads, especially at your age."

"You're not a little old fashioned, you are a lot old fashioned. No offense, but you're wrong; it's not realistic. It just doesn't work that way in the twenty-first century. Dad and I don't have unrealistic expectations of each other—well, that's not exactly true, he expects me to go to college and get a degree and I think that's unrealistic, at least for a person like me who is already on the rise without college. I can't afford to lose any momentum and gamble with my chance to follow my dreams. He followed his and I want to follow mine. We may fight about it but he must know I'm right and doesn't want to face it. At least he showed some support by getting me a first class ticket!"

"So your dad arranged this trip?"

"Sort of, it's partly for our show, and partly to keep me out of his hair for a couple of weeks while he puts the final pieces in place for the debut of his new technology. We both get something out of it as long as I promise to stay out of trouble."

"Are you prone to getting into trouble?" asked Agnes.

"That depends on how you define trouble."

CHAPTER 13

"Wow, level five security protocol," said Monica as she whispered loudly across the aisle into Brandon's cubicle.

"I'm not surprised," replied Brandon. "In fact, I suspected we would've reached that threshold sooner,"

"No doubt it's because we are so close to the deadline," said Monica.

"So what's different about level five anyway? I can't imagine tighter security than fingerprint scans, zero tolerance on outside electronics beyond the second checkpoint, zero electronics going out, body scans, and all communication recorded and archived. I think it must be easier to get access to the Pentagon."

"Don't you remember? Level five is the document we signed allowing our personal data outside work to be monitored for security purposes if necessary."

"Do you think there's a real threat or just nervous precaution?" said Brandon.

"It's hard to say but there were two official looking guys that Jeff rode with in the elevator and they were going to the tenth floor."

CHAPTER 14

"You have a very fascinating life," said Agnes.

Alex reveled in the thought that she was intrigued with his story, "It's manageable for now."

"So are you excited to experience a new culture?"

"Not really. I wish they would hold this event in LA but it's always in Seoul."

"Have you traveled overseas before?" asked Agnes.

"No, I'm not interested in other countries, I'm only interested in the event." Alex wanted to change the subject, "Anyways, now that you know most of my life story, you might want to start writing it down since you are somewhat of a historian. You could get a jump on the others that will come out of the woodwork once I'm famous!"

"That's an interesting thought, but back to Seoul, it's a very interesting city. You might be surprised."

"So you've been there before? And why are you going to Seoul? Are you going to the competition?" Alex was pleased with himself for what he thought was a good joke.

"No, I'm going to visit my daughter and son-in-law and some old friends"

"Some old friends?"

"Yes, I used to live in South Korea many years ago."

"You don't look Asian; were you or your husband in the military?"

"No, my husband and I were missionaries—"

"Missionaries? You mean you're one of those religious nuts who go around converting the pagans?"

"I wouldn't have described it that way—"

Alex cut her off again, "Well I hope you're not going to try and convert me because that would ruin an otherwise nice talk that we have been having. I'm not meaning to be rude but you would be wasting your time and mine."

Agnes just smiled pityingly at him without becoming ruffled.

"Now that I know where you're coming 'FROM,' I think we need a new acronym for this conversation like 'NO WAY,'" said Alex.

"Have you ever talked with a missionary before?" asked Agnes.

Alex paused to reflect on this puzzling question. He was bit perplexed; he wasn't even sure how he knew what a missionary was. He had never gone to church or anything like a church. His ideas must have come from television or movies but he couldn't recall anything specific. "I guess not," said Alex.

"Well, you're young, you don't know any different, but let me at least set the record straight. A Christian missionary is not just trying to make converts. It is only God who can change a heart."

"Well, if only God can change hearts then why would He need missionaries?" He was certain he had her cornered.

"That's a good question and I could give you an answer but it will lead to more objections and more questions that would need a response. You might accuse me of trying to convert you." She said this is such a winsome way that he found himself off his guard again.

"Well, you said you're not trying to make converts and I'm not convertible, so go ahead and fire away." Alex's obstinacy was sincere but he also liked talking with Agnes so he was willing to placate her.

"In that case, let me try to answer your question about missionaries, but I need to go back to the beginning, when God created Adam—"

"You don't really believe that fairytale do you? Science has proven that we evolved."

"One question at a time. You're going to need to keep a running list and I'll do my best to accommodate you if I can but let's get back to Adam."

"I guess you can go on with your story for now but I do have some objections already," said Alex.

"Okay, back to Adam. God created the world and everything in it. He gave Adam responsibility to manage it. Adam couldn't create something from nothing but he could cultivate what was already made. His work depended on other things out of his control, like the sun and water and soil and seeds."

Alex interrupted again, "So what does this have to do with missionaries? This sounds like a lecture on farming."

"Hang in there, I'm getting to the point. God doesn't need missionaries any more than God needed a planet or needed Adam and Eve. But from the beginning, mankind was given responsibility in his own domain, even though he needed help from another domain—"

"So you believe in aliens?" Alex interjected with new enthusiasm for the story.

"Alex, slow down, I don't recall mentioning any aliens just now, but I do believe in other domains like heaven."

Alex was a bit deflated at this and muttered, "You probably don't know anything about internet domains."

She was beginning to realize that she needed to compress her answers for Alex even though she would prefer to go a little deeper. "You'll have to teach me about those but getting back on topic, God often works through people, that's why there are missionaries even though God is the only one who can change a person's heart."

"So do you think there are aliens?" Alex was clearly not tracking with her.

"There are certainly other beings that God has created but they aren't called aliens in the Bible, and speaking of the Bible, have you ever read it before?"

"No way, are you kidding? I hardly read anything unless it's about gaming or entertainment. There's no way I'm going to read an outdated book that is boring and full of crazy religious ideas."

"How do you know what it's about if you haven't read it?"

"Hey, I thought it was my turn to be asking questions?" This was Alex's way of dodging the question.

Agnes remained unruffled and continued on, "Oh, before I forget—" she reached down to grab her bag and started fishing for something. "Here it is." She pulled out a small book not much larger than a deck of cards. "Here, Alex, please take this as a gift to remember me by in case our paths never cross again. It's a pocket New Testament Bible with the Psalms."

"Wow, that's pretty small."

"It's not the entire Bible but I would like you to keep it with you in case you get weary of your gadgets and decide to read something." She stopped talking for a moment and wrote a personal note on the inside cover page. Then handing it to Alex, he just stared at it, hesitating to receive it. She teased him, "It's not going to bite you, or blow up, or turn into something strange like your fantasy worlds."

Alex wanted to resist but he couldn't. This old lady really affected him in a way that he couldn't understand. "Well, okay, I guess," he said. "At least it's small," as he tucked it into his back pocket.

CHAPTER 15

All day long, Allison struggled with feeling distraught. Driving home, she thought she could try to unwind by getting on her beach cruiser for a relaxing bike ride to Marina Del Ray and then along the beach. The ride would not take long, the weather happened to be perfect, and she desperately needed something to divert her anxious thoughts.

Alex would be on the plane for several more hours before she could make contact with him and then hopefully smooth things over so they could be back to themselves again.

Is Alex feeling as miserable as I am, she pondered. *I don't know if I should hope so for my sake or hope so for his.* Her love for Alex teetered on the verge of idolatry. This distorted love often manifested through indulgence and leniency. She considered whether or not her continual pampering had fostered the ugly behavior that lashed out at her that morning. She mulled around a variety of alternative reasons in her mind for his outburst in an attempt to avoid the gnawing question, *Am I culpable for the incubation of a seventeen-year-old spoiled brat?*

Her little bungalow with a small manicured yard and fragrant fruit trees usually boosted her soul after getting home from work but not today. Alex wasn't there. *He's hardly here anyway, but when he's not here, he eventually gets here, but not today and not for several days.* It occurred to her that she might be experiencing the reverse of homesickness or maybe sympathy homesickness. She didn't fully understand the reasons for her emotional instability over this.

She was glad to find a parking spot in front of her house. She had asked

Alex to park his car on the street before he left so that she could use the carport while he was gone, but she covered again for him and gave him the benefit of the doubt that it must have slipped his mind in the excitement of his trip. It certainly couldn't be from a lack of consideration for others, especially not his mom!

Allison's distracted mind had no room to give any thought to the car parked in front of hers with two men sitting in the front. It didn't register that they got out of the car just as she was getting out of hers. She didn't pay enough attention to notice their approaching footsteps as she fumbled with her key in the door lock, trying to keep hold of her purse and a stack of work that she brought home from the office. A man's voice in close proximity made her jump.

"Excuse me, are you Allison Brooks?"

She let out a startled cry and whipped around like a snapped mousetrap, pressing her back tight against the unopened door. This made the two men jump and they quickly tried to remedy their poorly timed encounter.

"So sorry to startle you, we should have waited for you to get settled inside first then knocked," said one of the men.

"Yes, we are so sorry," said the other.

She was uncertain and confused by the unexpected visitors that seemed to emerge suddenly from behind her palm tree. She was holding her hand to her chest as she tried to catch her breath and calm her nerves while warily eyeing the strangers. They had an official look to them, which they verified as one of them flashed a badge and introduced himself.

"I'm truly sorry that we frightened you, I'm Special Agent Bill Hutchins and this is Agent Brent Davidson of the FBI. We need to talk with you about your son, Alex. May we come in?"

CHAPTER 16

"Hi Della, connect me to Greg in our security department."
With very little delay, Greg was on the line, "Hello Mr. Brooks, what can I do for you?"

"I just received a visit from the FBI and they're concerned about a potential plot targeting our product launch. They believe it may be coming through international channels but there is always the possibility of an inside connection. They've stepped up their surveillance and security measures but I need you to step up your own department's efforts. They said that vague bits of information have been exchanged on an online gaming site. I need you to scan all employees' business and private IP address histories for MMORPG sites, and once you have that pool gathered, then dig deeper and identify potential red flags."

"Yes Sir, consider it done," said Greg.

Mr. Brooks hesitated a little before he added, "And though he's not an employee, I want you to start with my son. My gut instinct tells me that this may not be as serious as the Feds think and it may have something to do with Alex. Remember two years ago when he and his friends attempted to hack our system to prove themselves and uncover imagined vulnerabilities?"

"How could I forget? What a mess in spite of their failure."

"I know, that was a major headache for everyone and cost us big time. I have no idea what he may be up to now, it could be as simple as a practical joke or who knows what that kid might try for his own kicks. If he's behind this, I'm going to..." Mr. Brooks stopped himself as he realized that he was losing composure and felt his blood pressure beginning to rise. He calmed himself and continued, "Sorry Greg for getting ramped up. I'm under a bit more stress than usual."

"No problem, Mr. Brooks, I understand. By the way, did you mention your son to the FBI?"

"Yes, I did, and when they learned he was on a flight to Seoul, they lost their unflinching composure for a moment, just long enough to give me some alarm. They're on their way over to his mom's house to confiscate his computer. I think they know more than what they're telling me. Anyway, I want a report by ten tonight."

"I'll have it to you sooner than that."

CHAPTER 17

Alex woke up to the gentle voice of the flight attendant. They were nearing their destination. He had left Agnes hours before to eat dinner then nodded off into a deep sleep. The thirteen-hour flight went much quicker than he had anticipated, considering his struggle the first couple of hours. It was nearing midnight by Pacific Standard Time, but it was almost 4:00 PM in Seoul and they had jumped a day forward.

Before long, the plane taxied to the gate and Alex was especially glad to be one of the first to get off the plane. His team was scheduled to rendezvous with the film crew at a meeting area after customs and baggage claim. He was anxious to find out if his dad had come through with a phone. He got to his feet as soon as the seat belt light went off. With his backpack strapped on, he made his move with a determined pace for the exit. He thought about the film crew waiting for him and the likelihood of some exclusive footage of his arrival ahead of his peers. His daydreaming halted as the voice of Agnes interrupted his thoughts. He had unconsciously walked past her seat on his way towards the exit. He stopped abruptly, and looking back, he noticed her warm smile and an outstretched hand.

"I will be praying for you, Alexander, that this will be a trip of a lifetime."

He gave her a polite nod and couldn't hold back a restrained smile for the old woman who had found a small soft place in his jaded heart.

"Don't forget this, Alexander, it must have fallen out of your pocket." She handed him the small Bible again that he accidentally or intentionally left lying in the adjacent seat.

"Oh that. Thanks." He slipped it into his back pocket as he continued walking. It wouldn't be long before he would look back and regret not spending more time with her and giving a little more attention to her wisdom.

As Alex walked into the airport, it occurred to him that the basics of the Incheon Airport were not so foreign after all, but some of the details and the atmosphere were unique. He found himself getting excited for once about his new environment and not just the gaming competition. He walked slower than usual, distracted by his surroundings. The passengers filing past him were like a line of impatient drivers on Highway 101 trying to get around a timid driver holding up a lane. A few hurried passengers bumped into him before he finally snapped out of his first foreign moment of wonder. He got back to business.

He would normally be on his phone by now, sending text messages and taking selfies. Now that his phone was dead, he found himself taking in his surroundings as he walked. He noticed a lot of glass. Big windows let daylight flood the immaculate environment and revealed a blend of modern and ancient aspects of the Korean culture. He was amazed at all the live plants and flowers and water fountains intermingled with state of the art visual displays and other artistic attractions.

A rapidly increasing noise of traditional Asian music alerted Alex that he had wandered into the path of a reenactment. Actors and musicians played their part of the royal procession of a king, queen, and princess of the Joseon Dynasty. The unfolding scene captivated him as he drew aside and stopped to watch. He instinctively reached for his phone to take a picture but realized he would have to take a memory instead.

Finding the luggage claim area was not too complicated. The routine was similar to other airports: look for the signs with the baggage icon, walk towards the arrows, keep track of the signs, ride a moving walkway, take an escalator, walk some more, and success. Alex had been too lazy to pack a suitcase; he thought it would be easier to do some shopping after he arrived. This gave him a fast track to customs. Thanks to the flight attendant, his forms were filled out properly during the flight, so getting through customs went quickly. Afterwards, he took a short walk and escalator ride down to the passenger welcome area.

A large group of people were assembled behind a railing, most of them holding signs. He looked for the film crew but something unexpected caught his attention. In the front of the crowd, an Asian man standing in a tailored black suit held a digital tablet with bold white letters on a black background that read "ALEX BROOKS." He looked intently at Alex with an expression of recognition and seemed to be waiting for a response. Alex acknowledged him with a questioning look while pointing to himself to confirm that the sign was intended for him and not some other Alex Brooks. The man smiled and nodded, motioning him to come in his direction.

He guessed, *This must be the contact from my dad's office with my new phone.*

The man politely shook Alex's hand and in very broken English said, "Please follow me," and turned, starting off at a determined pace. He did not even look back to make sure Alex was following. Alex did follow, but not easily. The man was on a mission to get them through the remainder of the airport quickly. Alex attempted to ask him a couple of questions in his effort to keep up, but it became apparent that he was being ignored in their haste or that the man couldn't understand English. Alex expected him to lead him to the film crew so it surprised him when they went through a door leading to an outside curb. Before he could raise a protest, it suddenly became clear—a black Mercedes limousine waited for him at the curb and another man in a tailored suit stood at the rear passenger door.

Wow, I wasn't expecting this! Someone really came through. It must be Dad, Alex thought to himself.

A man opened the car door for him and motioned him inside. Alex still had a flood of questions in his mind, including his concerns about the missing film crew and his new phone but he figured he should just roll with it. Another man slid in behind him and shut the door while the limo took off.

The swirling questions in his mind came to an abrupt halt. Two men suddenly pinned Alex against his seat while a third quickly duct taped his mouth and secured his wrists together with large zip ties.

One man began patting him down while another grabbed his backpack, dumping the contents onto the limo floor. He quickly rifled through the pile and pulled out the laptop, the tablet, and the broken phone. They spoke to one another in a foreign language but Alex could discern that they were intent on the electronics. In a few seconds, his devices were dismantled with the objective of wresting the batteries out.

Alex, in a state of shock and unprepared mentally for this unexpected turn of events, didn't attempt any resistance. His fear and confusion paralyzed him more than the gag or the zip ties, and just as he was about to make an effort to snap out of his stupor, he felt a sting on his forearm, horrified to realize that he had just been stuck by a needle and injected with something. The pain that took the forefront of his thoughts quickly faded. His head started feeling strange, followed by a spinning sensation, and then all went dark. From that moment, Alex's world would be forever changed.

CHAPTER 18

Alex started regaining consciousness. He could not fully comprehend what had happened, where he was, or where he had been. He felt as if deep under water, only able to see light and shapes above him as he slowly rose towards the surface and muffled noises steadily became clearer. He heard the sound of the ocean and foreign voices mingled with the clamor of sea birds. Now he sensed ocean air and the strong smell of fish. In this state of slow awakening, he had a vague recollection of being on a plane but could not be certain of anything in his dazed mind. The drug used to knock him out finally wore off. He began taking note of his present reality.

The subtle and continual motion confirmed that he was in a boat on water. Small waves of water gently lapped against the side of the vessel. He lay in a small cabin and the boat seemed to be docked. There was a small door, which opened to the cockpit area, and Alex could see a couple of men loading supplies and paying no attention to him. They must have presumed that he was still unconscious.

Alex's storehouse of limited experiences had not prepared him to comprehend his situation except for the plain facts. He began to take inventory: someone tricked him, bound his hands, and drugged him.

I've been kidnapped!

The duct tape was no longer on his mouth but his wrists remained immobilized by the zip ties. It occurred to him that he had watched a ton of action movies with heroic characters who always figured some clever way out of their predicaments, but it didn't seem realistic in his situation. He knew how to fight his way through digital challenges, but this was real life.

I should think of something now that my head is clearing up.

So many other things were affecting his ability at present for focused thought. His whole body ached, especially his sore neck and wrists. He felt hungry and nauseous at the same time. His head throbbed with a dull headache and he felt terribly scared. He didn't feel like a heroic action hero but more like a helpless little boy who needed to be rescued.

The only idea that came to mind was to pretend to be unconscious until he could think of something better. A moment later, the men's voices became more distant and seemed to be on the dock rather than the boat.

If I'm going to do something, it should be now. But what if they are still on the boat but just out of my sight? What if I did something stupid and got myself into more trouble? Maybe there will be a better time later to make a move. What move anyway?

While these thoughts wrestled one another, each attempting to pin its opponent in his troubled mind, a small puny thought stepped into the ring and vanquished all others with a reasonable and safe idea. Alex studied the small cabin windows on each side, which might give him a little more scope to his situation if he would take this window of opportunity to make a move.

Yes, that should be safe.

He was lying down on a padded bench in the hull of the boat. Sitting up proved to be more challenging and painful than he anticipated. He guessed that this might be only a brief opportunity. Adrenaline started to kick in while he propped himself up and staggered to his feet. He let out an audible groan as his body recoiled in pain and his rubbery legs gave way under him. Thankfully, the area was so small that there was no room to fall far and he kept himself propped up.

I'm glad my hands are tied in front and not behind my back.

He moved his face carefully towards the closest window and did his best to take in the limited view. He couldn't see much, the window was cloudy from being exposed to the salty spray of the ocean. He could see that the boat was in a harbor with a variety of other fishing boats. He stumbled to the other window in hope of discovering more, but no luck. He kept his ear tuned to the faint sound of the voices, which hadn't changed.

So far, so good.

Then he noticed a hatch above him that opened to the front deck of the boat. He wondered if he should stand on the couch and try sticking his head through the open hatch or try peering out the open cabin door. Both options scared him.

What if they saw me? What will happen?

The hatch was closer and he mustered some courage to go for it. The cockpit blocked his view of the dock towards the stern. It was a closed cockpit and had a flybridge above that. To his right and left, he had a better view of the line of boats and the environment. It was an eclectic mix of normal looking boats and a lot of rustic but brightly painted boats that seemed to Alex to belong to another century. The nicer boats looked like commercial sport fishing boats ranging from thirty to fifty feet in length with variations of cockpits and bridge decks.

The letters on the boats were recognizable but the spellings were not readable. Many of the rustic boats had foreign lettering that didn't appear to be Asian. These letters were more squiggly looking to Alex. In small letters under the name of the boat closest to him he read "Manado, Sulawesi." Alex didn't know the fifty States in the US and his geography knowledge beyond his native soil was woefully limited. He wasn't sure if Manado, Sulawesi was a place or the name of the boat. For all he knew, it might be the captain's name.

If he could have Googled it, he would have learned about the island of Sulawesi about three thousand miles south of Seoul, South Korea. It was part of the Indonesian archipelago consisting of seventeen thousand islands, a region once known as the Dutch East Indies or the Spice Islands. He knew none of this. If he knew how far he was from Seoul, he would have been dumbfounded by how he got there.

He shifted around to look towards the front of the boat and could see a wide bay opening to the ocean, flanked by a lush and mountainous landscape. There were a few of the crazy looking boats coming and going. A faint view of the people on them gave Alex the impression of a third world environment.

He heard the sound of the voices getting louder and dropped back down to the couch in panic, pretending to be unconscious. He was just in time. The activity continued on the rear deck of the boat and Alex heard steps coming closer. His heart pounded harder as a man peered into the cabin to check on him. Alex held his breath and exhaled with relief when the man went back to the cockpit and barked a few foreign words to the others. How many others? Alex couldn't tell. He thought he identified at least three different voices communicating back and forth.

A shock jolted Alex as he heard the sound and felt the vibrations of multiple outboard engines starting. The distinct smell of diesel fuel began wafting into the cabin and overriding the embedded smell of fish. He had no inner courage to attempt anything other than to lie there and wait— await what? He couldn't imagine. He couldn't hold back the tears that began welling up in his closed eyes as a new unknown terror gripped him and he had no mental resources to act.

CHAPTER 19

Allison would not have been able to sleep if she had wanted to. The visit from the FBI and the confiscation of Alex's computer rattled her despite the agent's efforts to assure her that it wasn't anything to be worried about, just protocol.

She planned to stay up until the plane landed and anxiously kept checking the flight status online, hoping that Alex would reach out to her. She had sent him a text apologizing for the morning mishap and asked him to call as soon as he arrived. She refreshed the webpage and her heart skipped with anticipation as the status indicated that the plane had landed. She knew Alex would turn his phone on immediately and check his messages. Hers would be only one of many. She waited a couple more minutes and began to grow more anxious, trying to downplay his silence with imagined excuses for the delay.

Ten minutes passed. *Is Alex still angry with me and intentionally ignoring me?* The thought cut deeply and she felt her heart aching under this unknown weight. After fifteen minutes, she couldn't bear it any longer and called his number, it went straight to voicemail. In the tumult of the day, she had completely forgotten about the other three onboard and her sudden re-awareness of their existence and proximity to Alex gave her hope of reaching him through them. She knew well enough that they would not willingly be in collusion with him against her. She sent a group text asking them if the flight went well and if any of them could ask Alex to give her a call.

What a relief when she started receiving a barrage of messages about

Alex's broken phone, the long flight, and their excitement about being in Seoul. They hadn't seen Alex because first class had already deplaned and they were still waiting to get off. They assured her that they would tell him to call as soon as they found him. If he didn't have his new phone yet, he could use one of theirs.

Allison was elated. Tears of relief were streaming down her cheeks from this revelation about Alex's phone. The emotional turmoil of the day acted like a clogged kitchen drain that caused dirty sink water to back up until the obstruction was removed. She thought she could lay down on the couch for a few minutes to rest until he called, certain everything was okay now. She quickly drifted off into a deep sleep.

CHAPTER 20

Allison dreamt about her son. In most dreams, very few things would make sense if you were reading about it or watching it on a screen while awake. This dream was different. Alex sat with her in the coffee shop, angry and not wanting to talk. She tried to get his attention by texting him but that didn't work, so she tried calling him but he wouldn't answer. He ignored the calls and turned his back to her. Just then, the two FBI agents walked in through the front door and grabbed Alex, put him in handcuffs, and started dragging him away. Alex turned to her and cried out, "Help, Mom! I'm sorry! Please don't let them take me! Help me!"

She couldn't speak. She couldn't move. She tried to say something but she could only make a deep throaty groan, like trying to talk with a mouth full of cotton balls. She reached for her phone to try and call Alex again as they escorted him through the door and out of sight. She could hear his phone ringing and noticed it sitting on the table in front of her. It kept ringing and she didn't know what to do. Suddenly, the dream faded as she started coming to a groggy consciousness with some faint comprehension that something was actually ringing. *An alarm clock? No! Oh, my phone!* She fumbled in her dazed state to find it lying on the floor. She didn't check the contact information, "Alex, is that you?"

"Miss Brooks? No, this is Paige"

"Why hasn't Alex called?"

"We don't know. We haven't found him. Nobody has seen him. We are here at the meeting area with the camera crew but they got here late.

We were waiting for a while before they arrived. We don't know what to do now."

"Have you asked for help from the airline in case he is in a lounge somewhere or getting a bite to eat?"

"Yes, they said that he got off the plane and they have paged him several times. He didn't check any luggage."

"It could be that!" said Allison. "He intended to do some shopping so he might be in and out of the airport stores."

Paige posed a suggestion somewhat hesitantly, "We thought that maybe you could call his dad to see if he knows anything. He was supposed to send someone to the airport to meet Alex with a new phone."

Allison thought out loud, "I don't know why I hadn't thought of that— he would be anxious to get his phone and hopefully his dad has the new number, which I'll need anyway. But if he has his phone, why wouldn't he call?"

"Well, he may not have anyone's number unless they were able to load his contacts to his new phone," said Paige.

"I hadn't thought of that either," said Allison. "So let's not panic…yet, just stay put for a little longer and I'll get back to you."

"Okay, but no one is in a panic, we're just tired and want to get to the hotel. Bye."

Allison hesitated for a moment before calling her ex-husband. They had very little interaction and the awkwardness of calling him at such a late hour made her uncomfortable, but it couldn't be helped. She tried her best to keep calm and rational and to convince herself that this was just an unfortunate misunderstanding on Alex's part about his responsibility to meet up with the team. As she thought about talking to his dad, she knew she couldn't even hint that it might be Alex's irresponsibility that had put them in this uncomfortable position so she would play it cool. *After all*, she thought, *this one phone call might clear up everything in one moment, it's worth the awkwardness.*

The number rang and rang and rang, then went to voicemail. She chided herself, *What made me think he would have his phone on this late? He's probably in a deep sleep with his phone turned off and completely ignorant of his son's whereabouts.* Before she could nurse her frustration any longer her phone rang.

"Hello Alex," she said timidly.

"This is unexpected. Is something wrong?" He said this in that unmistakably slow and distant way that people talk when woken from sleep just moments before.

"I hope not but I can't get ahold of Alex. The plane landed over an hour ago but nobody has seen or heard from him. The kids told me that you were getting him a replacement phone and I hoped you might have the new number so I could call or text him."

Mr. Brooks was silent for a moment, seeming to process the information, "Hmmm, I'm sorry to say that I don't know. I'm assuming my contact in Seoul has followed through but I didn't think to have him forward me the new number. I'll have to make a phone call and get back to you."

Allison was afraid to ask him if he planned on doing that right away so she just said, "Oh okay. I'll just wait to hear from you." And then she bravely added, "I hope you hear from someone soon, I'm really worried about Alex; I know he's probably fine but it's my mothering instinct I guess and—"

"I'm sure he's fine, I'll call you back soon," said Mr. Brooks.

"Bye," said Allison, but he had already ended the call. She now recalled the disturbing dream and her compounding anxiety was fueled. Her stomach took the brunt of that nervousness and she dashed off to the bathroom.

She eventually made her way to the kitchen to boil some water and steep some herbal tea, hoping to soothe her churning stomach. The dream still haunted her and her uneasiness increased. *Maybe I should call Paige back though I don't know what to tell her. Talking to someone would be better than pacing around.*

She inadvertently left her phone on the couch when making her mad dash earlier. When she finally sat down with her mug of hot tea and reached for the phone, she was surprised to see her notifications, "Two missed calls? How is that possible?" talking out loud in frustration to herself.

The first call was from Paige and the other from her ex. She was stuck for a moment not knowing what to do first, listen to the messages or just call back? And who to call first? She impulsively dialed Mr. Brooks first—no answer, just straight to voicemail. So she called Paige—no answer, just voicemail. "Ughhhhhhhh!" she vented and then listened to the messages starting with the one from Mr. Brooks.

"Hi Allison, my contact arrived at the airport shortly after the plane landed and waited for Alex with the new phone but he has not been able to make contact with him yet. I've asked him to talk with airport officials and track him down immediately. Who knows what he's up to but he has to be in the airport somewhere. You'll probably be hearing from him soon, I'll make sure he gets his phone and your number." His tone sounded perturbed—at their son, no doubt.

Paige's message was not helpful either. "Hi Miss Brooks, there's still no sign of Alex. We ran into the man who brought Alex's new phone and he has left to go talk with the airport people to get some help finding Alex. We are really, really tired and bored so the film team is going to send us to the hotel so we can check in and they will send the camera guy with us to get some B-roll, and then he'll join the rest of his crew back at the airport which they say is not far away. They plan to get an interview with Alex about his stupid antics that have inconvenienced everyone. I'm going to crash when I get to the hotel so I won't be answering my phone, but I'm sure Alex will call you once they find him. Bye."

Allison didn't know what to think. *Is my son really being a jerk like everyone assumes?* Her instinct unnerved her with a sense that something was wrong. *It could be a mother's irrational worry,* she thought. *What else can I do now but wait? Hopefully not much longer.*

CHAPTER 21

What's happening?

Paralyzing fear made it hard for Alex to ask that question in his mind, much less ask the other men in the boat. He couldn't avoid several more frightening questions, which seemed so bizarre to be asking himself: *Have I been kidnapped? Am I a hostage? Is this like one of those ransom stories unfolding?* He tried to think of alternatives. *This can't be a prank, it's too cruel.* He agonized with the thought, *Is someone going to rescue me out of this? Who will help me?*

The other thought vying for attention kept gnawing at him, *Should I just take a bold step and ask the men on the boat?* The increasing agony of not knowing became more of a burden than his fear of asking. He decided to sit up and see what would happen. The others in the boat didn't pay any attention to him. He again thought to himself, *What if I just step out of the cabin? What if I just ask them?*

He stood up and shuffled slowly to the open door. The movement of the boat on the ocean caused his legs to be more wobbly than they already were and he held himself up by leaning into the doorway. The pilot at the controls of the boat ignored him. He could see two more men sitting towards the back of the boat. They observed Alex but didn't react, which gave him a little more courage.

"I was wondering—" he began to ask but his voice was hardly audible to himself over the noise of the boat and his throat and mouth were dry and constrained. He realized he would have to try and shout but he didn't feel he had enough strength. He had gone this far, he decided to make a second effort and raise his voice. "I was wondering if you could…" he hesitated for a few seconds, "if you could give me something to eat?" His voice trailed off on his last few words as he ran out of energy.

It wasn't his intended question. He chickened out and felt he needed to break the ice.

They didn't respond. They were looking at him but Alex had a hard time reading their foreign expressions. They couldn't seem to make out what he was saying or they didn't care.

He tried again, "Can you speak English?"

One of the men got up and moved towards him in order to hear him better. "What you said?"

"Oh good, you speak English." Alex was relieved to get that question out of the way. He didn't mind broken English as long as they could understand each other.

"Eh, I speak a language, only me, no them. What you said?"

Alex got the gist of his question. "I said I'm hungry, do you have any food?"

He nodded yes, "Go and I will get for you," as he pointed inside the cabin.

None of these men appeared to be the ones from the airport. Their faces looked different in origin and there were certainly no tailored suits. They didn't seem to be threatening or mysterious but at ease in their boat. Alex felt somewhat relieved as he turned around and made the few steps back to the couch.

Maybe there isn't anything to be afraid of after all.

The man came back with a bottle of water and a bowl containing cold rice with pieces of cooked fish and some spices. Alex was glad to have some food but the man neglected to bring him a fork or spoon.

"Do you have a spoon?" said Alex while making a motion with his hand to the bowl as if he was using a spoon.

The man was confused for a moment then seemed to understand his request.

"You have already," and held up his fingers.

Now it was Alex's turn to look confused. The man reached down, grabbed some rice in his hand, and put it in his own mouth then said, "You have already. See!"

"Oh okay." Alex was disgusted at the idea of eating this way but his hunger prevailed. The man turned to walk out and Alex stopped him, "Wait! I have another question."

The man stopped and looked back.

"Can you take the ties off?" as he held up his fettered hands.

The man shook his head no.

Alex decided to ask his most feared question, "Well, can you tell me what's going on? Why am I here? Where are you taking me?"

The man didn't hesitate giving an answer, "Camping."

"Camping?"

CHAPTER 22

"What do you mean he's missing?"

Mr. Brooks was on the phone with Min-jun, his South Korean business contact. It had been more than two hours since he showed up at the airport with the phone and still no sign of Alex. Airport security had been alerted and the next step would be to file an official missing person report, which would get local authorities involved and also alert the US Embassy.

"What would you like me to do?" asked Min-jun.

Mr. Brooks didn't know. Part of him struggled with anger and certainty that this was a result of some irresponsible foolishness. His son would likely show up soon with his cavalier attitude, blaming someone else and expecting everyone to cater to his every whim. *But what if I'm wrong?* he pondered. *What if something is wrong?* It seemed so unlikely to him. *But what if?*

"Min-jun, can you wait a little longer?" said Mr. Brooks.

"Of course."

"I'll call you back in fifteen minutes with a decision."

Mr. Brooks needed to stall while he sorted through the tumble of emotions and provoking thoughts. It had been a long time since he had any personal thoughts that involved Allison beyond the necessary interactions about their son. He had an uncomfortable feeling of wishing he wasn't alone in making a decision. He was generally confident and unflinching when it came to business relationships, but for some reason, his impenetrable fortress of self-assurance experienced an unexpected breach. He rarely thought about life without Allison. He convinced himself years before that the relationship was a dead end for both of them, but at a vulnerable time like this, loneliness found a way to escape from its dungeon of suppression. It now intruded into a space in his life that he kept off limits.

He seriously thought about calling Allison for her input but his pride couldn't bear the idea for long. *Besides*, he thought, *she would be too easily convinced that something was wrong and not even try to be rational or consider that Alex might be the only factor to something gone wrong.*

A switch in his mind flipped and he was back to himself again. *No, I won't call and I won't entertain any notion other than the fact that Alex will show up soon and have some stupid explanation, or worse yet, not bother giving an explanation.* He called Min-jun back.

"I've decided to wait this out a little longer. Alex is in the airport somewhere and he'll show up sooner or later. He can't live much longer without a phone so he'll be looking for you."

CHAPTER 23

The foreign man attempted to answer Alex's question about this supposed camping trip that appeared more like a kidnapping in Alex's mind.

"Somebodies want you gone for two weeks and then we get you back."

"Who wants me to be gone?"

"Don't know. We are hired for big monies. They want no questions."

"Why are my hands tied?" said Alex.

"You might give trouble so we wait until the island."

"What island?"

The man smiled at this question and let out a short laugh, "Hah, you do not know anything. Many, many islands all around us. We are finding a lone one in time. Nobodies living on many islands. Are good to get away and nobodies know."

He continued his questions since the strange man seemed to be free with giving out information. "So you don't know who hired you to take me away?"

The man shook his head no.

"What are you planning to do for two weeks?" said Alex.

"Stay far from troubles."

"Will you take the ties off when we get to the island?"

"Yes, if you make no troubles. We get you back and we are paid more monies."

"But I can make sure you are paid more than what you were offered if

67

you take me back! My father is very rich and he will pay you much more! If you only take me back right now."

The man looked very soberly at Alex, "You are not knowing much. We all die if we do not keep the contract."

"But you will have so much money you can just leave your country and go somewhere else and whoever hired you will never know," said Alex. He did his best to try and convince him.

The man scowled, "You are not knowing anything. You do not know about powerful men who always know how to find somebodies. We would all die." He was unyielding and seemed perturbed by Alex's appeal.

Alex could sense a change of demeanor in the man so he backed off a little and changed his questioning. "What's your name?"

"Hariyono"

"Hariyono, okay. So when do we get there? At the island?"

"It may be soon but not today. Night will come soon and we take care to land on island in daytimes."

"Can I come out of the cabin for now and look around?" Alex wanted some fresh air.

Hariyono didn't like that question and gave him a stern answer, "No!" and left the cabin.

Alex's gnawing hunger compelled him to eat the rice no matter what it tasted like, but to his surprise, he actually liked it. What he didn't like was using his fingers, he felt uncivilized and it was challenging to manage the task with his hands bound. As he ate, he tried to analyze Hariyono and decide if he was safe and reasonable or if he was really villainous and capable of doing harm if push came to shove. He seemed to lean towards the second idea. *I don't trust him, why should I?* Alex wondered if Hariyono knew more details than he was letting on.

He felt certain that every effort was being made to find him and he wouldn't be surprised if a helicopter came swooping in at any moment with a team of Navy SEALs. He noticed that Hariyono had a pistol in a holster on his belt and assumed that the others had weapons also. *It is probably best that I stay in the cabin in case there's a shootout.*

He had troubling doubts about the possibility of a ransom demand. He wished he could be certain that his dad would pay whatever was asked. *After all*, he thought, *a son is surely more important than money.* So he hoped.

After his meal, and the much needed bottle of water, he felt unusually tired and decided to lay down again. It was hard to get comfortable with the constraint of the ties, not to mention another strange occurrence causing him a little discomfort—the little Bible from Agnes was still in his back pocket. He had no desire to try and fish it out but it was a small comfort to him that it was there. It baffled him that it had been left alone or ignored by his captors. He thought of it now as a good luck charm. This ordeal would all be over soon and maybe he could still attend the gaming competition. It would definitely be some good press for their show once he was rescued.

Chapter 24

"Ughhhhhh! I can't believe that man! That insensible blockhead!" Allison just hung up after a brief call from Mr. Brooks. She vented in her mind, *At times like this, I regret not changing my name back to Griswold!*

Alex voiced his resolution to let their son fend for himself since he was so thoughtless and inconsiderate of others. He even sent Min-jun home with instructions to leave a short note and the cellphone with airport security.

Her infuriation dissolved quickly to make room for her motherly worries now teetering on the brink of panic. *Something is wrong and someone needs to do something, but what?* She thought about the two FBI agents and the card they had left with her. *Would they take this seriously? It is doubtful that they would be answering a phone in the middle of the night. I could at least leave a message,* so she started there. She also left a message with her boss and tried reaching the Incheon Airport security and US Consulate in Seoul without success. Then the waiting game began. It felt like the longest night of her life, a life inevitably changing as the night unfolded but she had yet to comprehend it. She was only aware of her fear, anxiety, and sense of hopelessness. Allison spent the rest of the dreary night checking on possible flights to Seoul. *If nobody is going to do anything, then I will try.*

Morning dawned without news of Alex's whereabouts. The surreal revelation that something had gone very wrong began to embed in the fresh cement of her soul, mixed and poured in the last twenty-four hours. *My son is really missing.* And just as the sun began waking the birds, some bleak hope rose when her phone began to ring.

"Hello Miss Brooks? This is Agent Hutchins from the FBI."

"Yes, you got my message?"

"Yes, we did and we have already started an investigation into the disappearance of your son. We are considering this a high profile missing person case."

"Is my son in danger?"

"At this point, we only know that he is missing."

"But how? Why? Will he be alright?"

"Miss Brooks, we don't have any of those answers at this time, but we are taking this with utmost seriousness."

"I'm sorry, I've had a long restless night."

"Would you be able to stop by our offices in Los Angeles later this morning? We would like to get as much information about Alex as possible. You are our greatest source of details since he lives with you."

"Yes, I can come."

"We would like you to bring a thumb drive with recent photos. We already have a copy of his passport photo, driver's license, and images off his social networks, but you might have something more suitable."

Allison arranged to stop by around 11:00 that morning to give her time to make a couple more critical calls to her boss and the program crew. She hoped to have some time to spare to rest a little before trying to drive anywhere with her sleep deprived body and unstable state of mind.

Her phone rang again. She could see on the screen that the number was Mr. Brooks. She resisted the strong temptation to let it go to voicemail in disdain for him. *But what if he has news of Alex?* She answered, but not warmly.

"Hello?"

"Allison, look…I don't know how to say this…"

Her heart began to sink as he continued, "I made a bad call on this one—I was wrong. I should have taken this more seriously." There was a silent pause before he finished with, "I'm sorry."

This admission stunned Allison. Mr. Brooks, the man who never admitted being wrong and who never apologized for anything. A small trickle of tears followed the established path of their recent predecessors, but these were unique in their chemistry. They were part shock at the unexpected apology, part heartache from the sincere tone of concern in his voice, and part anguish with yet one more confirmation that something terrible was happening beyond their control. She was struck silent for a moment before giving way to uncontrollable sobs.

"Hello Allison? Are you still there?"

"Yes…I'm still here."

"Look, I'm really shaken by this. And I'm terribly sorry if I…if I was not thinking as clearly as I should have. I realized that if I'm this troubled, how must you feel? I was hoping you wouldn't mind if I stopped by and picked you up since we both need to go to the FBI office. I'm on my way to the airport to pick up the next flight to LA and I have a car waiting for me. I probably had a little more sleep than you did…plus, I would really like to talk."

Allison could hardly believe her ears. She had trouble sorting through her mixed bag of emotions and couldn't discern if this would be helpful or a really bad idea. *This is my son's dad, and if anyone could sympathize with my fear and anxiety, why shouldn't I find some solace in sharing his own turmoil?* But this was truly out of character for her ex-husband and might only be a flickering moment that would quickly burn out and just bring more regret and heartache. *What right does he have to come waltzing in during this crisis and start pretending to care for my feelings?* Allison worked hard to convince herself that Alex was totally blind to his own self-deceived notion of concern for her. And yet she considered the remote possibility that she judged him wrongly and this emergence of civility revealed a genuine breakthrough. She questioned her own prejudices, *Is this reason to hope or a potentially disastrous step that would tear open old scars and pour salt into fresh wounds?*

She felt a twinge of guilt from diverting the smallest amount of anxiety away from her missing son as if it would place him in peril and disrupt the efforts to find him. She not only became strangely angry with herself but also with her ex.

"I'll have to call you back with an answer." And hung up.

CHAPTER 25

Allison couldn't bring herself to call Alex back just yet so she sent a text. "I'll be ready at 10:30 if you still want to ride together."

He responded immediately, "I'll be there."

She looked at the clock and realized that she didn't have much time to get ready. She found herself surprisingly frustrated with what to wear, what to do with her hair, and wondering if she had enough time to do her nails. *But why does this all matter? My son is missing.* She felt guilty and tried to chase her insecurities out of her mind. But it wasn't that simple, she and Alex had not seen each other for over a year. He usually hired a driver to get his son for visitations and his personal assistant handled all of the necessary communications. It would be an awkward meeting, but they had at least one thing in common now, something stronger than the innumerable forces keeping them apart.

She couldn't explain it but she really needed her ex-husband right now, regardless of his years of neglect and living in the lonely shadows of his self-centered focus on business. She determined to bury the past for the time being and sign a ceasefire treaty in her heart.

CHAPTER 26

Mr. Brooks pulled up to the curb in a rental car. Allison watched for him and wasted no time getting out the door to meet him. She needed his presence but she wondered, *Does he need mine?*

She opened the passenger door and witnessed a sight she had never seen. He had clearly been crying. She had spent the last ten minutes before he arrived thinking about what she would say to him and what he might say to her. Now she realized that words would be too difficult right now. He couldn't raise his eyes to her. He gripped the steering wheel with both hands as if it kept him from falling over. His head bent downward with an expression of despair. Allison slipped into the seat. She couldn't help feeling overwhelmed with a strange compassion for this man whom she formerly despised. His apparent grief for their son touched her. She leaned towards him and put an arm across his slumped shoulders. He burst into a fresh sob at this gesture of tenderness towards him.

"I'm sorry, I'm so sorry," he said, his broken voice was barely audible.

Now Allison was crying and she didn't try to pull herself together. They momentarily shared their common grief over their missing son until the wave of emotion finished crashing upon their shore and subsided, leaving a shallow wake.

They sat together in silence as their hearts and minds calmed down. It began to reach an awkward stage and they both knew that one or the other needed to break the silence. It seemed to each that they would be trespassing on sacred ground.

Allison's gentle voice tiptoed into that delicate space. "I guess we should go to our meeting now."

"Yes, you're right," said Alex.

They were not only free to start driving but also found themselves free to start talking. It helped Alex to be occupied with driving but it didn't keep him from glancing from time to time at his former wife as they made their way to the FBI office.

"I'm really scared," said Allison. "I've had an uneasy feeling about this trip before he left and I pushed it back in my mind. Where could Alex be?"

"I don't know. We have the best people working on our behalf. I'm sure they will find him soon."

"Do they have any idea, any clues to his whereabouts?" said Allison.

He struggled again to keep his composure and had to wrestle the next words out of his mouth. "I received an update on my flight here…" he stalled. He had something bottled up that was too hard to get out. Allison just stared with panic on her face, reading something ominous in his unspoken words. He took the nearest exit and pulled into a convenient store lot to park for a moment and try to get his words out.

"They've got security footage from the airport." His hands gripped the wheel again as his head went down. He struggled to continue. He seemed to be choking on his words. "The footage shows him following someone out of the airport—and—and then getting into a limousine."

"A limousine? What limousine? Whose limousine? Who was he following?"

"They don't know the identity of the other men in the video, but they said Alex voluntarily followed the man but showed signs of confusion…"

"How many men? Who were they? Did they get the license plate number?"

"No, they don't know anything else. I mean, yes, they have security footage of the license plate but it's not a registered plate."

Allison could tell there was more he needed to say and she could hardly bear what he had said already. "Alex, you have to tell me! There's something else, isn't there? What do you know?"

"I'm so sorry."

"Tell me! I have to know. You've got to tell me!" she said.

Alex swallowed hard, "The FBI are almost certain he—he has been—abducted."

"No! No! No! No! No! This can't be!" Allison slapped the dashboard repeatedly, an outburst full of fear, anxiety, and anger. "This can't be happening! Oh please, please tell me they are going to find him and save him. What do they want with him? They will find him won't they? Alex, please tell me."

"Yes, yes, they will find him, of course. The FBI thinks we will hear from them soon."

"You mean a ransom?"

"Yes, they think they are likely holding him for ransom."

"You'll pay it of course. Won't you?"

"Yes, of course, there's no question about that; whatever they ask, I'll pay it. I just want him home safe."

Now that this great burden was off his chest, he could speak a little more freely as he explained his earlier conversations with the FBI, but it became apparent to Allison that another shoe was about to drop. It did.

"Allison, it's possible that they don't want money."

"What do you mean?"

"It's possible that they want the plans to my technology."

She burst out in a crying rage, "No! No! No! I can't believe this! You and your stupid technology! You've ruined us! You've ruined our family and now our son. What have you done to my son? God help us!"

CHAPTER 27

The remaining drive for Alex and Allison was as cold and silent as a graveyard. The only sounds were stifled sobs from Allison. She had no more energy to give vent to the emotional flurry inside. Each suppressed cry cut Mr. Brooks to the heart. *How can I ever redeem myself from this? I'm a terrible person, I've really blown it this time.*

Arriving at the FBI office, they pulled themselves together as best as could be expected. Allison wouldn't speak a word to Alex or even look at him. They entered the building, got through the security screening, and were ushered into a small meeting room.

Agent Hutchins greeted them with a somber tone as they sat down together at a table. An awkward silence hung in the room for a moment as they experienced a moment of paralysis brought on by a mixture of fear, anxiety, questions, regrets, and confusion. They needed to hear something hopeful. Hope that the government would have quick success at the recovery of their son at all costs.

"Have you found him yet?" asked Allison. "What can you tell us?"

Hutchins looked to Mr. Brooks. "Does she know what I have already shared with you?"

"Yes, I told her what I know. Is there anything new?"

"I'm afraid there's nothing new."

"What are you going to do?" said Allison.

"First of all, we will be able to work best if the news media stays ignorant, but we cannot guarantee it won't get out."

"But how?" she said.

"With all of our expertise, that is the greatest unsolved mystery," said Agent Hutchins. "There are a thousand ways these things get out. You have people watching both of your lives. Do you usually go places together? Do you make regular visits to our offices? Are you usually out of your office and not answering your phones? The slightest tip and the news hounds find ways through small cracks like cockroaches. Brace yourself, it's not if but when the story breaks. And when that happens, it's ten times more challenging for all of us."

"Understood," said Mr. Brooks. They both nodded their heads in agreement.

"Do you have anything hopeful for us?" he asked.

"Our online agent has been contacted for a virtual meeting tonight. We expect to receive the ransom terms and instructions. This is very complicated business because we do not give in to ransoms and it is against federal law for you to pay a ransom."

"What? That's ludicrous! Alex, tell them you'll pay, they can't stop you!"

"You didn't give her that information?" said Hutchins.

Mr. Brooks swallowed hard, bent his head down as his voice cracked, "No. No, I didn't."

"Alex, this can't be true! This is unbelievable"

"Miss Brooks, if ransoms are paid, then it would foster more abductions. Not paying ransoms is one of the greatest deterrents," said Hutchins.

"Then why would they take my son hostage?" her voice rising in anger and frustration as she shot incredulous looks at both men.

"They know US policy but they also know that some people will break the law and go out on their own."

Allison shot an inquisitive glance at Alex to see if she could read his expression

"So you sacrifice a seventeen-year-old innocent boy on the altar of US policy to appease yourselves?"

"Allison, they're not against us, they're here to help us."

She broke down in sobs, "Then how will you save my son?"

"That's why we asked you to come. In half an hour, we will be joining our regional director who will help assemble a special team consisting of the Critical Incident Response Group, Crisis Negotiation Unit, Legal Attaché, and Hostage Rescue Team."

"What does that mean?" she asked.

"It means, short of paying the ransom, we will do whatever it takes to get your son back safely and apprehend the perpetrators. *'Pax per conloquium'* is the unit motto—'resolution through dialogue.' Less than twenty percent of our resolutions are strictly tactical."

"Who are these villains?" asked Allison.

"We don't know yet, and we may not know until we apprehend them."

"But how?" she asked.

"The catch is that they often require the ransom to be in hand before releasing a hostage. It's an intricately choreographed dance and each is trying to lead. We will gather as much intelligence as possible during the negotiation process."

"What are you negotiating if you don't pay the ransom?"

"We make sure they believe we are considering making an exception to the general rule."

"Don't they know you are lying? Won't that put my son in greater danger? What is your success rate anyway with this approach?" she asked.

That seemed to be the question he didn't want to be asked and didn't want to answer. Allison picked up on it immediately. She slapped her hand repeatedly on the desk in vehemence as she cried. "You're not going to do this and let my son be killed!"

Mr. Brooks scooted his chair a little closer and tried to put an arm around her but she snapped. "Don't touch me! Don't you dare touch me!"

He recoiled as if he had accidentally touched the hot burner of a stove. She stood up, stormed out of the office, then stopped in the lobby and collapsed into a chair for a good cry.

Mr. Brooks gave Agent Hutchins a perplexed look. "I'll go try and help her calm down before the meeting starts." And left to join Allison in the lobby.

CHAPTER 28

"Mr. Brooks, Miss Brooks, we're here to explain the precarious path ahead of us in the recovery of your son," said Special Agent York, leader of the Crisis Negotiation Unit. They were joined by other key agents from the Critical Incident Response Group, liaisons from the Legal Attaché, the FBI Cyber Division, a representative from the US Department of State, another from the Pentagon, and the commander of the Hostage Rescue Team. Agent Hutchins and his partner, Davidson, sat on each side of the parents.

"Allison and I are in agreement that I will pay their ransom as long as we can be assured of his safe return."

"The solution to this problem goes beyond the thought of paying ransoms," said Agent York. "An exchange must take place, which usually means that once a deal is made, a location will need to be revealed. Once we know the location, our first priority is recovering the victim safely on our own terms."

"But don't they know you will try to get our son without giving them what they want?" said Allison.

"Miss Brooks, we must assume that they are trying to get what they want without ever releasing your son. This is very much like a game of chess, but we've played the game more often than they have, and as long as we are one or more moves ahead of them, we have a chance of getting your son back, but you'll need to trust our process."

"How can we be certain that Alex is alright and will be kept safe?" she asked.

"The first step is for us to refuse all negotiations until we have proof of his well-being. They must give real-time evidence that your son is alive and well. If we are lucky, they will tip their hand and we can start zeroing in on where they are holding him. We don't think they remained in South Korea."

"Where do you think he might be?" said Allison.

"We don't know. It could be North Korea, Russia, China, it's impossible to say. They seem to be an extremely savvy group, most likely connected with organized crime."

"Then maybe they have played this chess game more than you know," said Mr. Brooks.

"Possibly. We don't know. But back to our plan of action. The perpetrators have contacted Mr. Brooks through his office with instructions for a virtual meeting tonight on the Dark Web; he has given us permission to act as his proxy, especially since this is a cyber contact. It is likely that they will lay out the details of their ransom demands. We will expect proof of Alex's safety before going any further with negotiations. We believe their priority will be to keep him hidden from all possible attempts of a tactical recovery. We will have our best hackers working during the meeting tonight in the hope of decrypting the path and tracing the origin of the connection but the Darknet's anonymity structure of layered encryption is extremely difficult to crack. There are various special ops team stationed around the world on the alert and ready to deploy if we do get a location tonight."

"Excuse me, what is a tactical recovery?" said Allison.

Hutchins turned to her and explained, "That is when they send in a SWAT team and retrieve him by force if necessary."

"But why play this game when we are ready to give them what they want and be done with it. We just want our son back safe. Just tell them we are ready to meet their demands, give them my cellphone number for all I care," said Mr. Brooks.

"They certainly already have that, Mr. Brooks, if they wanted to call you directly, but they won't; we could trace the call within a reasonable distance throughout most of the globe and they know it," said Agent York.

"You're missing my point. Let's just give them what they want so they will release Alex. How difficult can that be?"

The room was deathly silent for a moment while the numerous personnel in the meeting room exchanged glances with each other. Agent Hutchins turned to Alex, "It is more difficult than you realize. Let's just say we told them tonight that we are going to upload the blueprints and processes of your Mockingbird project to them. They will be cautious and look for any Trojan Horses, Backdoors, or Malware embedded in the file. How long do you think that will take them on a file as large as this would be? And then they are likely going to wait to release Alex until they can authenticate the plans you send as genuine and complete. If they release him—"

"But that would take weeks, possibly months, or more! That would leave Alex vulnerable to them without any incentive to return him," said Mr. Brooks.

"Now you are beginning to understand this catch twenty-two," said Agent York. "They will try and assure you that they mean no harm to him unless you fail to follow through. Then they will promise to keep their word as long as you keep yours. But remember, they are professional criminals; they don't play nice and they almost always have their fingers crossed behind their backs.

"We can't imagine any possible scenario that will work as a simple hand-off exchange. Even if they wanted cash, they would want to take the time to make sure it was authentic and unmarked, but this demand is a thousand times more complex. We are guessing that they will expect you to trust them during the time it takes to verify any delivery and then promise to drop Alex off at some distant location and then tell us where."

Allison and Mr. Brooks both absorbed the raw truth of the situation and realized their own plight and their son's dangerous position.

"It seems hopeless," said Allison. She put her head down into her folded arms at the table.

"We are sorry that we can't put a brighter outlook on this for you. It is better you understand the stakes and realize they are not in your son's favor," said Hutchins.

"But what if we call their game and refuse to give them anything unless we have Alex back home alive?" asked Mr. Brooks.

"You will likely never see your son again," said Agent York.

"So are you advocating that we give them what they want and hope against hope to eventually get our son back after weeks or months of them testing the information? Whatever they think they know about Mockingbird, they obviously don't know enough. If they had the entire set of plans, explanations of the processes, and access to the extremely specialized equipment, it could take a year to have their first fully functioning prototype. It took us much longer and we knew what we were doing. Why can't they just ask for money?"

"To answer your question, no, we are not advocating you give them anything. We will perform all the tedious negotiations as if you are considering meeting their demands in hope of a slip. Our goal is to discover his location quickly during the process and send the Hostage Rescue Team to get him out. And be assured that our negotiators will appeal to them to consider a ransom payment of money."

"I suppose that makes sense. They seem to have me cornered," said Mr. Brooks.

"We are also concerned for your safety and Allison's. Our recommendation is to place both of you at a secure undisclosed safe site for a few days. It is similar to the Federal Witness Protection Program except ours is nicer and only temporary until we get this resolved for you. You can stay together or we can take each of you to different sites if you would prefer. We can contact you tonight as soon as the meeting is over with an update."

Mr. Brooks looked over at Allison with her head still buried in her arms on the table in deep anguish. "I can't give you an answer yet about the housing until I can talk with Allison privately."

"You two are welcome to use the smaller conference room across the hall. Take your time."

CHAPTER 29

"Hello Della, I need you to arrange an emergency board meeting tomorrow morning at 10:00. Everyone will need to be on location in the secure room. I can't be there but will be calling in from a secure FBI line. Also, after this call I'll not be using my mobile phone and it will be nearly impossible to reach me for an undetermined time. Make sure everyone adheres to the discreet code to keep all media in the dark. If, for some reason, you must reach me before then, you'll have to use a number from Agent Davidson. That's all for now."

"I will carry this out immediately, Mr. Brooks."

"Thanks Della. Bye."

Mr. Brooks looked out the dark tinted windows to see if he could recognize the neighborhood they were in. Not long after his call with Della, the driver pulled over and a similar black SUV pulled up beside them. The windows rolled down and Alex handed his cellphone to Agent Davidson in the other vehicle. Any slight possibility of GPS tracking had to be eliminated and the FBI needed his phone to monitor any remote attempts to breach its encryption.

He turned to Allison, "Are you ready to hand your phone over?"

"It's such a strange feeling to turn it over and be without it, but for the sake of our son, I should be able to survive without it for a few days."

She handed him her phone and her smartwatch which he passed through the window. This bizarre exchange was a compromise to allow them part of the drive to make some critical last minute calls before going dark. Once the handoff took place, their driver left the neighborhood, drove the opposite direction from where they had come, and took another route.

"We are concerned and extremely cautious about tracking," said the driver. "This group that is holding your son hostage is apparently more than tech-savvy and we don't want to take any chances. Now that your phones are going in the opposite direction I can get you to the safe site. I'm not even allowed to have a cellphone and this vehicle is GPS free with a modified chassis computer to make it hack proof and tracking proof."

The driver took them to an exclusive neighborhood and pulled up to a gate. The entry box had no numbers, just a thumb scanner. A long driveway lined with palm trees and accent lights led to a spacious home with a stucco exterior and red tiled roof. He parked and walked them to the door for a quick tour before leaving them.

"You should find most everything you need. The fridge and pantry are stocked but if for some reason you need something you can't find, here's the secure phone that's off the telecom grid and patched directly to our offices. An operator is on call twenty-four seven. They will be able to patch you through to your conference tomorrow. Do you have any questions?"

"When will we hear about the results of the meeting tonight?" asked Allison.

"There will be a follow-up meeting among the department immediately following tonight's contact and you'll receive a call from Agent Hutchins right after that. We won't keep you waiting any longer than necessary."

The driver left them and Mr. Brooks and Allison were now faced with their agreement to stay together for the sake of their son and make a mutual effort to get along.

At least the house is big enough to have some space if this ends up being a bad idea, thought Allison.

CHAPTER 30

T he clock on the wall read 11:08 when the phone rang. Mr. Brooks and Allison didn't have far to go in order to reach it. They were sitting in dining room chairs perched next to the phone as they anxiously waited for the last two hours based on the original time indicated for the meeting. They both stood up and Alex realized at the same time as his ex-wife that they would need to share the handset in order to listen together. They made a split second decision to bear with the awkwardness of being cheek to cheek as each kept an ear close to the receiver.

"Hello."

"Mr. Brooks?" said Hutchins.

"Yes, we are both listening."

"I'm sure you've been on pins and needles so I won't beat around the bush. I want you to trust that I'll always shoot straight with you, so I'm just going to get it all out on the table then we can talk about it. Are you good with that?"

"Yes," said Alex. Allison nodded in agreement.

"They began with a threat against you launching the Mockingbird project before they receive the plans. They said it is a sure way to never see your son again. Next, they asked for the plans to be delivered via the Dark Web and given the necessary time to authenticate. If they find a Trojan Horse, Malware, or any other tricks up our sleeve, then you can say goodbye to Alex Jr. forever. Once there is a preliminary agreement, they will allow you to speak to your son for sixty seconds from an encrypted satellite phone.

Afterwards, you will have twenty-four hours to deliver the Mockingbird files. Just so you know, satellite phones, especially encrypted signals, are difficult to trace, but not impossible. They must know that sixty seconds is not enough time to help us find a location so they will not budge on the time. They also implied that your other board members and their families could also be at risk if the stakes are not high enough already. We have twenty-four hours from now until the next meeting to give our answer and make the arrangements. That is the gist of it."

"This is worse than we thought," said Alex.

"So if we make the arrangements then we will be able to speak to Alex?" asked Allison.

"Only for sixty seconds to confirm he's alive."

"Were you able to decrypt their Darknet path?" asked Mr. Brooks.

"I'm afraid not. They were using an unfamiliar encryption sequence that we have not encountered before. Our cyber unit will be working around the clock to analyze it and see what they can do."

"Did you try to offer them money instead?" said Allison.

"Yes, we suggested a large sum of crypto currency as an alternative and tried to explain the challenges of delivering the plans for Mockingbird. They would not budge."

"Agent Hutchins, I've been pondering our meeting earlier today and the reality has sunk in that they have us over a barrel. I can see no other way than to give them what they want and hope that they will honor their end of the bargain," said Mr. Brooks.

"The US government will not allow you to simply hand over the Mockingbird plans to this criminal gang."

"There's nothing simple about it," Mr. Brooks' voice ramped up. "It's critical for the life of my son!"

Allison stood stunned at the recent news but also by her ex-husband's unrelenting tenacity to forsake his project for the sake of their boy.

"Mr. Brooks, our next step is to formulate a response that appears like you are ready to meet their demands as long as they can confirm your son's well-being via satellite phone. Once that is confirmed, we will have twenty-four hours—that's approximately forty-eight hours from now. They will indicate the transfer location once you are ready to upload the plans. That upload process needs to take as long as possible even with the fattest pipeline available. That will be the window for our cyber unit to try and decrypt the path to their actual IP address and breach their wall of anonymity."

"But what are we uploading if it's not the Mockingbird plans?"

"We need your team to prepare a file that is an intelligently jumbled version of Mockingbird and we will encrypt the file requiring a key. If we can find a chink in their armor during the upload process, we send them the key at the end. It will take half a day to decode the encrypted file and then weeks to authenticate it. By then, we will have your son back."

"But what if you don't find that chink in their armor? You will be signing a death sentence for my son."

"There are risks no matter what we do or don't do. But the encryption program we have developed allows parallel files to be packed together in a hidden format. There are two keys and whichever one we send will unpack one file while simultaneously deleting the second file or vice versa. It gives us two options depending on the outcome."

"But what is the second file you are sending if you don't trace their path?"

"That is classified information that I cannot divulge."

"What do you mean you can't divulge? This is not your company, your technology, or your son to be putting at a greater risk than already exists. Don't you dare send them a Trojan Horse no matter how clever you think you will be able to conceal it. Just give them the real Mockingbird plans when I hand them over to you. It will take them weeks to authenticate the real deal, and once they see the processes laid out, they will realize that there is no one on the black market who can sell them the equipment needed to build it because the equipment doesn't exist outside of our company. Nobody has the specialized technology to create Mockingbird except us. They're obviously not going to give me an address to ship it to them. Just give them the plans!"

"If we did what you are suggesting, it means they will have the plans and your son with nothing to make them give him back and we don't believe they intend to release him."

"You don't know that!"

"Our realistic hope is to crack their shield and find out who they are and where they are then deploy special forces to get him out. Please have your team prepare an alternate version of the Mockingbird plans; we cannot send them the real ones. This is a matter of national interest and security."

"Let me sleep on it. I have a meeting with my board tomorrow morning at 10:00, I'll call you before then."

Alex hung up and Allison just folded into his arms, unable to say a word. Alex was concerned that she might be on the brink of a nervous breakdown. He whispered in her ear, "I know you're tired and extremely fragile right now, but I need you to follow me into the next room without saying a word. We need to be somewhere where we can talk privately."

She looked up at his face with confusion and whispered, "What do you mean?"

"Just trust me. Please."

She leaned her head back into his chest for a moment and whispered, "Okay."

He let her go from his embrace and turned towards the living room and entered the bathroom. She hesitated for a moment but sensed something imperative to their missing son's safety in this strange proceeding. He had left the bathroom door slightly ajar. She gently knocked and went in, closing the door behind her.

CHAPTER 31

Mr. Brooks reached into the shower and started the water. He turned and mouthed a few words that could barely be heard, "Don't say anything."

He searched the cupboards in the bathroom as she watched, confused with his strange behavior. He found a package of paper hand towels and pulled one out. Taking a pen from his shirt pocket, he began to write while hunched over the vanity. Allison drew next to him to read his message.

"This home is under FBI surveillance. Cameras all over but not in bathroom. Audio likely but unsure. To be safe let's only write."

She nodded in agreement.

"I think they want us here to be kept safe from doing something 'rash.' The FBI means well but we have different interests. I think we need to take things into our own hands for the sake of Alex. Can you trust me?"

She nodded again.

"Good. I don't think the FBI plans are good. I want to deal directly with the people who are holding Alex but I need the help of my company. They are loyal."

Allison grabbed the pen and wrote, "How?"

"This is going to take a while to write out, but be patient and I'll do my best to be succinct and explain my plan."

A single tear rolled down Allison's cheek while he leaned over the paper towel and wrote. She leaned over and gave him a kiss on his head.

CHAPTER 32

"Hello operator, this is Alex Brooks. Could you please connect me to my secretary, Della Robinson? You should have her number on file."

"Yes, we have her number. Is there something we can help you with at this late hour? Or a message we can pass along to her for you?"

"No. This is an urgent company matter I need to deal with right away or else I won't sleep. You won't have any problem reaching her, the number is a dedicated phone and she'll be ready to answer."

"At this hour?"

"Not even a question," said Mr. Brooks.

"Hold on one moment," said the operator on duty.

He waited longer than expected. He assumed this unexpected action would get the attention of the Bureau. He finally heard Della's voice.

"Hello Mr. Brooks, this is Della."

"Hello Della. I know this is an uncommon hour to bother you but I need you to reschedule our meeting with the board of directors immediately. I need as many assembled as possible at our headquarters within an hour. It's regarding my son and the ransom demands and time is of the essence. Once again, I'm sorry I'll not be there but will call in from this secure FBI phone line."

"Mr. Brooks, everyone in the company is ready to do whatever it takes to help you in this crisis. I know you're not a religious man but a few of us are praying for you and your son."

"Thanks, Della, you're right, I'm not a religious man but I truly appreciate your thoughtfulness. I know you mean well. If there is a God, I'm not opposed to help right now."

"You can count on me to alert the board and I'm sure you can count on them to do all they can to get to headquarters as soon as possible."

"Thank you again," said Mr. Brooks, "and stand by for any further instructions if needed."

"I will certainly do that, Mr. Brooks."

Alex hung up then asked the operator to connect him to Agent Hutchins. He explained his desire to hold a meeting with his board that night to discuss the plans for preparing a file for the FBI.

"Time is of the essence," said Mr. Brooks.

Agent Hutchins agreed and they set a time to talk again in the morning.

Most of the following hour was spent with short clandestine meetings in the bathroom with paper and pen offset by a seemingly casual exploration of the house.

The time came and Alex called the operator again who connected him to the private company conference line. Della, who had arrived early to welcome the board, answered, "Hello Mr. Brooks, everyone is here except for Sherrie Mendall who is out of town this week with her family, and Nathan Gray who is recovering from a bout of the stomach flu. Would you like me to give the signal to Mr. Swanson to call the meeting to order?"

"Thanks, Della, that would be helpful."

The meeting was called to order and Mr. Brooks was given the floor via the conference line. A picture of him appeared on a large screen on the wall at the head of the large conference table and his voice came through an integrated sound system with remarkable fidelity.

"I cannot tell you how grateful I am for your undying support at this dark moment in my life as a parent and as the founder of this company. I hope that no one will ever have to experience such a gut-wrenching crisis as having a child kidnapped and held for ransom. But if any of you were to ever experience a personal or family crisis, I only hope that I could show to you the same loyalty and friendship that you've shown to me and to Miss Brooks, especially tonight."

Alex could hardly keep his emotions in check. His voice wavered as he struggled to continue his speech. "I have called this emergency meeting tonight to inform you of the plan laid out by the FBI and the role we need to play as a company to try and secure my son's release. But before I do that, I've asked Alex's mother to give you the update on what we have learned and what we don't know about the abduction. I will resume my part of the meeting afterwards with the technical details."

By this time, Mr. Brooks was no longer in control of his emotions. He choked up and handed Allison the handset then rushed off to the bathroom.

"Hello everyone. As you know, this is a very emotional ordeal for us as parents and this has really shaken us, especially Mr. Brooks who, even now, had to dismiss himself for a moment to try and pull himself together, which, as you know, is completely out of character for him. Alex has asked me to give you the latest information from the FBI."

Suddenly, all of the lights went out in the house and Allison, being startled, gasped. "Hello? Is everyone still there?"

"Yes, we're still listening. Are you alright?"

"Oh…I'm sorry, this is a little unnerving," said Allison with a hint of panic noticeable in her voice. "All the lights just went out and Mr. Brooks is not back yet. Excuse me for a moment…" and Allison began addressing the FBI in case they were surveilling the conference line. "If anyone in the FBI is listening in, this seems very unusual for the power to go out all of a sudden. I'm a bit frightened and concerned about it. Can someone check on this right away?"

Just then a familiar voice came on the line, "Hello Miss Brooks, this is Agent Hutchins. I'm sorry to interrupt your meeting but I wanted assure you that everything should be okay. I'm not sure why the power dropped but we have a couple agents stationed in a vehicle near the entry gate of the house and they will come check on it right away."

"Thank you," she said, addressing Agent Hutchins but then turned her attention back to the board members. "Please stay put for now until Mr.

Brooks gets back in touch with you as soon as this is cleared up. I'm sorry for this strange interruption."

Allison hung up and went to one of the windows that faced the front yard. She opened the blinds to get a look at the driveway and gate. She could see a black SUV passing through the opened gate and up the driveway. In the faint glow of the rear taillights, she saw a person's figure slip past the gate with stealth as it slowly closed behind the vehicle. Her heart pounded with anxiety.

Allison heard a knock and quickly unbolted the front door. An agent stood, holding a flashlight and a drawn gun, and in a no-nonsense manner, ordered her to stand aside and stay put adding, "There's an agent going around the outside of the house so don't be alarmed. Where is Mr. Brooks?"

"He went into the bathroom a few minutes before the lights went out."

The agent found the bathroom door and knocked. No answer. He checked the door, it was not locked, and when he opened it, Mr. Brooks was not there. The agent continued to search the house. A few moments later the lights came back and shortly afterwards, the second agent stepped through the front doorway.

Allison just sat in a chair and waited patiently until the two were finished with their search.

"Miss Brooks, do not panic but we are not able to locate Mr. Brooks. The main electrical breaker was shut off. Please come with me, we are going to get you to another location. We have backup on the way."

The agent escorted Allison to the SUV and the two agents stood outside conversing.

"I don't believe he was abducted, it looks like he left on his own."

"Why do you say that?"

"The main breaker box is in the garage and the door between the utility room and garage was unlocked. The window in the back bedroom is also not latched and left partially open."

"Why would he leave in that manner, he's not on house arrest. Isn't this just for their own safety?"

"I don't know all the details of this assignment but I've called Agent Rodriquez and she is checking the security footage now."

"It's bizarre behavior. Is Mr. Brooks suspected in any way?"

"Not that I'm aware of."

"Well, we'll just wait here until Hutchins and Davidson show up. I really don't think there is any danger for Miss Brooks."

"You're probably right but I'm going to ask that they get a couple teams to search the immediate neighborhood ASAP and alert local police. I don't know what his motivation is but it looks suspicious."

CHAPTER 33

"Hello Della, this is Mr. Brooks again. I know this phone is not a listed number, I borrowed it for a minute from a nice guy standing here with me at a convenience store. I need you to charter a jet through McMillan's company ASAP. I need to be at this meeting with the board. I'm going to call for a ride after this and should be at the private air strip in fifteen minutes since there is very little traffic to fight at this hour. Have James pick me up when I arrive. It should take no more than forty-five minutes to get there once we take off. Now let me speak to the board for a minute and you jump on those calls. And oh, you'll likely be getting a call from the Bureau. I need you to keep my visit classified for now."

"Yes, Mr. Brooks, right away."

"Hello team. I'm sorry for that dropped call earlier, I'll explain when I arrive. I'm on my way there and want to talk to you in person. Please do your best to make yourselves at home for the next hour. I'm very sorry for the inconvenience but you'll understand the desperate situation we are all in and the necessity for this."

The young man standing next to Mr. Brooks outside the convenience store was wide eyed at the conversation he had just overheard.

"Do you mind if I make one last call for a cab?"

"Whatever you need, my man. When a friend like you palms a bro a C-note like that, you make all the calls you want."

Minutes later, Mr. Brooks waved goodbye to Jermaine as he jumped in the cab. His next stop—the private airstrip, catering to wealthy business men who bought shares in a small fleet of jets exclusively used to shuttle the club members from LA to the Bay Area.

They were expecting Mr. Brooks when he arrived and the flight was ready to leave as soon as he was on board.

An onboard phone allowed him to reach out to Della to gather his top engineers to join him after the board meeting. In less than an hour, a company driver was shuttling him to the Mountain View headquarters in the heart of Silicon Valley.

CHAPTER 34

"**S**o that is all we know up to the present," said Mr. Brooks as he debriefed his board members. "Now, does anyone have any feedback regarding the FBI's plan?"

The board members were disturbed and, one by one, voiced their opinion the FBI plan was a terrible one.

"I didn't want to influence you to that conclusion," said Mr. Brooks, "but I agree. It is why I've come here in person tonight." He then explained his adventurous exit of the house and about his strong suspicion that the FBI, though well meaning, was trying to keep him from doing something "rash" like what he was about to do now.

"The life of my son is at stake, and I feel the need to take charge of these negotiations in order to save my son as the number one priority, and if possible, save this company from the devastating theft of intellectual property like ours."

Everyone agreed and was ready to hear Mr. Brooks' plans.

"Let me share my thoughts for moving forward but I need your collaborative help to find unnecessary weaknesses and bolster confidence for the strongest action forward."

For the next couple hours, the team devised an operation they called "Day for Night," a technique for filming a night scene during the day. The board arranged for Mr. Brooks to be moved to their own version of a safe site where he could have access to his team and make direct contact with the criminal group they code-named "Anaconda." His vice president agreed to act as proxy to the FBI due to Mr. Brooks' "nervous breakdown" and "disturbed and irrational state of mind," and relate to them that the board had allowed Mr. Brooks temporary leave and they would work directly with the Bureau to provide the fake Mockingbird plans.

Mr. Brooks and a small team of three others made their way to a vacation rental in Pacific Heights, an exclusive San Francisco neighborhood. They quickly settled in to the three-story Victorian home owned by one of the board members and conveniently blocked out for several weeks for new interior decoration and maintenance. They took cues from the FBI and avoided use of cellphones, opting for encrypted internet calls until their satellite phone arrived. His team consisted of Greg from his security department, Greg's top assistant, Liam, and Miles from the engineering department.

As soon as their secure communication link to headquarters was up and running, they received news that Anaconda had already responded to their inquiry. Their first attempt using the original Dark Web meeting site and authorization code didn't work, but in a matter of minutes, they received a query link to vet the source of the digital knock at their door. "They have provided a new site address and single use password to make contact as soon as you are able," said Liam.

"Give us twenty minutes," said Miles, "to get the router installed and the software up and running." The link and password took them to a private chat window being monitored by a real time gate keeper ready to vet him. The anonymity existed both ways and each side must determine the authenticity of the other for the meeting. Either one might be a rogue third party crime syndicate, the FBI, or an adventurous lone hacker.

"They're not going to trust that you're the real Alexander Brooks without layers of confirmation and it will be up to you to do the same with them. You should take the lead to make sure you're not tipping your hand unknowingly to the FBI or some other party," said Liam.

Mr. Brooks took the advice and typed in the chat window, "I know you need to verify my identity but I also have reasons to verify yours before I give any personal information. Neither of us are interested in a third party right now."

He received the reply, "Would a picture of your son's phone suffice?"

The four men huddled and agreed it might be sufficient if Mr. Brooks could identify it. He told his team, "I pay for his phone so go ahead and access his account and check the model and serial number."

In the meantime, Mr. Brooks typed, "A picture of the phone and a picture of the serial number on the SIM tray would work."

He received the reply, "Stand by."

They got into the phone account and pulled up the device information right about the time that a file transfer link appeared. After the digital handshake between computers, Mr. Brooks downloaded two files: one was a picture of his son's cracked phone in the model and color listed on the account, and the second picture was a close-up of the serial number on the SIM tray. They cross checked the number with the account. They matched.

Seeing the image of Alex's phone caused an unexpected quake of emotions in him. It took him a moment to gather his wits and keep his head clear for the task at hand. He typed, "Verified."

Now it was their turn to authenticate his identity. He read, "Does your computer have a web cam?" The team was reading over his shoulder.

"Say yes without delay," said Liam.

He did so.

"They're going to ask you to give them access to this computer," said Liam.

"Should I?" asked Mr. Brooks. "What kind of risk can that put me in?"

"No risk," said Greg. "This laptop is new out of the box with zero personal data other than some generic company info for registration that we use on any outside company equipment."

"They will likely send you a program for remote desktop access," said Liam. "Once activated, you will be giving them control of this computer including the webcam and microphone. They will be able to see and hear you until they give control back to you. We can delete the program and scan for malware later, but they will see it's not an FBI rig and see you live. The FBI would certainly not let them breach one of their computers."

Just then, another file transfer was initiated. As Liam guessed, it was a remote desktop application. The other three moved to the other side of the laptop and coached Mr. Brooks.

"Once you've installed the program," said Miles, "they will likely lock you out until they give control back. I'm guessing they will initiate imaging of the entire computer for their own records, but you've got nothing to lose and they have nothing to gain because there is nothing to find on this laptop."

It went exactly as they said.

The chat window read, "Now rotate the computer around the room."

As if a sixth sense had already alerted them, the others quietly moved into an adjacent room to keep out of view. Not that it would have been an issue but mostly to keep things simple and keep their own faces from being identified and used later. Once he set the laptop back on the dining room table, the others slipped quietly back. The controls of the desktop were returned to Alex and he read, "Verified."

He closed the remote desktop application and deleted it. Greg came back in with a piece of electrical tape to put over the onboard camera and microphone then double checked the system to make sure they were free of intrusion for now.

"All clear," said Greg.

The screen read, "Stand by."

After a few minutes, they read, "Tell us what this is all about."

Mr. Brooks told them of his plans to bypass the FBI and negotiate directly with them. He requested that they would continue interacting with the FBI to keep them in the dark. He hinted at the possibility of a modified plan that they might transfer and his readiness to send the actual Mockingbird plans as long as he could be assured of his son's return. He tried to explain the overwhelming complexity of the Mockingbird project with a few technical explanations. He likened it to having plans to build a nuclear warhead but not having a means to acquire weapons-grade uranium or the ballistic missile technology to launch it. He tried to assure them it was not from an unwillingness to meet their demands but from an openness to explain the hurdles that he could not resolve for them once the master plans and processes were in their hands. They agreed to reconnect after the Bureau's scheduled meeting with them.

"You must give his mother the sixty second phone call with Alex as agreed when you talk with them tomorrow and then another sixty seconds with me after we finalize the time and place for the upload of the plans."

"You will have to split the time. Thirty seconds for her and thirty for you. Take it or leave it. And beware of any tricks or your son will be thirty seconds from the end of his life."

"If I wanted to pull a fast one, I would have stuck with the FBI. I just want my son back safe," typed Mr. Books.

"If you keep your end of the bargain, we'll keep ours. Understood?"

"Understood."

They ended the session and the team performed a deep scan of the laptop and found an install of spyware.

"Leave it be. We'll shut this computer down until tomorrow's meeting, and if they think they'll find anything, they'll be disappointed," said Greg.

"I've copied the two images they sent to a thumb drive and will see if I can find any embedded metadata they might have forgotten to purge," said Miles.

"It's doubtful," said Liam, "but it doesn't hurt to check."

"Liam," said Mr. Brooks. "Have our team calculate how large the files are for the complete library of Mockingbird plans and how long it will take to package it for delivery."

"I'll take care of it."

"Mr. Brooks, when's the last time you ate or slept?" asked Greg. "You don't look good and you should get some rest. I can't imagine that there's anything else you can do with what's left of this night, as it is, it's almost morning. You really ought to get a bite to eat and get a nap at least."

"Maybe you're right. I do feel pretty tired."

CHAPTER 35

The sun disappeared into the sea. Hariyono received a call on a satellite phone. He spoke in his native language, "Hello, what is the news?"

"Have you found a suitable island yet?"

"Not yet. Tomorrow morning we will land on one, I wanted to get further off the beaten path as they say."

"What is your present location?"

"Ah, very funny, that is a good one. You know as well as I do that I'm not allowed to divulge that information to you. The less people know, the safer everyone else remains. Those are the orders from above and I'm sticking to them."

"Whatever Hariyono! You've always been overly cautious. But here's the news, the boss wants to make certain the boy will be ready to speak on the phone tomorrow around noon, your time. There will be two separate calls, thirty seconds each. He must be informed not to mention anything about you or his surroundings. Warn him that if he doesn't comply, you will cut the call off immediately and things will not go well for him. Tell him that he is only allowed to let his father and mother know that he is alive and in good health and treated very good."

"No problem, we will be sure to be settled by then and ready for the call."

"Good, don't mess this up."

"What is there to mess up? This is an easy job," said Hariyono.

CHAPTER 36

A new day in the Indonesian archipelago brought a new liberty for Alex. He was allowed to sit out in the open. His captors knew that their present location was remote enough to shield them from any notice. Alex felt the warm air and it occurred to him that it hardly seemed to change much. The refreshing spray from the ocean lifted his spirits a little. A few small and distant islands were visible in multiple directions. Some islands seemed wider, some taller, but all of them in this region were uninhabited according to Hariyono. They were too far from the bigger islands and off the beaten track of established trade routes which were centuries old.

Alex had also learned that they had brought enough food and water to last two weeks. Hariyono was confident that any number of the islands in this area would have plenty of edible food available, both plant and animal. It perplexed Alex to think that such isolated places would have animals other than birds.

The pilot started slowing the boat down significantly and seemed to be zeroing in on one of the larger islands suitable to them. It wouldn't be long until they were on land again and Alex couldn't wait for the zip ties to come off. They must have thought he might be desperate enough to try something violent, but for all of the video game violence that Alex had been immersed in, it didn't give him courage or actual abilities to know how to take three men on in an altercation. It hadn't occurred to him that one of the three captors was always at the controls so the odds were not impossible if he had any real ideas. He thought about the innumerable times and hours he had fought a host of enemies in fantasy games or military simulations. Somehow, it didn't seem to transfer in this case. Plus, his game characters did not have their hands tied together and could come back to life if killed.

As they neared the island, it was uncanny that he could no longer see any of the other islands on the horizon. He could see a sandy white beach, palm trees and thick tropical vegetation, and a fairly high elevation. Alex began to wonder how they would land the boat, so he asked Hariyono who merely replied, "You will know soon."

The risk of mortal danger seemed to pass. Even though Alex felt perturbed to be missing the gaming competition, something about the island sparked a sense of adventure. He had never really camped before other than staying in a tent once on the beach not far from home.

As they neared the beach, the pilot turned the boat so that it faced away from the island and then put the motors in reverse. The other man went to the bow and dropped an anchor while letting a loose coil of rope unwind while they inched closer to the island. Now only twenty yards from the beach, the motors idled and Hariyono climbed over the side into the shallow water with another anchor and a long coil of rope. He waded to shore and secured the anchor beyond the high tide line and waded back. They lashed the ropes taught on each end of the boat as Alex watched with keen interest in the activity of landing the boat and the knots that they tied.

As soon as they were satisfied that the boat was secure from being beached at low tide or drifting at high tide, they began the tedious work of unloading. Even now, they were hesitant to take the zip ties off of Alex and employ his help.

Alex thought, *Maybe they're afraid that I'll try to commandeer the boat and leave them stranded. If they only knew how harmless I am, I might have been freed from these ties by now.* Instead, they helped him out of the boat and into the water to wade to shore after he insisted on removing his shoes and socks to keep them dry. The warm water reached about mid-thigh. Once he got to shore, Hariyono told him to sit under the shade of the trees at the border of the beach.

Alex understood the advantage of the shade but he could hear all sorts of bird sounds and other noises that were unfamiliar to him. His imaginations and fears were not anchored like the boat that brought him here. His mind drifted as a mental tide encroached upon him. The jungle made him nervous and uneasy. Thankfully, the location of the sun provided long enough shadows from the thick wall of tall palm trees. This enabled Alex to keep some distance from the imagined threat of unknown creatures waiting to take advantage of his vulnerability. He positioned himself in order to keep his eye on the men unloading the boat and the forest of palms. He wished he had another set of eyes behind him.

Without warning, a startling scream came from one of the men. Alex looked up and could see the man crouching on the sand and struggling to stand up. The cry sounded like an exaggerated response when someone accidentally smashes their thumb with a hammer or is stung unexpectedly by a wasp. The other two men looked bewildered, not knowing the cause of this sudden outburst. He continued yelling something at the others through gritted teeth as they instinctively ran over towards him. Their partner, on his knees, tried twisting around to see the back of his thigh.

To their dismay, they could see the shaft of an arrow protruding from his leg. Hariyono knelt down and quickly gave his friend some instructions as he grabbed the shaft and got ready to give it a pull. The other man took his pistol out and stared wildly into the jungle, looking for the unseen menace. At the same moment, the characteristic sound of an arrow in flight was heard for a fraction of a second before the more disturbing sound of it hitting its target, followed by a sharp cry from Hariyono. Pandemonium broke loose as randomly aimed gunshots began ringing out towards the jungle to ward off the unknown attackers. The next few seconds were filled with a barrage of arrows mixed with the shouts and cries of the unprepared victims. The few remaining bullets were fired haphazardly in the chaos and came to a stop.

The surreal scene unfolded before Alex in a flash and he scrambled up from the sand and bolted towards the jungle in a wild senseless manner. His heart burst through his chest and every ounce of his being rocketed into the foliage, ducking and weaving around palm trees, falling several times but driven on like a madman. Suddenly, the ground disappeared under his bare and bloody feet and he tumbled end over end into a steep ravine. His body came to an abrupt halt as he crashed into a thick woody bush. On his back looking up, he stayed deathly still, listening for the sound of any pursuer. All he could hear was the deafening sound of his pounding heart, seemingly so loud in his state of terror that he was afraid it could be heard echoing through the jungle like a homing device for the unknown assailants.

His whole body ached. He could not tell if anything was broken but didn't want to move a muscle anyway. If he had thought that his capacity of fear had been maxed out at some point before this, he was now proven wrong. His gasping breaths and uncontrolled sobs seemed amplified and he desperately tried to calm himself. Carefully shifting to his side, he painfully drew up his knees to his chest. Alex buried his head into his knees in a fetal position and wept. The faint sound of his muffled but high-pitched cry escaped this attempted barrier of concealment. He closed his eyes tightly with the false hope that it would help him stay hidden.

CHAPTER 37

Fifteen hours to wait. Such a long time until Mr. Brooks could get his thirty-second phone call with his son. He dozed a little but his exhausted body and troubled thoughts made it impossible to succumb to his need for rest against the tumult of his mind. He thought about Allison and how she must be feeling. His one consolation was that she would get the first opportunity to talk with Alex. He sat in an elegantly furnished room with tall ceilings trimmed with ornate crown molding and big bay windows with sheer curtains drawn. The morning sun lit up the large room with warm tones. Miles brought his boss a large cup of hot coffee and a breakfast sandwich fetched from a local café. The others left him alone as much as possible as they continued their correspondence with headquarters on project Day for Night. Only on a few occasions did they interrupt his malaise to ask a critical question and relay his thoughts to the engineers working nonstop on the daunting Mockingbird plans.

This quiet but restless morning gave Mr. Brooks time to sort through some disturbing thoughts about himself that he was obligated to suppress in the last twenty-four hours due to the desperation of the sudden crisis. But now, these previously caged thoughts slipped quietly into the room and haunted him. They were relentless.

What have I done to my family? Do I even have the right to use that word family? I once thought I did all this for them, to provide a comfortable life, to make them proud of me, to assure them that my dreams were not in vain. I thought they would join me in my passion to become one of the elite men of the century. How did they know the truth that I haven't admitted to myself until now? It wasn't for them, was it? They know it. Allison knows it. Alex knows it. I marginalized them. How is it that I felt and showed no real love for my son while he was within reach? I never entertained the idea that I was failing in something. It feels like waking up from a good dream only to realize I'm in a prison and discovering that I'm some sort of a criminal. I hate these men who have robbed me of my son, but are they worse than I am? I hate myself for not caring about him when he was not being held for ransom and his life was not in danger. How did I become such a horrible father? I've sacrificed him. I've sold him, but even if I buy him back with everything I possess, I won't have him anymore than before. I'm sure he hates me, why shouldn't he? He sees right through me. He knows that I haven't loved him. He knows how I've treated his mother. I must try to redeem my son, but who can redeem me?

He felt as if anguish were wringing his soul like a dirty dish rag and his tears felt dirty like the water left after a sink full of dishes. With his head leaning back on the plush chair, his emotionally drained mind finally nodded off. He slept deeply for several hours, waking up with a sore neck from an unnatural sleeping position. His stomach felt slightly nauseous from the strong coffee he drank earlier.

His body gained a little rest but not his mind. The troubling thoughts seemed to reverberate back and forth in an echo chamber. All of his grief and regrets overlapped each other and he couldn't keep track of where one thought ended and another began. It was maddening, but he felt as if he deserved no better and should embrace this self-inflicted mental torture.

The day dragged on with mounting anxiety over all his perplexities, his son's unknown situation, and the turmoil Allison must be going through as she waited. It seemed like the clock would never advance but it did, slowly. The moment finally began drawing near for the first meeting to commence between the FBI and Anaconda. It had been arranged that a report from his vice president would be relayed as soon as the meeting was over.

The call finally came.

"Mr. Brooks, we are at a loss to know how to proceed or what steps to take. Everything seemed to go well and the call with your son was about to take place as planned. Then nothing. No call, no follow up, no messages. Not a hint of anything."

"What did the FBI do? They have screwed this up somehow. Oh, why did I let that meeting happen at all? Hopefully our meeting will go as planned and I will be allowed to talk with Alex, I hope that is their plan."

But he was wrong. The meeting never took place that night and neither he nor Allison heard from Alex. Their worst nightmares seemed to be manifesting.

CHAPTER 38

On the island, Alex woke up from a deep sleep, feeling extremely sore and groggy. He wondered, *Did I pass out?* He didn't know, but sensed that some time had passed and it seemed to be late afternoon. The dense jungle made it hard to discern the position of the sun, but everything appeared to be a shade darker than he remembered. He suddenly recalled much more, especially the terrifying scene from earlier that day. It caused him to shudder and his mind and emotions were rapidly trying to process the unfolding of events.

Pain began pushing its way to the front of the line. He stopped mulling these things in his mind to take stock of his aching body. His wrists were raw from the chaffing of the ties. His muscles were stiff and sore from lying too long in an unnatural position. His head ached and his mouth was dry. He needed to sit up. He was facing the trunk of the bush, so he slowly rolled over and found himself staring sideways into the face of a crouching man holding an upright spear.

Alex swallowed his compulsion to scream and tried scooting back further under the bush. His heart thumped convulsively again. He couldn't hold back a whimpering cry, unconsciously pleading for mercy.

Alex shut his eyes in vain. It didn't stop his tears or make the jungle man disappear or cause his fears to vanish. He tensed up in anticipation of being speared. But it didn't happen. Instead, the strange man spoke a few unintelligible words. Alex thought he might have perceived a compassionate tone in his voice, or could he be fooling himself in ignorance? He barely opened his eyes to peek at the crouching man. The remnant of water in his eyes made this a challenge, but now he stared at the man's face staring back at him. The man spoke a couple words again acknowledging Alex's gaze. This time, the combination of his tone and facial expression gave Alex hope that the man may not be aggressive or angry or ready to spear him after all.

"I don't understand what you are saying," said Alex, his voice raspy and barely audible.

Again the man spoke without any perceivable anger.

"I'm going to try to sit up," said Alex in a sheepish manner.

He made very slow movements doing what he could to send a nonverbal sign of nonaggression. His movements were necessarily slow anyway because his stiff and sore body. Alex grimaced as he awkwardly sat up, cradling his knees to his chest by his fettered hands, his head peering over this semi-sheltered posture.

The jungle man didn't react. As Alex sat, he felt an uncomfortable lump underneath him so he shifted his weight and the lump shifted with him. *That's strange,* he thought. *I can't believe that it is still in my back pocket.* How the little Bible from Agnes had remained with him seemed a mystery. For now, it was merely one of several circumstances causing him discomfort.

Being afraid to look too long at the jungle man for fear of making some unknown mistake, Alex looked away. He didn't want a foolish move to get him skewered with the spear or hacked to death with the machete he saw tucked into a sash at the man's waste.

The man spoke to him again so Alex looked up. He noticed for the first time the man's old age with a long scraggly beard streaked with white hair. His leathery, weather-worn face intimidated Alex. The man held out a container made of bamboo that resembled a large tumbler. No doubt, it was something to drink but he doubted what kind of strange concoction might be in the container and if drinking it would be another mistake in his vulnerable ignorance. Too many outlandish movies in Alex's past made it hard to consider that it might be water.

He reached out with his fettered hands and took the cup. Peering into it, he skeptically thought, *It looks like water but what if it's poison? Or some strange drug? What do I do?* The jungle man made gestures with his own hand to his lips, coaxing Alex to drink. Alex took a very small sip and to his surprise, it was just water—the most memorable drink of water he would ever have. The combination of his extremely parched body and the simple act of mercy stamped an indelible memory in his mind. The water refreshed his dry mouth and gave him a drop of hope.

He looked at the man and humbly said, "Thank you."

The jungle man certainly didn't know the words but he seemed to know the meaning. The man replied with more unknown words but Alex seemed to know that they meant: "You're welcome."

Alex considered this, *I think this man means to help me and not hurt me, though it doesn't make sense after seeing the attack on Hariyono and the others.*

The jungle man reached out and grabbed Alex's hands and lifted them up to look at the thick plastic bonds. Alex still held the empty water container. The man seemed to be thinking deeply and then stood up from his crouching position and motioned for Alex to stand also.

Alex didn't entirely distrust him but being so weak, he wasn't sure he could stand. In spite of his doubts he struggled up onto his wobbly feet but not for long. He began to fall. The skinny but strong arms of the jungle man caught him and kept him propped up. Alex gave him another "thank you" and the man gave him another "you're welcome" in his native tongue. Unbeknownst to Alex, this was his first immersive language lesson.

Alex focused on staying upright as the man slowly walked him forward step by step. Being so near the man also made him aware of his earthy and wild smell, not rank but strong smelling nonetheless. The spear and water container were left behind and the jungle man looked around the immediate vicinity in search of something or someone. He continued helping Alex hobble along until they reached a large fallen palm tree.

He gestured for Alex to sit down and straddle the log, motioning him to stretch out his hands. He drew out the machete. There didn't seem to be a comfortable enough distance between his hands for error, so Alex closed his eyes and imagined the man taking a high and wild swing that would sever more than the ties. He missed the opportunity to witness the deft handling of the machete as the man raised it about six inches from Alex's wrists and brought it down with a precise snap—an easy task for a man with years of experience splitting coconuts, sago palms, bamboo, and a host of wildlife. Alex started breathing again when he realized his hands were free of each other and the fragments of the zip ties dropped to the jungle floor. All that remained were swollen rashes around each wrist, but that didn't bother him, his hands were free and his heart a little less heavy.

The jungle man went back for the things he left behind and returned to help Alex get to his feet again and off they went. They were at the bottom of a small but steep ravine and precariously climbed up the bank. The old man nearly carried Alex up the slope with one hand holding the spear and cup and the other hand wrapped around Alex. Alex held on with one arm around the man. Once out of the ravine, the trek through the jungle was not as difficult, and in a short time, Alex felt more steady and able to hobble along on his own behind the man. Twenty minutes later, the jungle man stopped and surveyed his surroundings intently. Alex could not see the beach but he could hear the ocean not far away.

The man said something unintelligible to Alex and when Alex didn't respond, he repeated his instruction and motioned for Alex to sit down. He walked off leaving Alex alone. Alone with uneasy doubts and new fears.

CHAPTER 39

Alex's present threat of dying subsided and his mind began to rest enough to give attention to the jungle sights, sounds, and smells around him. The rumbling in his stomach from hunger prevailed over all other interests as he noticed a palm tree with bananas. He had never given any thought about how they grew. It shocked him to see such a large bunch sticking upside down, or really right side up. He wondered, *Do they always grow pointing upwards or is this a rare and confused species? There must be fifty or more bananas on this one tree!* To the delight of his eyes, the uppermost bananas were bright yellow. He didn't delay, he got up and grabbed a couple. The jungle man had motioned for him to sit down before he left, but Alex was certain he meant to stay put, not necessarily sit indefinitely. But just in case, he thought it best to sit back down to eat his bounty.

The first banana he peeled and stuck in his mouth gave him a shock. This experience set a new standard far beyond the store-ripened counterfeits. He gave an audible "Wow!" muffled through his stuffed mouth.

In his mind, he just tasted real fruit for the first time and anything that posed as fruit prior to this must have been imposters. It felt so good to have food again in his stomach. He got back up on his feet and reached for the cluster. Altogether, seven banana peels were flung into the neighboring brush and Alex's observations now expanded beyond food.

His knowledge base grew as he took in his new surroundings, surprised that he hadn't noticed many of the sights and sounds around him. He became aware of a cacophony of bird sounds as they sang their various calls and flitted through the jungle causing a steady rustling of palm branches and tree leaves. He felt that he had been previously deaf until now. His ears could finally tune in to the environment now that his heart started to settle down.

He also noticed the varied colors of birds darting across his field of view. They were captivating—brilliant red, bright yellow, blues, and iridescent greens. The rustling sounds at ground level disconcerted him a little. He couldn't identify the sources and wasn't sure if he really wanted to know what moved along the jungle floor.

He spotted several camouflaged lizards on the palms, then a strange spider repairing a web on a nearby bush. Countless insects created a jungle chorus, easily tuned out as white noise until something close or much louder demanded a spotlight for a solo act.

The continual rolling of a gentle surf provided a comforting sound in the mix. *I must not be far from the beach,* he thought. It brought back the recent memory of three dead or seriously wounded men and his mental list of unanswered questions.

Why wasn't I killed?

Do they have worse plans for me?

Why did the jungle man seem kind?

Why did he leave?

Where are the others?

Am I going to die soon?

Should I have been dead already?

These thoughts echoed through the deep, unexplored caverns of his soul and they disturbed him. He previously lived with a lot of ignorance about death. In fact, he lived in a lot of ignorance about the meaning of life. He shuddered. An instinctive fear of the unknown lurked inside but now a new fear emerged that had nothing to do with an island, or a jungle, or a pack of thug kidnappers, or an assaulting tribal group. This fear had something to do with himself that remained unknown.

Once more, the little book tucked into his back pocket started making him uncomfortable as he sat. He pulled it out as an easy remedy. He stared at it for a moment and got it oriented right side up and front forward. He opened the cover and saw the handwritten note from Agnes in very small cursive writing to accommodate the limited amount of room available on the flyleaf of the pocket Bible. He read with eagerness:

Dear Alexander,

I'm so grateful to God that we met. I hope you will read this. It is not an ordinary book and I believe God wanted you to have it. It has the answers for the big questions in life and will be a light in times of darkness.

Love, Agnes

Transfixed with these personal words to himself, Alex didn't notice the jungle man's presence. The man spoke abruptly and startled him out of his wits. Alex screamed. The rush of adrenaline and sudden shortness of breath caused him to feel faint and nearly pass out. He fell over from his sitting position and continued to cry out in short bursts of terror while curling into a fetal position again, reacting in shock.

The jungle man crouched beside him and gently patted him on the shoulder in an attempt to help him calm down. This gesture proved effective and Alex recovered quickly from the unnecessary fit of terror.

CHAPTER 40

The nameless man who continued to show small signs of kindness to Alex looked at him with great inquisitiveness. Alex looked at him with equal intrigue as he pushed himself up from the jungle floor and sat back up. The man's eyes shifted from Alex to the little book clutched in his right hand. The native seemed to be stunned with his own version of shock. He slowly lifted his hand, pointing to the book and turned his gaze back to Alex's face. He said something that was clearly a question that meant, "What is that?"

Alex had momentarily forgotten the small Bible and looked in the direction of the pointing finger to discover the subject in question.

"Oh this?" he said hesitantly. "It's a book—a Bible."

He held it out to the man. The jungle man stared with obvious amazement and carefully reached over to touch it. Alex let him hold it. He gently handled it as if it were a priceless treasure. He carefully moved a few pages then handed it back to Alex with an apparent new regard for this young stranger to the jungle.

Alex slipped it back into his pocket, then took unusual initiative by asking a gnawing question, "What is your name?"

The man stared blankly. This time, Alex pointed to him and asked again, "Name? What's your name?"

The man did not comprehend him. This time Alex pointed to himself and said, "I'm Alex."

Still nothing.

Alex pulled the Bible out again and pointed at it with his other hand, "Bible." Then himself, "Alex." Now at the man.

He finally understood what Alex was attempting to do. Alex could see the faint light in his eyes, hinting at some progress. He tried again. "Bible," then "Alex," then he pointed again to the man and paused.

"Setiawan."

Alex tried his best to repeat it, "Set-ee-a-wan."

His pronunciation must have been close enough because Setiawan smiled and repeated his own name once more.

That acknowledged smile brought so much hope to Alex, more than knowing a dictionary full of foreign words could have done. This foreign smile needed no interpretation. Its universal response crossed all borders and cultures. Alex smiled back with sincere delight and repeated, "Set-ee-a-wan."

Alex excitedly pointed again to himself, "I'm Alex"

"I-mal-lekus," said Setiawan.

"No, just Alex."

Setiawan looked confused but made another attempt, "No-jus-a-lekus."

Alex realized his mistake and tried again. "Alex."

Setiawan, still confused, but determined, replied, "A-lekus."

Alex smiled, "Alex!"

Setiawan smiled, "Alekus!"

Alex thought, *Close enough, I'm probably saying his name wrong.* He pointed one more time to his new jungle friend and said, "Set-ee-a-wan."

Setiawan pointed to Alex, "Alekus."

Alex just completed his second immersive language class.

CHAPTER 41

N ow that he and Setiawan were on a first name basis, it became clear to Alex that more work lay ahead of him beyond learning names.

Setiawan brought a clay pot containing hot coals which he used to start a fire. He motioned for Alex to collect wood to burn. The sun was going down and Alex didn't want to be tromping around the jungle in the dark, so he didn't waste any time despite his sore body and limited agility. He got the job done.

Setiawan set to work, cutting down tall bamboo shoots with his machete and making piles of palm fronds. Alex sat down next to the fire. The air temperature remained warm but the campfire was comforting now that the sun was going down. Setiawan joined him, handed him a palm frond and motioned for him to watch as he peeled a strand of fiber from the center. It was nearly two feet long and he laid it on the ground and indicated that Alex should do the same. Alex complied. It wasn't as easy as Setiawan made it look. He reached over and placed a pile of fronds next to Alex, obviously expecting him to keep going. Alex didn't know the purpose of this task but felt like he should do whatever this man expected from him. His collection of strands increased and the pile of fronds decreased.

Setiawan not only collected plants but also animals. He pulled out a lizard about a foot long and skewered it on a piece of bamboo. When he started to roast it, Alex's eyes got wide and he thought, *He's not going to eat that is he? That's disgusting. Uhhhhh!*

The dangling lizard was sizzling and an acrid smell wafted past Alex who nearly gagged at the thought. Then to his shock, Setiawan grabbed the smoking lizard in hand like a child taking a roasted marshmallow off a stick and tried handing it to Alex. He did not take it and looked at Setiawan with dismay.

"No way! There's no way I'm going to eat that!" He shook his head in disgust to try and make it clear he wanted nothing to do with the lizard. Alex's propensity for being obnoxious came to the surface again and his ignorance of the cultural grievance he provoked was not a forgivable excuse.

Setiawan's countenance changed immediately. He looked angry for the first time and said a few terse words with a sharp tone. Alex checked himself and suddenly realized that his little tantrum over the offered food was not a good move, but he didn't know how to remedy the situation. He already determined in his mind that he would not take a bite of that lizard, yet he realized it offended Setiawan. How much of an offense was it? He couldn't guess. *What do I do? I can't eat that thing, but what will he do to me if I don't?*

Setiawan's face still looked troubled and Alex knew he had better change his present course for the sake of peace and maybe his own life. He reached out to grab the lizard and spoke in a conciliatory tone, "Sorry, I just thought it needed to be cooked a little longer. I like my meat medium well, you know, to kill the bacteria—no you probably don't know. Do you have any salt?"

Alex knew very well that Setiawan couldn't understand a word he said but it was a ploy to stall and see if the man's expression would soften a little. Alex had effectively used this tactic innumerable times with his parents and others when they were upset with him.

Setiawan did relax a little but watched Alex intently as he held the steaming lizard. A thought went through Alex's mind, *I wonder if I could turn my head sideways and do that little trick like I was dropping it down my throat? That might be too risky. Little kids fall for it but I don't think this man will. Don't blow this, Alex!*

He decided to try to placate the man by taking a small bite of the tail. *I don't have to chew it, or swallow. Maybe it's not so bad.* He raised it to his mouth, holding it over his head in order to get at the tail. It was still a bit floppy and not as cooked as he would have opted if given the choice. The smell was even stronger now that it was so close to his nose while he bit down. His intention was to sever a small piece but it took more effort than he anticipated. The entire tail detached, leaving most of it dangling from his mouth. This was more than he could handle, his body recoiled and he suddenly doubled over and threw up a stomach full of bananas, along with the unfinished tail.

The shock of it, combined with the sheer exhaustion from this horrific day, made Alex lightheaded and he fainted.

CHAPTER 42

S everal miles from Alex and Setiawan, an agitated jungle village stirred
with frenzy like a large anthill disrupted by a child's mischievous stick.
Everyone seemed disturbed from their usual routines. The unexpected
arrival of foreigners made this one of the most unusual and alarming days
for the isolated tribe. This alone would be enough to cause anxiety and fear.
What made things worse, several of their tribal elders were away on a rare
trading expedition to the nearest populated island, which, in reality, wasn't
very near at all. They had been away for several weeks and were expected
back any day, and now several boats could be spotted as silhouettes against
the setting sun.

A young man came running from the beach and approached a hut on
the periphery of the village.

"Tomanti! They have returned! They are almost here! You must tell
them soon," said Gabiek.

"Of course, I will tell them, I know that! Who else must tell them,
Gabiek? Of course, I must tell them!"

"We were responsible to you," said Gabiek.

Tomanti seemed worried. He was not confident that his actions would
be acknowledged as heroic. As the youngest and newest member of the
tribe's leadership, he must now face his fellow elders.

The other four had left the island in an unprecedented manner, leaving
Tomanti in charge alone. They were not in the habit of sending so many
elders at once off the island but this year was a necessary exception. After

all, what could go wrong? Since migrating to the island over fifty years ago, there had been very little trouble from the outside, only petty community conflicts. The island remained unnoticed by the rest of the world, exactly as hoped. The vast network of islands in the region made this possible.

The community was conflicted about two major decisions that Tomanti had made that day. The first was to kill the foreigners who trespassed on their island. The second was the more scandalous decision to spare the captive young man at the request of Setiawan.

What would normally be a festive day of excitement at the return of the boats was now a moment of uneasiness. No one talked about the new fabrics for clothes or the replenished supplies of spices and other goods not attainable on their own island.

The village talk was all about the dead men and the young man. They talked about Tomanti's decisions. They questioned his wisdom but not his authority to call them to action or to keep them from it. Their doubts would soon be put to rest once the other elders were on shore.

The villagers could see the catamarans with their sails and canopies drawing very close to the shore. The men in the boats were in dismay, "Why is the village not greeting us with singing and dancing and the blowing of conch shells?" Something was clearly wrong. The entire community of about four hundred people stood in a tight mass with a look of dread. Tomanti stood out in front.

Several young men waded out into the shallow water to help anchor the boats. The team of men consisting of three of their elders and nine other helpers stepped onto the shore with sober faces. They could only guess that something terrible must have happened. Something tragic? Something... what was it? They were at a loss.

The oldest of the elders approached him. "Tomanti, what is this?" said Waniwan. "What has happened in the village?"

"Strangers came to our shore today. Do you want to sit down here and listen to my story or will you come to the community house and sit down to eat around the fire while I tell you the whole story?"

This made the elder pause. Waniwan knew that if they sat down now to hear the story, all of the people would be welcome to listen. They would also hear the elders discuss the matter. That was one of the main reasons most of the villagers were present, in hope of listening in. They would not be allowed to speak but they could listen. But if the elders chose to meet at the community house around the fire, then the rest must leave them alone until they were finished.

Waniwan could see their hopeful anticipation but not knowing the reason and gravity of the news made this scenario tenuous. How can four hundred people including children, dogs, pigs, and pet birds keep still and quiet for long? Of course, they were all on their best behavior now because they wanted the elders to sit down on the beach not in the community house.

The three elders huddled with Tomanti and quickly declared their decision. "We will sit down in the community house around the fire. We will eat and Tomanti will tell us the story."

A communal groan reverberated with disappointment. Nevertheless, they understood the authority of their chiefs and respected their decision. Some quick instructions were given to the people for unloading the supplies and the four men walked forward with a small procession behind them as they made their way to the village.

CHAPTER 43

T he community house stood on a large clearing in the jungle and could hold nearly one hundred men, but today, it was only available to the four elders. The villagers constructed the rectangular building in a similar way to their personal dwellings except for its larger size. Wood piers raised the structure off the ground about a foot or more and provided the upright framing for the walls. Each wall consisted of bamboo shoots running vertically and lashed together by several horizontal cords tied onto the piers. They used a similar construction method for the floor overlaid with a tightly woven palm covering. A thick layer of thatch covered a tall and steep roof. The overhangs of the roof extended at least six feet with supporting piers. This resulted in something like a covered porch that wrapped around the entire building.

Coals burned in a large clay fire pit in the center of the floor. The men sat around it while anxiously awaiting detailed news from Tomanti. They motioned for him to dispense with any protocol regarding the assortment of food laid out for them.

Gusti, one of the chiefs, spoke what the others were thinking. "We are not hungry for food right now, we are hungry to know what has troubled the villagers and about the strangers. Don't keep us waiting any longer. We have peace and quiet and can think now without covering our ears."

"This morning, we were looking carefully for your return. We spotted something afar off and thought we were seeing you. Then we began to hear the engines at a distance and could clearly see the boat sitting higher out of the water. We hoped it would pass by but it was aiming towards us. The men gathered and came to me for counsel. I had no one to consult since you were not here except old Setiawan. I know that we do not usually seek his advice but since he was older, it seemed right to get his input, though the final decision would be mine.

"My decision was to cover all traces of our existence on the beach and hide in the jungle, ready to strike if it appeared that the strangers were determined to stay. We watched them closely as the boat came near. There were only three men and one young white man with light hair. They landed and began to unload supplies, but the young white man was tied and appeared to be a captive. I decided we must kill them but old Setiawan made a plea for the white man's life. He made a hospitality claim, which you know is unheard of in regard to a trespasser. I didn't know how to answer but chose to wait until you returned. The young man was separated from the others and I knew we could kill him at any time if it was the council's wisdom."

"Where is he now?" asked Waniwan.

"He is with Setiawan several miles away on the opposite side of the island. He is setting up a shelter and will watch him until we decide."

The three other men seemed to communicate their approval with nonverbal expressions.

"We agree that we also would have ordered the men to be killed. You have acted rightly," said Gusti, voicing the opinion of the elders.

Tomanti breathed a sigh of relief on this one important point but wondered, *What will they think about the captive?*

"As for the young white foreigner," said Gusti, "that is not such a clear decision and Setiawan's actions make it clouded. We would not have questioned you had you killed them all. But it is hard to know if we should blame you for listening to that old man's foolishness. He should be wise at his age and respected, but he has forsaken wisdom and continues to hold on to his stubborn ways. If it wasn't for the knowledge that he was one of the few at the beginning, I would be tempted to set him adrift in a canoe and be rid of him once and for all."

"Be careful, Gusti, how you speak," said Suharto, the one elder prone to remaining silent. "Setiawan is to have the honor of his age regardless of his foolishness. Your frustration with him will not change the circumstances."

"No, it doesn't change anything but we can change the circumstances," said Gusti.

"But what about the hospitality claim? Can it be used in this situation?" said Suharto.

"I don't believe so," said Waniwan. "But the one who would know for certain is Agung who is no longer among us. If only he would have stayed and Setiawan gone."

"We can't change that either so we must decide what course of action to take," said Suharto.

"The young man cannot live, it isn't right! He doesn't belong here and his presence will only bring us trouble. It would be better to have the trouble now of killing him rather than more trouble later," said Gusti.

Suharto would not let his question go unanswered. "But what about Setiawan's hospitality claim? You all know how sacred and deep that claim runs among our people, ages beyond our own lives."

"What about it?" said Gusti. "How can it apply? The young white man is an uninvited trespasser. Setiawan is making things up, he is only pretending to have knowledge. I say the foreigner should die and spare us all. It will be an end of these disturbing events and we can start a new day with rest."

The men continued debating the matter late into the night without reaching an agreement among themselves.

"It is no use continuing like this, we must consult the sacred stones," said Waniwan.

"Are you sure?" said Gusti. "You know the decision would be binding on us all. Wouldn't it be better to act according to the wisdom of the council rather than submit ourselves to the fate of the sacred stones?"

"We do not have wisdom or else we would come to an agreement on what to do. But we might agree to let the determination be made by the sacred stones," said Tomanti in agreement with Waniwan.

It seemed inevitable to the four that it would be necessary to have the decision made by their tribal version of casting lots to determine a course of action.

"If the markings all agree, then he must live and we must deliberate about what to do. But if they are confused, then he must die," said Waniwan.

Tomanti, Gusti, Waniwan, and Suharto agreed.

"Let us make the preparations."

CHAPTER 44

Alex slowly stirred from an uncomfortable sleep. A rock kept jabbing his side. He watched the glowing bed of coals a few feet from him. In the faint light, he could see Setiawan still asleep. He wanted to get up and stretch, maybe grab a couple bananas for his empty stomach. A variety of noises filled all the quiet corners of the night. Yet Alex thought he heard the sound of something or someone moving beyond the reach of the ember's glow. A feeling of being watched overcame him so he laid still. Setiawan continued to sleep soundly. More rustling came from a different direction this time.

It's not my imagination, something or someone is there. What do I do? Why do I never know what to do? More rustling sounds. Alex cried out, "Setiawan!"

The rustling stopped immediately and Setiawan awoke and sat up. Alex didn't know how to communicate his fear, so he also sat up and pointed in the direction of the disturbing sounds in the darkness. Setiawan perceived his alarm and listened acutely. His authoritative voice broke the silence, *"Siapa kau!"*[1]

Several boys immediately stepped forward from various directions, looking sheepishly at Setiawan. He spoke harshly to them and, of course, Alex couldn't understand a single word. But he was familiar with the tone of an adult reprimanding kids. The old man stirred the fire and added sticks, making the immediate area brighter while he chided them. Alex got a better

---

[1] "Who are you?"

look at them. He was surprised that they didn't look too much different from boys at a beach in California. They wore long shorts cinched with rope, no shirts or shoes, and some handmade necklaces with a variety of charms hanging from them. They were medium dark skinned and their dark hair looked moppy but not overly long.

Alex thought they looked a bit younger than himself and were certainly frightened at Setiawan's harsh words. If Alex could have understood their speech, he would have heard the following:

"What are you doing out here? Do your fathers know you are out?"

"No, Setiawan. Don't be angry and don't tell our fathers. We were just curious to see the foreigner."

"You'll see him enough in the days to come!"

"How do we know that? The elders are deciding his fate."

"The elders are deliberating tonight?"

"Yes, they are consulting the sacred stones."

"How do you know this? Those meetings are secret!"

They were stunned and silent, realizing they had just incriminated themselves.

"You have been sneaking and listening haven't you!"

They shot glances at each other but did not answer.

"Go home now before I decide on your fate!"

They all scurried off. Alex wanted to ask what that was all about, but the language barrier limited their ability to carry on that kind of communication with any success. Setiawan just looked into the woods with a thoughtful countenance, then closed his eyes and murmured some words that sounded to Alex as a solemn and sympathetic plea, almost like a prayer or maybe some tribal incantation.

Who is he speaking to? Alex wasn't sure he wanted to know, but it made him think about prayer for the first time. He dismissed Agnes when she said she would be praying for him. He thought it was just empty religious talk, but now he wondered if she really did pray for him and if it had any real meaning. Alex reached into his pocket to make sure the little Bible was there, then attempted to get back to sleep.

Morning dawned and Alex enjoyed his breakfast of bananas. Without warning, a young island man appeared at their camp with an urgent message for Setiawan. Seeing Alex, he paused and stared for a moment with a look of disdain and contempt. Setiawan noticed his distracted glare and brought him to attention by calling his name.

"Kadek, what are you here for? What do you want?"

"I've been sent by my father to fetch you. You are wanted at the meeting of the elders right away."

Setiawan motioned to Alex to continue working on the pile of palm fronds before leaving. Kadek had been instructed not to say anything else on their trek through the jungle. Setiawan asked no questions, the answers would come soon enough. Neither of them needed help navigating the complicated path back to the village with the various forks and bends eventually leading to the network of clearings for the huts, each connected with more trails.

It was still early in the morning by the time they reached the village but people were stirring and going about their tasks. As Setiawan and Kadek walked past several huts, men, women, and children stared or whispered to each other but no one said a word to the two walking by. Not a single friendly greeting or attempt at small talk. A heavy blanket of dread covered the village. As they came to the large clearing for the community house, Kadek stopped but Setiawan marched forward and entered.

"Setiawan, please sit down with us and have something to eat," said Waniwan.

He received the food gladly out of protocol and from genuine morning hunger. Slits of light beamed through the vertical gaps in the wall of the hut and reflected off the smoky haze that filled the room from the smoldering fire.

Anxious to get right to the point, Gusti asked in an angry tone, "Setiawan, why did you think you could invoke the hospitality claim on a foreigner who has trespassed on our island?"

Setiawan remained calm and possessed an air of dignified authority even though he was not recognized as a village elder. He was as old as

Waniwan and Suharto. "The foreigner was not trespassing like the others. He was clearly a captive. We do not know if he is an innocent or guilty captive, but since we do not know, he is to be regarded as a guest."

"A guest?" said Gusti.

"Yes, a guest! You have forgotten our former life and customs. You have sheltered yourselves from the customs of foreigners and created new customs that are worse than the ones you fled from. We have chosen to shut the world out but it does not change the older customs of hospitality!"

"No, he is not a guest, we did not invite him!" said Gusti.

"No, we did not invite him but he is a guest according to our ancient customs. Did you receive hospitality on your voyage? Do you expect it of foreigners?"

The others were silent about this. Setiawan took advantage of their momentary stupor. "If you want to stay true to your new custom, then why do you depend on foreigners every other year? You must because we cannot be entirely independent. But you are one-sided in your thinking, and if you do not show hospitality, it may go bad for you and the whole village."

The others were provoked by this man they all despised who audaciously lectured them.

"You are a fool, Setiawan, you know nothing about these things. You should not put your hand to an oar when you are not asked," said Gusti.

"I am not foolish and your words do not alter the truth I am speaking. I'm weary of you disregarding me."

"You should have thought about that many years ago before coming with us to the island. You brought your unwelcome ideas secretly. You deceived us and we will not regard you!" said Waniwan.

"We will certainly not settle this matter today," said Setiawan, "but let me remind you that I have been a faithful man in this village since the beginning. When have I not carried my own load and helped others these many years? You can't answer without acknowledging what I say. But now, we are the few left from the beginning and we were all young then. You have treated me shamefully all these years, but now I am old and I will not die with the blood of an innocent person on my body. If you kill the foreigner, his blood is on you and it will not go unpunished."

"Stop your preaching!" said Waniwan. "We don't want to hear it. Besides, you should know that the sacred stones have determined his fate, so your preaching changes nothing. We will let the foreigner live—for now."

Setiawan, stunned with surprise at this revelation, pondered for a moment. "That's good. That's right."

"We cannot say that it is good or right! For all we know, it is a curse but we cannot go against the sacred stones," said Waniwan.

"So what will you do with him?" asked Setiawan.

"That is why we brought you here. We don't need you to teach us but you must teach the foreigner so listen carefully. We do not know about the future, but for now, we want him to live away from us. We considered taking another journey to leave him on another inhabited island, but is impossible to make another trip so soon. Finish setting up your camp and teach him to fend for himself. We will instruct the others to stay away from him until we can all agree what will happen with him in the days to come. He must know and understand the island rules and order. If he does not abide by them, then his blood will no longer be on our hands but his own—and yours."

CHAPTER 45

Work on their new camp began in earnest. Setiawan showed Alex how to use the palm strings to lace together fronds for a thatched roof. He kept trying to indicate something important to Alex through rustic sign language.

"I don't know what you mean," said Alex

Setiawan looked heavenward, pointing up, then followed by hand motions downward.

"Birds? Airplanes? Who knows? I don't understand you."

Setiawan didn't give up. He cupped one hand and poured a little fresh water from one of the bamboo containers. Without warning, he splashed it in Alex's face and continued his downward hand motions again.

"Okay! Okay! I get it! You don't have to splash me! I understand now—rain." He mimicked Setiawan's hand motions and repeated "rain." Without warning, he quickly grabbed the bamboo container and splashed the contents onto Setiawan, partly as a playful joke but partially out of retaliation for the sprinkling he received. As soon as his thoughtless action hit his target, he became suddenly terrified with the reality that this man might not think of this as a joke. *I'm such an idiot! Why did I do that?*

Alex's response stunned Setiawan for a moment and then the old man's eyes flashed and his face contorted into an awful scowl. Alex was just about to start running when Setiawan could no longer conceal his own joke. His stern face transformed into a huge playful smile. He let out a big laugh.

This caught Alex entirely off guard and he breathed a sigh of relief. He got caught up with the man's infectious laughter and joined him. It was a moment to remember. They instinctively knew that this was a going to be a special friendship.

The day continued with more work and more charades for learning basic words. Seti, as Alex began to call him for short, seemed quicker at learning the English words than Alex was at learning the tribal tongue. Setiawan was anxious to break through the language barrier as he thought to himself, *How will I teach Alekus about his testing period to prove himself and learn the rules of the island? It is life or death for him but he will be clueless until he can understand. How do I teach him about our ways and customs? He seems so ignorant of basic living skills and works so slow and clumsily. What if his own village banished him? He is lazy and weak.*

Alex's thoughts wandered in different directions as Setiawan lashed large bamboo poles together while he helped to hold them in place. *When will the Navy SEALs show up and get me out of here? How will they find me? What if they never find me? How am I going to get off this island? Does anyone know that I'm missing? Do they care? Does Dad care? Is he going to try and find me? Maybe he's glad that I'm out his hair. I'm sure Mom is worried and trying to find me. I can't believe this!*

The day flew by quickly with all the work to be done, and the next day, and the next. Slowly but surely, a hut finally stood complete and secure. After several weeks, a clear path could be seen beaten down to the closest fresh water source. Another path led to the beach where Seti taught Alex to fish. The new trail had to navigate around brackish waterways originating from the coast and mingling with fresh island streams. This network of swamps and canals formed a maze through parts of the island.

Everyday brought new discoveries for Alex: new tasks to learn, new plants, new animals and insects. Yet one unsettling reality sinking in was the conspicuous absence of other people. Besides the brief encounter with the curious boys and the one young messenger, no one else appeared.

"Seti, where are the others?"

"Don unstand." This was how Setiawan said "I don't understand your question" in his broken English.

Alex made a walking motion with two fingers using both hands then pointed to the jungle.

Seti seemed to get the gist of the question, *"Jangan lakukan itu, jangan lakukan itu!"*

To the best of Alex's comprehension, this short phrase meant something like, "Don't do that!" It was one of his earliest language lessons due to many innocent and some not so innocent missteps in the last few weeks. His first time hearing it was when he got tired of lacing palm fronds and slipped quietly away to take a nap. He awoke to *"Jangan lakukan itu, jangan lakukan itu!"* When picking a delicious looking berry to taste, *"Jangan lakukan itu, jangan lakukan itu!"* Or when he snuck away with a flaming stick to make a signal fire on the beach, *"Jangan lakukan itu, jangan lakukan itu!"*

It occurred to him that Seti probably meant they were not allowed to see the others or vice versa. It remained a complete mystery to him why they allowed him to live and why they were isolated from the others. On the other hand, he held onto the faint hope that a boat or helicopter or both would arrive any day now and his lingering questions would no longer matter.

His island food tolerance expanded slowly. Bananas were all he would eat at first. Then a little cooked fish or shrimp. Seti brought some starchy white substance like flour and cooked it over a fire wrapped in a banana leaf. This became a staple food in Alex's new diet. It was bland by itself like white rice, but an acceptable filler along with some fish.

Life seemed to consist mostly of hunting food to eat, gathering food to eat, fishing for food to eat, building fires to cook the food to eat, and digging holes to get rid of digested food they ate.

"You know, Seti, if we could get by without eating food, we could kick back and relax some more." Alex made a habit of talking casually with Setiawan even though he knew Seti couldn't understand everything he was saying. His habit branched out into thinking out loud due to the solitary existence they were living.

"Don unstand," said Seti.

"Yeah, I know, I just think we spend so much time just finding and fixing food. There's got to be more to life."

In some strange way, he seemed to grasp Alex's basic meaning to his jabbering.

"Wanita kerja."

"Okay, I understand *kerja*. I say 'work' you say *'kerja.'* But what do you mean *'wanita kerja'*?"

Seti reached down and grabbed a couple palm fronds and held them to his waist like a skirt and rocked his hips side to side.

Alex laughed, "Oh, a woman. A woman's work! I get it."

This made Setiawan smile. He didn't mean to be funny but he was affected by Alex's sudden levity. Yet in the back of his mind, he knew the sobering truth that Alex was in jeopardy and that was no laughing matter.

CHAPTER 46

AUGUST

A village woman sat outside a hut working tediously, weaving long slender palm fronds and transforming them into a functional basket destined to store sago flour. A young woman emerged from the doorway.

"Mother, do you want me to gather roots for you today?"

"You want to gather roots? Indah, what has gotten into you? You've never liked gathering roots before."

"I know, but today I feel like gathering roots."

"Let me feel your forehead."

"Mother, I'm not sick! I feel fine."

"I'm not opposed to you gathering roots, it's just strange behavior coming from you. You must admit that you like your status as a chief's daughter a little too much at times and are usually trying to get out of work."

"No, I don't. Stop teasing me. I work—most of the time—just not all kinds of work. But now that I'm almost at the age to be married, I think I had better start working harder."

"Really?"

"At least today," said Indah with a wry smile.

"Go. Get roots. Don't disappoint me."

"I won't disappoint you."

Indah was giddy about today's outing and skipped off after grabbing an empty basket from the hut. Her mother had no clue about her daughter's real motivation.

Indah whisked her way through the village, trying not to draw any attention to herself. The huts in the main part of the village were close together like the main street of a town, but many others were separated by short distances, each with its own clearing and interconnected by walking paths. Her family lived in one of these dwellings towards the outskirts of the village but she still had to walk past several more huts.

With a basket at her side and an uncharacteristic determination in her steps, she unintentionally drew the attention of little Aisyah, a younger cousin about seven years old who lived close by. She was playing with a litter of puppies and took notice of Indah's determined steps.

"Indah, where are you going?"

"Nowhere interesting, Aisyah."

"What are you doing with the basket?"

"I'm going to dig roots for my mother."

"You are going to dig roots? Do you know how?"

"Of course, I know, Aisyah! I was digging roots long before you were born or could even say 'root,'" Indah said with a smile.

"But I've never seen you dig roots before."

"What do you mean? Stop teasing me, of course I have."

"Can I go with you? I'm not doing anything now." Aisyah put the stick down that served as a chew toy for one of the puppies.

"No, not today. I'm going alone."

"But you need my help, I don't think you'll remember how to find roots."

"I don't need help today, Aisyah, but thank you for asking. Maybe next time."

"Next time? That may be years from now! Do you have a fever?"

"Don't be silly, I don't have a fever!"

Indah moved on, her heart pounding. She didn't want company. No one else stopped her but another set of eyes fixed on her as she disappeared into the jungle.

The island was covered with an elaborate network of trails. Her limited knowledge made her a little uneasy. Indah marked the trail each time she veered off in another path by tearing the broad leaf of a common jungle plant. She wanted to make sure she didn't get lost. She walked for nearly an hour.

The further she ventured from the village, the smaller and less trodden the trails became. She now walked on a faint path, yet her limited trail skills were good enough to recognize signs of recent use. She slowed her pace. The sound of the surf gently made its way to her present space. *I must not be far from the other side of the island.*

She slowed down and started stepping lighter, listening intently while scanning every direction for signs of a camp. She didn't want to be seen, she only wanted to get a peek at the foreigner. Her curiosity grew day after day and week after week since hearing the description of the light-haired young man from the boys who caught a glimpse of him. Her heart pounded harder as the reality of her precarious journey started setting in. *What am I doing here?* she asked herself. *What was I thinking? I'm such a foolish girl to come all this way alone. If Setiawan sees me, I'm going to get in big trouble. I should go home right now!*

A faint smell of smoke caught her attention and caused her wandering thoughts to vanish for the moment. *I must be close. I've come this far. It would drive me crazy for weeks if I don't try to catch a glimpse of him after coming this far.*

Indah used extreme caution as she moved through the woods with the stealth of a hunting cat. The smell of smoke grew a little stronger. She decided to get off the trail in case Setiawan or the foreigner happened to be walking her way. After a few more steps, she caught sight of the newly constructed hut, barely visible from her limited vantage point behind a barrier of plants and trees. She felt her stomach in her throat and struggled to temper her fear mingled with excitement. *What am I doing?*

She crouched down, keeping her head below the tall plants. Without a path, it was more challenging to inch her way closer. The jungle provided a few natural clearings around large sago palms and fallen trees. She sometimes peered around trees, other times, her head periscoping over tall bushes to keep the distant hut in view. Some of her movements placed her at a disadvantage, losing sight of the camp altogether.

A sudden rustling sound to her left startled her. She froze, casting a quick glance in the direction of the noise. *Oh, it's just a civet.* The small cat-like animal with a pointy face similar to a mongoose looked at her for a moment and went back to foraging for food. Indah admired its efforts. She lightheartedly thought, *I'll have to ask you where to find roots after I find what I'm looking for first.*

A new rustling sound behind her didn't startle her this time. *There must be a family of civets out gathering food.* She casually looked behind her and then screamed.

CHAPTER 47

Indah's startled scream quickly turned to embarrassment. She got more than a peek of the foreign visitor, there he stood not more than ten yards from her. Alex stared dumbstruck at her as she stared in awe of him.

He broke the awkward silence, "Wow, are all the girls on the island as beautiful as you? Or have I just met the winner of the Miss Island Pageant?"

He knew she couldn't understand a single word but he missed the company and conversation of females, so much that it felt satisfying to give voice to his thoughts anyway. She looked frightened so he decided to change his tactic. He tried using a few words in the local language.

"Ha-lo si-apa nam-amu?"[2]

She stared in silence.

"Siapa namamu?" Alex asked again, more unsure of himself than before.

"*Namaku* Indah," she said with equal parts shyness and intrigue.

"Indah?" he said. He couldn't help smiling, excited that she understood him.

She nodded.

"Alex," as he pointed to himself and slowly repeated, *"Nam-aku* Al-ex."

She just nodded. Her heart was still racing from being taken by surprise at a tense moment, her nerves wound tight while sneaking through the jungle. Now that her cover was blown, she just stared, paralyzed. Indah didn't

---

[2] "Hello, what is your name?"

144

have a contingency plan. She blurted out, *"Aku mengumpalkan makanan,"*[3] and slightly lifted her basket in a sheepish manner.

Alex caught her last word *"makanan." "Makanan?"* he asked. "Food? You are gathering food?" He was excited again to find that his limited knowledge of the language was useful.

She nodded and said, *"Talas."*

"Talas? You are gathering roots? *Talas?"* he asked.

She nodded again. Then a strange thing happened that changed the dynamics of this unfolding scene, Indah's eyes began to get watery and Alex thought she was frightened by him. He was so nervous about scaring her away that he made a quick decision to stop talking and immediately sit down, thinking this would be a nonthreatening posture.

She stared with confusion as a single tear ran down her face. She reactively wiped it off with the back of her hand and tried hard to stop another tear from welling up.

Alex looked on with sympathy. He thought she was the most beautiful girl he had ever seen. She wore a simple patterned tube dress that left her shoulders bare and was synched at the waist with a decorative cord. It was not a clumsy island frock but a graceful fit that didn't hide her figure. Her straight black hair was long and tied back. She had high cheek bones, almond shaped eyes, a pleasant rounded face, and lips like a magazine model. She wore a necklace made of large earth toned beads and metallic disc earrings about the size of a small coin. But the tears in her eyes troubled him.

As she made brief glances at Alex, now sitting on the ground, she couldn't help but notice his genuine look of interest and sympathetic blue eyes. He looked kind. She sat down and wiped another tear away.

Why is she crying? thought Alex.

Why am I crying? I'm so embarrassed, she wondered.

Alex pointed to the basket, *"Talas?"*

She nodded, surprised again that he knew some of her native tongue. *Maybe he can understand me.* She decided to explain herself in her own language.

---

[3] "I'm gathering food"

"I didn't mean to intrude, I was out collecting roots and you startled me. I know I shouldn't be here. I'm not sure how I came this far, I don't want to cause any trouble. I hope Setiawan won't be angry and tell my father."

Her voice sounded beautiful to Alex. He couldn't understand a word she was saying but he loved to hear her. He assumed she was explaining herself.

"Well, I don't know what you just said but I wouldn't mind hearing it again."

He noticed her basket was empty and suspected that she was not collecting food but snooping around from curiosity. He could tell that she was nervous and not comfortable in his presence so he concocted a plan.

"*Tinggal,*" said Alex. This was another word he learned early on, which, to the best of his knowledge, meant "stay here" or "stay."

Indah looked confused but nodded acquiescingly.

Alex got up, turned in the opposite direction and darted off.

Indah was an emotional basket case, overwhelmed with this turn of events. *What did I think was going to happen? What is going to happen? I'm going to get in trouble for this, I should get up and run home right now. He seems kind but how do I know? I don't understand most of what he says. Where is Setiawan? What if he finds me? I'm going to be in trouble, I had better leave soon. I had better leave now! But where is he. What did he say his name was? Why wasn't I paying attention? Why am I crying?*

Indah wrestled with these questions for several minutes, unable to make up her mind on what she should do. It seemed like a long wait but then Alex reappeared from the direction he left. He carried a large jungle leaf folded like a package and cautiously approached Indah, watching to make sure she didn't panic and bolt. He sat down directly across from her, much closer than before. He set the package down between them and unfolded it carefully.

"*Talas!*" he said with a big smile.

She looked at the pile of taro roots in wonder and looked up at Alex. His big smile touched her nervous heart and she smiled back at him.

Oh, that smile, Alex thought. He wished he could have taken a picture and stuck it in his little Bible to stare at any time he got discouraged. But he didn't need a picture. Her face, smiling at him with glistening eyes, and her shy, embarrassed demeanor, became etched into his memory as if his soul was equipped with a photo sensor and his gaze a shutter that let the light and image through.

Alex wasted no time trying to make a big impression on her. He motioned to her empty basket. She handed it to him and one by one, he transferred the taro roots until the basket was nearly full. But the basket wasn't the only thing almost full at that moment.

"I'm guessing you trekked a long way from your village to get here and I can only guess why," said Alex. "But you will probably be needing to get home soon. I hope this helps. I hope you come back some time. Soon. Bye." He got up again, waved goodbye and said, *"Kembali."*[4]

Indah didn't understand what he said or the gesture of his hand but she did understand *"kembali."* With her subdued voice and beautiful eyes gazing up at his, she replied, *"Salamat tinggal,"*[5] and whispered under her breath, *"Aku akan datang kembali."*[6]

Alex disappeared but not far. It was his turn to hide and spy as he secretly watched her get up, look around, and make her way back to the trail to begin her walk home.

Indah felt her heart pounding again, but this time, it was beating a different rhythm than when she began her venture.

---

[4] "Come back."

[5] "Goodbye"

[6] "I will come back."

CHAPTER 48

Indah skipped along the path towards home, daydreaming. In the back of her mind, she knew she needed to make haste to avoid unnecessary suspicion and questions. She rounded a tight bend and suddenly crashed into an unsuspecting person heading the opposite direction.

Her initial shock and embarrassment quickly morphed into exclamations.

"Kadek!" shouted Indah with exasperation. "Watch where you are going! You frightened me and nearly knocked me over!"

"You want me to watch where I'm going?" said Kadek. "What are you doing out here?"

"That's none of your concern!"

"What do you mean by that? I've always known what you are doing."

"We're no longer children. We're not playmates anymore," said Indah.

This seemed to affect Kadek deeply.

"Of course, we aren't children, but that hasn't changed my interest in you," said Kadek. He had a smirk on his face and a tone of romantic interest in his voice.

She wasn't amused.

"I'm a young woman now and can manage my own affairs, and if you want me to speak to you again, you'd better leave me alone."

Indah was not usually rude but he had startled her at a time when she wanted to go unnoticed.

Kadek didn't get the hint and blundered on, "Your father and mine would have a different opinion about that since they have plans for us to be together."

This was too much for Indah. "I am not a piece of property to be bargained over or traded. I will not marry anyone against my will, and if you don't believe me, you can find that out for yourself from my father."

He should have stopped there but his own stubborn streak kicked into to high gear. "I already know your reputation for being hard to tame, but you must get married soon and our parents agree that we are a good match."

Indah didn't respond. She shoved past him in anger and stomped off towards the village.

Kadek stared for a moment and realized that he needed to change his tactics. She was stubborn but she was also the most beautiful girl on the island. Regardless of what their parents thought, he knew that she could influence her father against him if she wished.

"Indah! Wait! Indah!"

She kept her pace without pausing or looking back.

He quickly caught up to her and pleaded while trying to keep up, "You know I'm only teasing. We have always been friends and I just wanted to know what you were doing. I saw you leave on the trail earlier, and when you didn't return, I thought I would look for you."

"You should mind your own responsibilities. I was digging roots for my mother!"

"Digging roots?"

She suddenly stopped and faced him with eyes blazing and her basket outstretched, "Yes! Digging roots! Now leave me alone!" With that, she turned and stomped off again.

Kadek just stood there pondering, *She has a temper and she's stubborn, but she's so beautiful. But is she worth the trouble?* He kept watching her distant figure marching off in a huff. *Yes, she's worth the trouble. Who knows what has set her off this time? Maybe she's sick with a fever. Something's not right because I've never known her to dig roots. I didn't know she knew how. I better keep a closer eye on her.*

CHAPTER 49

S itting across a fire that evening, Setiawan wondered at Alex's strange mood. "Alekus okay?"

Looking up, Alex shifted from his distant thoughts to his present reality and smiled. He had taught Seti "okay" and it made him feel more connected to hear Seti use his own English slang. Alex launched into one of his many lengthy monologues as if he was sharing his heart to a pet that couldn't understand. It was therapeutic to him. Yet he didn't stop to consider that Seti was not a pet but a man, a keenly interested man who understood more than Alex imagined. Seti gained an understanding of some basic English quicker than he could speak it. Beyond that, he interpreted Alex's tones, mood, and body language with astounding accuracy.

"I'm okay, Seti. I was just thinking about my mom…and my dad. You're kinda like a dad I never had. You're teaching me things and showing me how to survive, and I think you actually care about me though I'm not sure why. I never thought much about family and life before. I have time to think here. I miss gaming, I miss my bed and pillow, I miss drinking macchiatos, I miss my mom. But I feel like I've been missing something in life and I can't tell you what it is, but I feel it here more than ever. I think I felt it a little back home but my life was never quiet enough to give it much thought. It was like everything in my life was filling up all the space, and if things got quiet for a moment, it would freak me out and I would turn to my phone, or my computer, or my TV, or to my friends. But I think I've been running from something though I'm not sure I know what it is. So that's what I'm trying to figure out. I'm trying to understand why I try to drown out this empty feeling, whatever it is that's missing. I wonder if it has to do with my dad. He's been missing but I don't know if that's it. Almost all my friends have divorced parents and I don't know if they feel this way. I never asked, they never asked. Who knows? Do you think my dad is trying to find me? Is anyone trying to find me? Or maybe they're all glad that I'm missing and saying, 'Why should we look for Alexander Brooks? What's really so special about him?' In fact, I've been thinking that maybe I'm not such a great person after all, but I'm not really different from others. Nobody's good. I felt like I did something good today and wanted to be a good person when I met—well, maybe I better not tell you about her, you might not approve and I can't handle that right now. Let's just say I've been given a little motivation today."

Alex stopped talking but didn't expect a reply.

Setiawan couldn't understand most of the words, nevertheless, his gift to interpret the essential meaning didn't fail him. He got up and entered the hut and returned with Alex's pocket Bible and sat down next to him and gently said, *"Baca baca."*

Alex no longer kept the little Bible in his back pocket for fear of losing it. But he didn't read it either.

Seti repeated his words, *"Baca baca."*

"I'm not sure what *'baca baca'* means but I'm afraid to read it, Seti. I'm afraid I won't understand it, and worse yet, if I do understand it, I'm afraid I won't like it. But maybe you'd like to hear it read?"

Seti seemed eager for him to do just that.

"Well, I guess *'baca baca'* means 'read,' but how would you know about reading? Do you have a written language? Hard to know. Oh well, I guess it won't hurt."

He found the start of the first chapter. "The book of the genealogy of Jesus Christ, the son of David, the son of Abraham—oh great, what a start, a genealogy of all things! What kind of compelling opening is that?"

Seti looked amazed that Alex could read the words and then puzzled when he stopped. He looked at Alex with anticipation and enthusiastically said, *"Baca baca."*

Alex decided to keep reading in spite of his belief that it would be boring and confusing.

When he read the story of Christ's miraculous birth, he personally became interested. Then the story of the wise men from the east also kept his attention. Alex had seen nativity sets at Christmas time but they had no meaning to him. He now felt educated and informed. He was genuinely drawn in by the angels, the prophesies, and dreams.

"You know, Seti, I'm no school teacher but I could try to teach you how to read. It might take a while—wait a minute! Scratch that. I've got to get off this island. You know, that's another thing that scares me. I've been thinking, how is it possible for anyone to find me? Hariyono told me they were picking an island at random. How many islands are there? I'm not sure where we are. If the men on the boat were the only ones who knew our location and now they are all dead, what then? How is it possible to be found? What if I'm stuck here for the rest of my life?"

Seti looked on with sincere interest in Alex's distress. He only replied, *"Baca baca,"* and pointed to the Bible again.

"I think I've read enough for one day already, maybe tomorrow. But it's not going to help me get off of the island. What if I'm beyond help?" Alex slipped into a melancholy mood for the rest of the evening, pondering the possibility that this might be the only home he would ever know.

CHAPTER 50

SEPTEMBER

Indah couldn't get Alex out of her mind. She really didn't know much about him except his precarious situation on the island, his isolation with old Setiawan, and his gift of roots. She at least knew what he looked like now, and as she thought about him, an unconscious smile emerged. The novelty of a foreigner close to her own age was captivating enough, but the actual sight of him only increased her interest. His light skin, blonde hair, and blue eyes added to his pleasant face and features. She cultivated her busy mind like a garden and planted imaginations like seeds while daydreaming. Daydreams threatened with a potential nightmare if anyone guessed what was going through her mind—who was going through her mind.

This wasn't the first time she found herself intrigued with thoughts of foreigners, though no one on the island her age had ever seen one or heard much about them. Indah thought about the select group of older men who would go away every other year to trade with foreigners and bring back clothing, materials, and other essentials that couldn't be produced on the island. Even as a young child, it caused Indah to ask questions about the foreign lands and the people who lived in them. "What were they like?" "How were they different?" "Why didn't they come and visit to trade?" So many questions hushed by her parents time and time again until she learned to stop asking. But she didn't stop wondering. It became part of the fabric of her being and influenced her thoughts about the world outside her village. She was unique. None of her friends seemed curious about these things or else their parents did a better job driving it out of them.

Old Setiawan also caused great curiosity in her but she was not allowed to talk with him. He lived as an outcast among them under strict tribal rules to not spread his unwanted ideas. They continually threatened to remove him from the island. Indah thought, *What are his ideas that my father and the other village leaders don't like?* Her limited knowledge of her tribe's history was sufficient to drive her curiosity to higher levels in recent years. *How is Setiawan mixed up with the beautiful young man from another island where the strangers have light colored skin, light hair, and bright eyes?*

The evening fire was burning in the center of the family hut and Indah's mother worked late preparing extra food for tomorrow's community gathering to make sago flour. Her father, Tomanti, sat near the fire, carving spear tips. Her three younger siblings were lying down in various places but Indah couldn't sleep. Her mind kept working late. She shifted from thoughts of how to visit Alex secretly and what to make of their island's history. Her father's father was part of the original migration to the island from somewhere else. They wanted to preserve their culture from unwelcome foreigners with different customs and strange beliefs. People who didn't believe in the spirits of ancestors or the ancient spirits that dwelt in trees, rivers, stones, and some animals. Good spirits and bad spirits, malicious spirits, and jealous spirits. These native people were taught from generation to generation to respect and appease these spirits.

All she knew about Setiawan is that he was a young man during the migration who brought strange beliefs, influenced by foreigners. He did not reveal his changed views until years after the island was established. *But what are his beliefs?* No one was allowed to know and he was forbidden to tell.

Her thoughts drifted back to Alex, *How will I be able to see him again? Tomorrow begins the village's work of preparing sago, maybe I could slip away. Everyone's so busy and I am already known to disappear on these occasions and make excuses for not helping. Maybe if I worked for a little while then sneak away, nobody would miss me and everyone, especially Kadek, will be hard at work. Yes! I think that is a good plan.*

CHAPTER 51

The community effort to process sago starch took several days, followed by a feast. The hard work began months before when the men hacked down several large sago palms, then split them down the middle and let them lie on the ground untouched. They took this extra step ahead of time to cultivate one of their island delicacies called *"tombulu."*

Now the arduous work continued by chopping up the pith of the sago with axes, machetes, sharp sticks, or anything that could effectively break apart the woody pulp. Men, women, and children not only helped with this task but also carried baskets of the pulp up a small hill to dump into cloth laid out in a large hollowed log. This basin is connected to a sluice that runs down the hill to another hollowed log lined with cloth. At the top basin, women pound and knead and stomp the pulp as a steady flow of water is supplied by villagers who haul it from a nearby stream in bamboo containers. The starch is separated from the pulp as it filters through the cloth, runs down the sluice, and settles in a lower basin like silt. The dense starch is placed in cloth sacks and allowed to drain until it forms a usable cake of flour for cooking. This white substance provides the staple food for their diet along with starchy roots like cassava and taro.

Indah preferred hauling water because it afforded her the opportunity to appear and disappear at will. The village knew her habits. They wouldn't tolerate this from any other young woman except Indah, partly due to her status as a chief's daughter but more so for her rare beauty and charm. She was the island's version of a prima donna.

She made an extra effort to look useful this time in hope of gaining more leniency for a longer absence than usual. Her mother wondered, *Maybe my Indah is maturing and taking more responsibility like other girls her age. First, the root gathering and now she is working hard to help make sago.* But when Indah disappeared during the late morning work, she just sighed and thought to herself, *It's a good thing everyone loves Indah or else I would be shamed as a mother for her laziness.*

Indah planned her journey across the island and she didn't intend to go empty handed. She wanted to bring Alex a gift. Keeping her eyes open for an opportune time to slip away, she also slipped some of her mother's prepared food into a small basket along with a clump of sago. *If only I could get some tombulu,* she thought. There was presently no one near the collection of community provisions. She casually drew near, keeping a careful watch to make sure that no one was around. Among the baskets, she spotted a fresh harvest of *tombulu* and quickly grabbed a handful.

"Indah, are you hungry so soon?"

She froze, startled by the sudden appearance of Kadek. He had kept his eyes on Indah in hope of being near her for part of the day. He set his machete down and picked up an empty container to haul water. "What are you doing with the *tombulu*? You know that those are for the feast."

"I'm not taking *tombulu*, I'm putting more in the basket. You, men, missed these in your haste so I was asked to bring them." With that she reached into her own basket, grabbed the *tombulu* again, and put them back where she had snatched them from.

This confused Kadek who thought for sure that he had just seen her taking a handful out of the container. He changed the subject, "I thought you were carrying water this morning?"

"I was until I was given this small job," said Indah. She made certain in the tone of her voice that she felt put out that he was talking to her at all.

"You're not still angry with me, are you?"

"No, but I can get angry again if you keep me from my work!"

"When did you start being concerned about work?"

She scowled and stomped off not saying another word.

I guess I made her angry again but I don't know why. He set down the water container, picked up his machete, and left grumbling to himself.

Indah didn't stomp off far. As soon as Kadek walked away she ran back to the baskets, grabbed a fistful of tombulu, and darted off again.

Her trek to Setiawan's camp would take her an hour at a brisk walk. She wasted no time. When she reached the halfway point, according to her intuition, she paused, scanned the jungle intently, then slipped off the path into the dense foliage.

CHAPTER 52

"This isn't working, Seti!"

Alex, knee deep in the surf, held two short poles with netted material between them, trying his hand at dipping for small fish and shrimp but not having much success. Though Setiawan was not in earshot, Alex continued speaking out loud in frustration. "You make it look easy, I don't get it, this shouldn't be that hard!"

The thought often crossed his mind that there is a huge gap between racking up kills and points in a game and the real challenge of collecting enough food everyday by hand or spear or net. Seti tried teaching him how to use a bow and arrows, but those lessons were not going so well. The arrows had no fletching, the bow had no arrow rest, there were no sights, yet Seti could shoot a bird out of a tree or a fish in a stream. Alex couldn't hit a large palm tree with any consistency.

He looked both ways down the beach to see if Seti was near. He wasn't. So Alex took the opportunity to leave the shallow surf and sit at the edge of the jungle under the shade of palms. He thought, *What a difference since the first day on the island.* An involuntary shudder came over him as he recalled the death of Hariyono and the other two men. Just then, a rustling sound from behind startled him. Rustling sounds in the jungle were a regular part of daily life but he learned to not ignore them. He focused his attention in an effort to drown out all the other noises as he looked and listened in the direction of the noise. Nothing at first, but then he heard a unique bird call. He had a new and growing interest in making a mental inventory of the exotic birds, especially the remarkable birds of paradise, though he didn't know their name. He looked intently in the direction of the call but he didn't catch sight of the bird.

He slowly took cautious steps towards the sound. The call stopped and he stopped. It resumed and he resumed. *It must be close but I can't see it.* He had discovered that these birds often perched low in the brush or on the ground. The call stopped again. He continued his search forward, navigating around bushes, palms, and vines but he went too far, he heard the call behind him.

He turned around and finally caught sight of this rare bird of paradise. His heart leaped, "Indah!" he said with a huge smile. "You've come back."

She returned his big smile, but before he could process this happy encounter, she took off through the woods at a brisk pace, looking back briefly and motioning him to follow.

He hesitated a second or two, wondering if he was about to do something foolish by blindly following her. His second guessing didn't last long, he threw all caution to the wind and caught up to her. She looked back and gave him an approving smile. They soon stepped out onto the faint trail that cut across the island towards the village. Indah picked up her pace but Alex stayed close behind.

As thrilled as Alex was to be on an unknown adventure, there remained some lingering doubts that troubled his mind. These pestering thoughts dissipated every time he got a glimpse of the excited and eager expressions on her face. Yet the skeptical thoughts kept coming back the longer she kept going. He remembered what happened the last time he followed someone not knowing where they were taking him. That didn't go so well.

At last, she slowed her pace then stopped to peruse their surroundings. She spotted what she was looking for and stepped off the trail into the thick, dark jungle forest. She brought Alex to the base of a large outcropping of stone that stood about eight feet high and twice as wide. She led him around to the opposite side where the ground sloped steeply down, and more of the rock was exposed due to the slope. The most interesting feature was a decent size hollow in the face of the rock, forming a shelter big enough for at least two people to sit under comfortably, clearly Indah's intended destination. A basket of food already awaited them. She knelt down with a giddy expression, motioning for Alex to sit down next to her. He was on cloud nine.

Indah didn't waste any time with her agenda. She brought out a small clay jar containing a few smoldering coals and deftly started a tiny fire in front of them by gathering little sticks and dry leaves within reach. Alex, simply dumbstruck by the encounter, just stared at her in wonder, wishing they could talk. She brought out a piece of bark in the shape of a crude dish which she placed on the flames, and continued stoking the fire with sticks. Alex was familiar with the use of bark since Setiawan used the same technique. It got hot and sizzled but it didn't catch fire. She took some of the sago and carefully wrapped it in a banana leaf like a burrito and laid it on her steaming wooden dish. Her first surprise for Alex was a few prepared cakes that her mother had made from mashed taro roots mixed with spices and baked the night before. She handed him the treat and waited for his response. He took a bite and showed his genuine appreciation for the good cooking by making the universal sound of "mmmm." Setiawan was only a rustic cook and nothing he made was fancy or seasoned. He thought her food tasted great but it was her close presence and enthusiasm that fed his soul. She couldn't hide her delight at his enjoyment of the food, but she was almost ready to burst with excitement over the thought of her next surprise, the island delicacy known as *tombulu*.

She reached into her basket again and Alex's eyes got big when she pulled out a large wiggling grub, the size of a bite-sized breakfast sausage. Its fat white body full of ridges and dark reddish head made Alex woozy. Thankfully, she was so focused on admiring the size and fatness of this palm weevil grub that she didn't notice Alex's perplexed expression. She picked up a small piece of bamboo and stuck the grub like a hotdog on a stick and started to roast it over her fire.

She bashfully averted her eyes from Alex and kept her focus on the *tombulu* to make sure it was cooked just right. Her joy couldn't be stifled and it expressed itself through frequent smiles and a faint giggle.

This delay in eye contact gave Alex a needed moment to gather his thoughts and prepare his mind and stomach for this trial. *You can do this. Don't look at it. Don't blow this. Don't throw up, don't pass out. Just pretend you love it and don't disappoint her.* He was so taken by this girl that he was willing to try almost anything, but this certainly stretched the boundaries of chivalry.

She slid the steaming grub, now glistening in its own fat, off the bamboo and handed it to Alex, her face radiant with exultation.

Alex's mom always hoped that he would take up acting but he continually disappointed her by swearing he had zero interest in that line of work. But this small part that he was about to play would have made her proud. He gave Indah the biggest smile he could muster then popped the tombulu into his mouth, closed his eyes as if savoring it and gave a hearty "Mmmm." He didn't bite into it, hoping he could swallow it whole, but his gag reflex was kicking in. He opened his eyes and one look at her face brought the needed inspiration to go for broke and chomp into it.

To his surprise, it wasn't a repulsive taste, but the textures on the other hand drove him to the brink of gagging. His determination paid off with success. He ate it and she was clearly pleased, but the ordeal wasn't over. There were more grubs in the basket, and before he got the first one completely swallowed, she skewered three more, anxious to roast them as soon as possible. He eventually ate everything she brought him and once the meal was over, they just stared at each other not knowing what to do next since they had no easy way to communicate to each other.

Alex decided to break the silence, "I've not been this far from our camp but I'm glad I'm here. I like this spot. I mean, I like you in this spot. I wish we could talk. I want to know if this is an official first date or if you treat all castaways this way. Or maybe, in your culture, this is a marriage proposal." He said this in a joking manner for his own amusement, but once it was out of his mouth, it occurred to him that it might be something he shouldn't take lightly. "Maybe I shouldn't joke about that," he said sheepishly.

Indah appeared to enjoy hearing him talk, so he continued. "Anyway, I wish I could tell you—I mean, I'm going to tell you, but I wish you could understand that I'm really thankful for your kindness. I don't think you would understand how scared I am of being stuck here for long, worse yet, maybe for good. I'm really missing my mom and my friends and a bunch of other things that you would have no clue about anyway. But getting back to my point, I'm glad we met because it's a boost for me and I've been thinking about you a lot, even though I don't know anything about you except you're very pretty, and I suppose you're a decent cook in your village and you seem to be interested in me. As far as I'm concerned, that's something to bring a little bit of uplift to a miserable exile on your island."

When he began his little speech, he spoke playfully, but as he kept going, his voice got lower and without premeditation, his mood became more serious and he unexpectedly found himself pouring out his heart to her. "You couldn't imagine how surreal this is for me. I'm worse than nobody here and I'm sure that I'm not welcome except by you and Seti. And I don't want to be here, I didn't ask to be kidnapped and held hostage, or for those men to be killed on this island by your people. And I can't help but think that every day may be my last. It's terrifying and..." At this point tears began to well up in Alex's eyes, and once the first tear broke away and formed a path down his cheek, others quickly followed behind it.

"I don't want to die, I don't want to be here, I didn't ask for any of this, and I don't know what to do. And then you show up and are kind to me. I'm not sure I believe in miracles yet, though I'm reading about them, but it's hard not to hope that they still happen."

Indah's heart overflowed with empathy. She was not used to seeing a young man cry, or any man cry. She was used to comforting her little brothers and sisters when they were upset or scared and now instinct led her to move closer to Alex's side. She cradled his drooping head under her arm and drew him close to her. It was more like the action of a mother than an affectionate girlfriend. Alex did not resist her, he felt like a little child. She patted his head gently with her other hand as she did when consoling her little siblings. This touch of kindness reached Alex's troubled soul and caused a short burst of quiet sobs before he pulled himself together. A peace came over him as he continued to lean against her quietly, no words, no anxious thoughts for a moment.

The nearby sound of something moving in the jungle brought the special moment to an abrupt end and caused both of them to be alert, neither of them breathing. Seconds passed and they didn't hear anything else unusual so they both relaxed. Even though this disrupted their quiet moment, it reminded Indah of her need to get back. Surprisingly, there was no awkwardness between them after such an unexpected emotional moment. Alex noticed Indah's sympathetic dark eyes, misty and full of compassion.

He looked deep into those eyes and taking her hand into his, he said, *"Terima kasih,"* the equivalent of "thank you." It was all he knew to say in her language that would be appropriate. He continued in English but used hand gestures to try and explain himself. "I know we both need to get going. How will I know when to meet you here again?"

She interpreted his meaning and looked up to the sky and waved her hand in an arch that clearly indicated the rise and set of the sun. She held up three fingers.

"Three days, but what time of day?" asked Alex, enjoying this game of charades.

She didn't understand his gesture as he pointed to his wrist. Realizing his dumb mistake, he tried a different gesture by making the arch but stopping at intervals with a questioning look on his face. She understood and pointed straight up.

Parting seemed hard for both of them. Alex was hopelessly glued to the spot but Indah reached for her basket, got up, and disappeared in the jungle, giving once last glance behind her.

CHAPTER 53

Indah did not get very far down the trail when she suddenly stopped in her tracks and froze. A man blocked the way.

"Indah."

"Setiawan," said Indah with trepidation.

"You and I must have a talk," said Setiawan.

"I cannot stop now. I am expected back soon."

"This cannot wait. We must talk now. Sit down." His voice was firm but not angry.

"Sit here on the trail?"

"Yes, there is no one else around. This will work as good as any place."

Indah sat down on her knees and he crouched down low but kept to his feet and folded his arms about his legs.

"I was just out looking for roots," said Indah.

"You were not looking for roots. I know why you are here. I followed you and Alekus."

"Please don't tell my father! I didn't mean to do anything wrong." She teared up from fear and anxiety.

"What I decide to do cannot be determined now. I must warn you that what you have chosen to do may decide the fate of that young man."

"What do you mean? I only took some food to him out of kindness."

"His life is in danger from the elders and that includes your father. If they knew he was meeting with you secretly, Alekus would not see another sunrise in his short life."

"No! That couldn't be true, they wouldn't kill him."

"They would, Indah. And I believe they are looking for a reason to justify themselves."

"But why? What has he done?"

"Nothing. He has done nothing. Yet."

"I was only showing him hospitality."

"I am not blind, I saw your faces. I could almost feel your pounding hearts through the ground I stood on."

Indah looked down, abashed at his insight into her heart.

"I meant no harm," she said with tears in her eyes.

"There's more you need to hear so listen well. When I followed the two of you, I kept my distance so I would not be known. When you stopped at the stone and I stopped not far off, I had an intuition that you were not safe or hidden as well as you thought. I have keen knowledge of this jungle after so many years and I knew that someone was on the trail coming this way from the village. I could hear them walking afar off so I left you and Alekus to go meet whoever it was before it was too late. I stood in the path and along came Kadek."

Indah gasped.

"I knew he must be looking for you. I pretended not to know his purpose and reprimanded him with much anger for seeing him on this side of the island since everyone knows it is forbidden." He said this with an emphasis on the word "everyone." "I did not give him a chance to talk or explain himself but made him turn around and return immediately."

"What am I going to do? He might be waiting for me somewhere along the path."

"Yes, I think he will be waiting. He suspects you and has a jealous look. He must have watched you come this way."

Indah breathed a sigh of relief, "Thank you, Setiawan. I don't know why you would help me but it must be to protect Alekus."

"Yes, he needs protection and so do you."

"What do I do now?" asked Indah.

"I am going to lead you another way across the island to the opposite shore. You can rejoin the village from there on your own. No one will suspect that you came from here. But we must leave now and I must speak some words of wisdom to you as we walk."

"I will follow you and listen. But will you also answer some questions I have about your past and our village history."

Setiawan gave no reply, he simply stood up and began walking. Indah followed close behind as he left the trail and began leading the trek across unfrequented terrain. Very few islanders had the skill and knowledge to go off the trail far without getting turned around and possibly lost. He was mindful of the young woman and did his best to minimize the difficulty of the journey in the direction he chose.

"Indah, you must not meet Alekus in secret again."

This time, it was Indah who didn't answer.

"You will get him killed."

"Because I gave him food?"

"Because you are a chief's daughter. He would not like you to meet alone with any young man at your age, much less a foreigner whom he despises."

"Why does he despise him?"

"Because he is a threat to our village's customs and beliefs. He is an uninvited intruder."

"Do you think that way?" asked Indah.

"No."

"What do you think about him?"

"I think he was stolen from his own island and carried here against his will. I saw him when the boat came. His hands were tied and his skin and hair a different color from the men who were killed."

"Why was he stolen and brought here?"

"I don't know. We don't know enough words yet to understand each other, though he talks much."

"Why did you help him?"

"It is the right thing to do according to our tribe's ancient customs and according to my own beliefs."

"Setiawan, this is the first time we have ever spoken to each other besides customary greetings. The elders do not want us to talk with you. Why?"

"They believe I betrayed the tribe."

"Why do they believe that?"

"You just said they don't want me talking with you. I could be banished from the island for talking with you about it."

"But you are holding my secret within you. You must know that I will hold your secret within me. I have thought about you and our history since I was a little girl. I have so many questions that burn like a fire in me. This is meant to be."

"Hmmmm." Setiawan kept leading the way but stopped talking for a little while, seemingly in deep thought. He finally replied, "You are right, it is meant to be. I will tell you my story and I must not fear the outcome."

CHAPTER 54

"The leaders of our tribe chose a treacherous path by not teaching children the history of our nation. They keep our tribe ignorant of the realities beyond these shores. The past is forgotten and the present is hidden," said Setiawan.

"What is hidden?" asked Indah.

"Knowledge of the world beyond our small island."

"Please, tell me about the world beyond our shores."

"Our trek is not long enough to answer all the questions in your curious and restless mind. But you should know something about our history. Did you know that there are thousands of other islands around us?"

"Thousands? I don't understand what that means?"

"It is like the number of palm trees on this island."

"How can that be?"

"It is true and many of those islands are like this one before we came, no people, just birds and other living creatures. But many others are full of people, more than the sand on our shore."

"Setiawan, are you speaking truth or have you injured your head?"

"I am speaking truth, and the islands of our nation are only a small part of the bigger world." He stopped, looked intently at Indah, held up a hand and grabbed the tip of his little finger. "Not even this big in the world."

Indah's eyes opened wide.

"And the world is full of different people with different customs and beliefs," said Setiawan.

"Are they light people like Alekus?"

"Some are lighter and some are darker than you or I but we are all related."

"Related? You must have spent too much time in the hot sun!"

"No, I am not crazy, but I don't have time to explain everything to you. You said you want to know, are you going to listen or question me?"

"I will listen, but it's hard to believe what you are telling me."

Setiawan looked sympathetically at her for a moment before continuing their journey.

"Did you see the foreign boat that brought Alekus to our shore?"

"Only a quick glance. My father made everyone stay away from the beach."

"Do you remember the size of the boat?"

"Yes, it was very large, much larger than our boats."

"Did you see sails or oars?"

She thought about it for a moment, puzzled. "No," she replied.

"That boat doesn't need oars or a sail, it swims fast on its own and doesn't need to rest. It is small compared to the ones that travel the seas from other parts of the world to our group of islands. This is not new to our generation, they have been travelling here for generations, not just to visit and trade but to settle and take control. The Muslims, the Dutch, the Japanese—"

Indah interrupted, "Who are they?"

"Indah, I told you we don't have enough time for all your questions, I will explain what I can. "Our people may not be the first people, but we have deep roots in the islands. We were only one of many tribes that existed on our former island. It was much larger and lay along a shipping route. Long before I was born, many generations ago, visitors from other countries came to trade goods among the islands and began settling. They were merchants who held to a belief known as Islam. Over time, they gained influence and prominence on many islands, but they were not the only strangers who came to live among us.

"Among them were people called Christians from another land who came to live with us to learn our language and teach us about their beliefs. At first, this was not welcome and the elders warned the tribes against them. Our people harassed them but they would not go away. Some of the tribes were more receptive because they helped cure sicknesses and taught children to read and write. They provided clothes and new kinds of tools for work. By the time I was born, some tribes and villages adopted the Christian beliefs but not ours. Our leaders resisted Islam and would not be influenced by Christianity, they feared the spirits would be angry and do terrible things to us if we did."

"Did the spirits do terrible things to the other tribes?" asked Indah.

"Not that I know of."

"How do you know all of this?"

"When I was a boy, a few of us were educated in schools by teachers with understanding. But our tribe wanted to preserve our heritage and believed that isolation and ignorance of the rest of the world would be the way. They had enough of the encroaching people and their foreign customs, religions, and wars. They chose to leave the island in search of our own, far away from the shipping routes and modernization and away from visitors."

"That is why we moved here?"

"Yes. They sent out a few able men to search out islands who came back with news of this place."

"Is this knowledge the reason you are shunned and kept silent?" asked Indah.

"No, it is not the main reason. There are others on this island who know all that I have spoken."

"Then why are you not allowed to speak to us?"

"Because one of the many things our leaders wanted to get away from was the foreigners' knowledge of our Creator."

"Our Creator?"

"Yes, the One Great Spirit who created the world and everything in it. The Christians had knowledge of Him and His Son who came down from the heavens and lived as a man to teach the world."

"But we believe in a great spirit and many other spirits. How do they know something that we don't?"

"The Son of the Great Spirit came many generations ago in a faraway place. We did not hear the report of Him until ships came to trade, and people called missionaries travelled the world to give the report and pass along His teaching to us."

"That must be good. Why did our people not listen?"

"Some of us did, but not many."

"Why?" asked Indah. "I don't understand."

"After many generations of living in ignorance, our own beliefs were poisoned by evil spirits and we were deceived. The deception is so deep that our leaders would not open their ears to hear."

"How is it that you opened your ears to hear them?"

"I was a simple child, an orphan living with an aunt and uncle. I was a burden to them so when a school started by Christian missionaries opened near our village, my relatives took me so I would learn to read, get a meal every day, and medicine for sickness. I spent many years going to school and I also learned about God and His Son."

"Why did you come with the tribe if they were trying to get away from the foreign ideas?"

"I was sixteen years old when my uncle died and my aunt needed care. Her children had their own families to feed, so I left school to work and take care of her. It was close to the time the village leaders decided to migrate."

"You must have known they wouldn't want you to come if they knew you held foreign beliefs."

"Listen carefully, Indah, they are not foreign beliefs, they are the true record of God, His Son, and the people of the world. If you knew that your tribe was ignorant of truth and believed lies from evil spirits that keep them away from the true God, wouldn't you want them to know for their own sake?"

Indah couldn't answer this question. There were too many new ideas that troubled her mind. They frightened her. She didn't know if Setiawan could be trusted. *What if he was the one listening to evil spirits and my father and the other village leaders are right to forbid him from speaking about these things?*

Setiawan sensed the conflict from her silence and could see her troubled face when he looked back to see if she was going to answer. Her initial enthusiasm for knowledge of the world had introduced a real dilemma and she didn't know what side she should be on. Ignorance was still and quiet like an undisturbed pool of water, but this knowledge, if it was true or false, brought trouble to her soul. *Maybe the leaders are right,* she thought to herself, *even if they are wrong.*

"You are troubled and that is why I am forbidden to talk. It does disturb what has been taught and believed for generation after generation."

"So why would you disrupt our people's understanding?"

"Because, Indah, if you go deeper and search out a much older generation, you would learn that they understood differently. It was to help us get back on the right path that the foreign missionaries came. We should thank them, not run from them, or worse, harm them."

"Is Alekus a missionary?"

"No, I am."

"You?"

"At least I hoped to be one when I came here, but I'm an old man now with few years left and I have not helped one person to see the truth. Maybe I will be able to help Alekus in time."

"Do you mean Alekus believes like us?"

"No, I don't think so. I don't know what he believes or understands. He has a Christian Bible with him. It is the only thing he brought to the island but he doesn't behave like a Christian."

"A Bible? What is that?"

"A Bible is a sacred book. It is the history of the creation and how we can know the One True God and His Son."

"Have you read this book before?"

"Yes. I have a copy that I received in school. It is old now and hidden but I still bring it out and read it."

"May I see it sometime?"

"I don't know if that would be safe and you do not know how to read."

"No, but you could read it to me."

"Hmmmm. I would like to do that for you but it may be too difficult to keep it secret."

The two travelers were now close to the opposite side of the island not far from the shore. They could hear the surf and the distinct sounds of the seabirds. Seti stopped.

"It is time for you to go back to the people from here. I'm sure you will have an excuse for your disappearance since that is your known pattern already."

"Thank you, Setiawan. I made a plan with Alekus to meet him again in three days."

"Don't worry about that, I will do what I can to explain it to him."

"Do you talk to him?"

"He has learned a little of our tongue and I have learned a little of his. We struggle to get our words understood."

"Can you tell him that I didn't mean to put him in danger? And I would meet him every day if I could."

Setiawan was surprised at her feelings for the foreigner and didn't know how to reply. "You had better go, the sun is going down."

She went on her way but paused and looked back once last time, "I will consider what you have told me today."

CHAPTER 55

The evening fire cast a warm light upon Alex as his island mentor sat across from him, pondering the young man's expression. Setiawan understood that the glow radiating from Alex emanated from a different flame. As for Alex, he remained oblivious of the goofy smile across his face as he relived the events of the day in his mind.

I don't know how I'm going to stay focused on my work the next few days, thought Alex. *I wish Seti would give me a couple days off. Maybe I'll ask for a sick day. After all, I'm lovesick.*

They ate a scanty meal of cooked fish. Alex tried to cover for his absence earlier in the day by going back to the beach after his unexpected lunch date and try his hand at netting fish again. He was thrilled to have a little success and even more surprised when Seti returned late with nothing.

"This is a first, Seti! I came home with a bigger catch than you."

He understood Alex's boast and gave him a quick smile.

"Kejutan untukmu."

"Kejutan? Let me think, what did that mean…I remember now—'surprise'! You have a surprise for me? It's not even my birthday today, at least I don't think it is, but it's sure full of surprises."

Setiawan went to their hut and grabbed a small basket, not much bigger than a lunch box.

"Oh, I hope it's not grubs. Been there and done that."

He sat down next to Alex and untied some jungle twine holding a makeshift palm frond lid over the woven container. He carefully reached in and pulled out a young cuscus.

"Oh wow! Is this a pet?"

The small furry animal seemed frightened and lost but it did not try to get away from Alex's hands as he held it in his lap. He got a good look at it. It wasn't exactly like a cat but it resembled one closer than anything else he was familiar with. It had little hands and feet like a raccoon. Its face was long and pointy with a funny pink nose and perfectly round eyes like a stuffed animal toy. It had light cream colored fur with a darker shade on its face and some blotches elsewhere. Its long furry tail curled at the end. The fur, like on the rest of its body, looked and felt like short thick carpet, as if it had a crew cut all over. It clung to his shirt and then crawled up to his shoulders and finally perched on Alex's head. Alex and Seti both laughed.

"Wow, I never had a pet before other than a goldfish I won at the carnival. This thing is cool. *Siapa namamu?*"

"*Kuskus.*"

"What does it eat—I mean, *makan*—*apa makan?*"

"*Buah.*"

"That's easy enough, I'm always eating fruit. One more mouth to feed, though."

Alex tried to pluck the animal off his head. It held tight to his hair.

"I hope it will stick around and not run off. Is it a boy or girl?"

Seti didn't understand the question and Alex was not in the mood to play charades.

"I guess I'll have to give it a neutral name. How about Macchiato? It's Italian but it sounds like it fits on an island."

That evening before going to sleep, he put the cuscus back in the basket and tied the lid down out of caution, but in the middle of the night, he woke up and discovered that Macchiato had somehow escaped. He wasn't concerned for its whereabouts. He could feel the cuscus nestled up to next to his head.

CHAPTER 56

Morning light diffused through the thick blanket of jungle vegetation. Unless a person stood on the beach, they would not see the sun rise or set. The only time it would bear down on anyone was in the afternoon if they happened to be in a clearing, otherwise, it simply peaked through the leaves and fronds overhead. The most notable indication of morning was the increase of ambient noise. Everything but the nocturnal animals woke up and had their unique way of greeting the day.

Setiawan left Alex alone early the next morning to make an unexpected trek to the village. The hour of walking gave him time to think through his plans and to pray. The habit of walking alone and praying to God gave him consolation through his lonely years as a despised member of the tribe, always kept at arm's length. His requests seemed unanswered yet he faithfully offered petitions. But most of his time was spent seeking communion with God through simple yet sincere thoughts of worship and gratitude. He lacked friendship on the island from his own people but he was not friendless and he knew it in the depth of his soul. He understood that his life was a temporary sojourn in a broken world. That brokenness being manifested in this far away island among a people who wished to be forgotten. He had faith in an eternal home filled with friends. In the meantime, the island had been a lonely place for him until Alex came into his life.

Setiawan arrived at the outskirts of the village and began walking past the huts situated at the perimeter. The tribe stirred with anticipation of the community feast in celebration of their hard work the day before.

As he encountered people, he kindly greeted them as he always did. Few responded, most simply looked away and ignored him. He watched two men haul a dead pig suspended upside down on pole, heading towards the village to be roasted. He walked past a small group of children racing palm grubs on the parallel ridges of a large banana leaf, prodding them along by poking their back ends with small sticks. The race was not a fast one. Setiawan smiled at them as he reminisced about the times as a child when he raced grubs. He passed little Aisyah playing with her puppies while their mother lay under the floor in the shade of the hut raised about a foot off the ground.

He made his way to Chief Tomanti's hut and found Indah sitting in the clearing, cutting taro roots into a basket. She looked up at Setiawan with surprise as he gave her a friendly greeting. She acknowledged him with a slight smile and inquisitive eyes. *What is he here for?* she thought.

"Is your father home?"

"Why?" she asked with uneasiness.

"It does not concern you," he said.

Was that a hint or simply an elder putting me in my rightful place for an inappropriate question? she wondered. She got up and went inside, her heart overcome with trepidation. Her father, Tomanti, came out.

"Setiawan, what are you here for?"

"I must speak to the elders."

"Today?"

"Today."

"Why today? Why couldn't you wait? Can't you see we are all preparing for a feast?"

"Do you want me to join you for the feast and wait until you are ready to speak with me? I will wait."

"Hmmm—I better ask the others what they want to do. Wait for me at the community house while I go and find them."

As the two men walked off in different directions, Indah could barely be seen peering out of the doorway with a look of fright.

CHAPTER 57

S etiawan stepped into the community house and the presence of the other three village elders caught him by surprise. Even more surprising was the pale looks of the men who stared at him with a stunned expression.

"Setiawan, how did you get here so soon?" said Waniwan.

"I left early this morning," he said, somewhat confused.

"But how did you know we wanted to speak with you?" asked Waniwan.

"I didn't know, I was compelled to come speak to you after having a dream last night, so I came."

A strange silence came over the place as the eyes of the men shifted back and forth to each other. Gusti finally broke the tension, "We sent my son, Kadek, a short time ago to find you and ask you to meet us here and another child to go find Tomanti."

"I did not see Kadek, he must have taken a different trail. I just met Tomanti at his hut and now he is looking for you."

Just then, Tomanti stepped into the community house, equally surprised. "I just heard that you were asking for me."

"Yes, we are all here now, sit down," said Waniwan. "And since I am the oldest among us, I will speak first. Last night, I witnessed in a dream a sea turtle. It swam to our shore and died. From under its shell emerged a small bird, a kind I have never seen before. It had a broken wing and was unable to fly. It climbed up an old sago tree and took shelter in a hole and was nourished by the tree and its wing began to heal. Four men from the village came to the sago with machetes to chop down the tree, but when they began to cut the tree, the sky grew dark and cold rain like stones were hurled upon the men and they could no longer hold their machetes. The men drew near to the tree for shelter and the sago bent it palms to shield them from the cold rain. The frightened bird flew to the top of the sago. Then a voice came on the wind, 'Ask Setiawan, he will tell you.' Then I awoke from my sleep. Before you tell us what the dream means you must also know that Gusti also had a dream."

"In my dream," said Gusti, "a fire spread through our village and threatened to destroy everyone, but the tide rose higher than ever before and flowed over the island and quenched the fire. But that was not my only dream. I had a second dream. In that dream, a pack of wild dogs pursued all of the children on the island. They fled to this community house and were surrounded. Their cries were drowned out by the howling of the dogs. Many black drongo birds flew into the shelter and pecked at the eyes of the children and they were helpless. Then I awoke from my sleep."

"I also dreamed last night," said Suharto. "A great egret visited our island and built a nest. A komodo dragon swam to the shore and climbed the tree to eat the eggs. Setiawan shot the dragon with an arrow. It did not die but it left the island. The egret flew away and left its nest. I awoke."

"We have not heard if Tomanti has a dream to share," said Waniwan.

Tomanti looked extremely troubled at this question. All eyes were on him now. "No, I did not have a dream."

The others wondered why they had significant dreams but not Tomanti.

"None of us can understand the meaning of the dreams. Tomanti may have the answers since he has a clear mind with no troubling dreams," said Gusti.

"I am the youngest here and least experienced as a leader. How can I have insight if you do not?" said Tomanti.

"Setiawan will help us understand. Your name was mentioned in one dream and you appeared in another. Do you have an answer?" said Waniwan.

All eyes were now on Setiawan.

"I have an answer to one dream without doubt, but like yourselves, I am puzzled about the others and must give it more thought."

"Then tell us about the one you understand and how you know it," said Waniwan.

"I know it because I came today to talk with you about something in your dream. The wounded bird is the foreign boy brought to our shores by men from our nation who intended no harm to us though they meant harm to the foreigner. I alone have sheltered him and you wanted him dead. You are facing catastrophe if you continue your plans and do not give shelter and show hospitality to him. You have treated me shamefully and have not treated the foreigner as a guest. I have learned some of his language and he has learned some of ours. He is able to contribute to the community and I can help him to be woven into village life. Beware if you fail to do what is right. You have been warned in your dream. If you will not listen to me, then you should consider your dreams.

"There is another reason I came today. You know that I have kept my part of your plan to keep the boy on the other side of the island but you have not kept watch over the village. You do not even know that there has been a steady stream of children and even some adults who sneak away to get a look at the foreigner out of curiosity. I am constantly chasing them away. It will do you no good to keep us on the other side of the island. I may have some understanding on one of the other dreams, but for now, I am sure about this one. The dream said to 'ask Setiawan, he will tell you,' so I have told you but it is up to you to decide. My thought is that all your dreams are somehow related, but I'm not certain until I ponder them."

"What was the dream you said you saw last night?" asked Waniwan.

"I mean no disrespect to you, elders, but you know that I am not recognized as an elder in this community. So how can I tell you my dream since it is not to be regarded if not from an elder?"

A feeling of contemplation and inner conflict hung heavy in the quiet room.

CHAPTER 58

Kadek hustled through the jungle on a mission to give Setiawan the message from the elders, his father being one of them. He felt important and wanted to please them. In order to save time, he ventured off the main paths to cut a few corners until he reached the less travelled route to the new camp. This would have served his purpose well except that he missed Setiawan heading towards the village without knowing it.

As he neared the dwelling, curiosity distracted him for a moment from his mission. He knew that several groups of children had attempted to get a glimpse of the foreigner but they were always detected by Setiawan and chastised by him before chasing them away. Setiawan was known as one of the keenest woodsmen on the island. Kadek had the recent embarrassment of being stopped by him the day before when he carelessly tromped through the jungle on the trail in search for Indah. He now wondered if his own skills, if applied carefully, could prevail over the old man's senses. He was also curious to see the foreigner again. His first encounter was brief and awkward.

He made it to the perimeter of the camp undetected. He spotted Alex feeding a young cuscus a banana. He shifted his position to try and discover Setiawan's whereabouts. Just then, a small tree branch snapped under his feet. In a panic he crouched low.

The noise did not go unnoticed by Alex who became alert and instinctively called out, "Seti? Is that you?"

No answer.

"Indah?"

Indah, Kadek thought. *Why would he be calling out her name?*

"Is anyone there?"

No reply. He went back to feeding Macchiato when all of a sudden, Kadek stood before him, giving him a start. Kadek stared, saying nothing.

Alex got a good look at his visitor who seemed to be near his own age. He had long dark hair tied back in a ponytail. He wore a modern pair of olive colored cargo shorts cinched at the waist with a jungle rope. He didn't wear a shirt, only a rustic necklace strung with beads and what looked like animal teeth. Though he seemed similar in height, he was definitely more muscular, though Alex did notice his own body becoming stronger and his muscles more defined since coming to the island. He felt insecure sitting while his visitor stood in front of him so he set Macchiato down near his feet, stood up, and made an attempt at being friendly.

"*Siapa namamu? Namaku* Alex."

Kadek was confused by this stranger's ability to speak his language. He took offense at the friendly greeting and got to his business.

"*Dimana orang tua itu* Setiawan?"[7]

Alex only understood half the words but he got the gist and was put out that the young man wouldn't tell him his name.

"If you're looking for Setiawan, he's not here. Of course you can't understand me and that's a little awkward, but we might as well get it out in the open since two can play at that game."

Kadek was more confused than before and his face showed it.

"Setiawan?" asked Kadek. He spoke with a less than friendly tone.

"*Pergi,*" said Alex, which meant he was gone or away.

"*Dimana?*" asked Kadek,

Alex understood that he wanted to know where Setiawan went. He pointed to the trail, "*Desa,*" the simple word for village. He asked the stranger once again for his name, "*Siapa namamu?*"

No reply. Kadek just stared him down. During this bold stare, the small

---

[7] "Where is the old man, Setiawan?"

cuscus inadvertently wandered under Kadek's feet, and when he suddenly turned to walk away, the small animal got caught in his path and caused him to shift his footing, almost tripping him. He reacted in frustration and embarrassment of the awkward departure in front of Alex and kicked the cuscus out of his way.

Alex snapped and without thinking gave the visitor a violent shove from the back. Kadek stumbled forward but caught himself from falling to the ground.

"What did you do that for?!" yelled Alex.

Before he finished his short outburst, Kadek, with well-trained precision swept Alex to the ground and immediately had him in a headlock, unable to breath. Alex didn't know what hit him, it happened so fast. He was near passing out. The strange position limited any movement except for his eyes which could see the small curved blade protruding from his opponent's fist being held inches from his throat. Kadek must have been watching for his eyes to start rolling because as soon as things started going dark, Alex was released in a heap on the ground, gasping for breath. By the time he recovered his senses, the young man was nowhere to be seen.

Dazed and angry, Alex looked around for Macchiato. During the brief altercation, his new pet crawled up a tree, frightened with no intention of coming down any time soon.

CHAPTER 59

N ight settled in quietly at the remote camp but Setiawan hadn't returned.
Alex sat next to his fire alone and talked out loud to Macchiato, still
up in a nearby tree, making no effort to come down.

"I don't know where Seti is Macchi. He didn't tell me why he was going
but told me that he would be gone awhile. I didn't think it would be this
long. Don't you want to come down for some banana?

"Tell me, you were born on this island, what in the world did that kid
do to me? Some sort of Jackie Chan business? How did he learn that kind
of fighting? I'm sure he's never watched *Karate Kid.* I think he wanted to
kill me. All for sticking up for you, little guy. You really ought to show your
appreciation for my heroic defense and come down the tree. If I wasn't so
sore right now, I'd try to climb up to get you. If you're still up there tomorrow, I'll give it a try. There's some food down hear waiting for you."

Alex didn't want to go to bed just yet but didn't know what to do with
himself. In his former life, it would be an easy decision involving some type
of screen. On the island, there wasn't much to do after the sun set. He
gravitated towards his little Bible in these moments of boredom. He was
still reading the Gospel of Matthew.

*Again, the kingdom of heaven is like a merchant seeking beautiful pearls, who,
when he had found one pearl of great price, went and sold all that he had and bought it.*[8]

"Now that's what I'm talking about, something that finally makes sense.

---

[8] Matthew 13:45–46

184

This guy is going all out for the one thing he wants. I can understand that. I want so badly to go pro and I'm willing to give up everything else, but where has that got me? I'm a little nervous, Macchi; if they haven't come to rescue me yet, I wonder if they will ever come at all. I'm not a little nervous, I'm a lot nervous. I'm scared to think about the possibility of being stuck here forever. I'll have to build a boat or something. I just can't accept that this my fate. My pearl is professional gaming, but I haven't found it yet and I can't find it here, and I have nothing to sell to get it. It's who I am, without gaming, I'm nobody.

"And yet, as strange as this might sound, I'm losing my hunger for gaming and it scares me. What scares me is that I feel okay with that right now but I feel that I shouldn't. I feel like I'm betraying myself to just let it go and find a new identity in something else. I'm afraid of it fading away in me, that drive, that passion is fading. But what am I without it? "By the way, that guy who kicked you scares me. He had a knife at my throat, I'm not sure where it came from, I didn't see it in his hand before. He was lightning quick. I wish he was a gamer and I could go one on one with him, he'd find out soon who would be gasping for breath. It makes me wonder what this tribe is really like. Seti is nice, Indah is nice, but maybe they're the only civilized people around. Maybe the rest are violent murderers or worse. It creeps me out. "Hey little guy, keep coming, you're half way there. I've got some nice ripe fruit for you. I don't know what these hairy looking things are called, but once you peel the crazy looking skin off, they're super yummy. "Hey Macchi, you haven't asked me yet about Indah. But now that we're on that subject, I think she really likes me and I really like her, but I'm not sure what I'm getting into. You wouldn't believe what I ate just to make her happy. She's amazing and definitely a pearl in her own way. I'm going to meet her again the day after tomorrow. My social schedule is improving.

"I think my neck is going to be stiff and sore for a few days. I really don't like that guy. I know Jesus says I should love my enemies but I'm not convinced it's realistic or even possible. I'm sure that kid understood me and knew that I was trying to be friendly. I really tried. He never gave me his name so I'm going to make one up, like a gaming name generator. Let's see, he's definitely an opponent…a jerk…my enemy…a rival—Rival! That will work. It's got a ring to it. Rival will be his official tag but to mock him, I might resort to calling him Ravioli for fun. I better find out if Seti can teach me some island judo or whatever Jackie Chan sauce that Ravioli is baked in.

"I took karate when I was little until I achieved a yellow belt. But we never sparred and hit anyone or got hit. I think it must have been a yuppie hybrid program. Everybody gets a smiley face sticker for showing up. I dropped out as soon as I discovered video games.

"I don't blame you for wanting to stay up in that tree. I would be doing the same in your situation. Too bad, you don't bark and could alert me when someone was nearby. Oh well, I'm not sure if you make a noise but be sure to make an effort if someone else comes. I thought Seti would be back by now, I can't imagine what is keeping him so long. He'll probably be back later. I'm going to bed."

CHAPTER 60

A hazy mist rose from the jungle floor as the sun emerged. Beams of light slipped through the walls of the hut, sharp and distinct due to the humid morning air and the haze from the smoldering fire. Alex woke up sore from yesterday's incident. He could see through the doorway that Setiawan was back, tending the coals of the fire and cooking some sago. He was glad to find Macchiato asleep at his feet. He pet the sleeping cuscus, who opened its eyes for a moment and decided to shut them again, content to sleep. *Maybe he's sore also*, Alex wondered.

"Good morning, Seti"

"Good morning," Seti replied in broken English then continued in his native tongue. *"Kita akan desa."*

"What? You're kidding? The village? We are going to the village? *Akan desa?*"

"Kita akan desa."

"Whoa, that's unexpected. How did that come about? I mean, why... why...oh yeah—*mengapa?* No wait, that's not it. I remember—how? *Bagaimana? Bagaimana?*"

Setiawan just smiled and pointed upward.

"The sky? That doesn't make sense. What would the sky have to do with it?"

"Bible," said Setiawan.

"The Bible in the sky? That's even more confusing."

Setiawan could tell that Alex was confused, but he didn't know how to

187

explain to him all that had transpired in the last twenty-four hours. He knew it was nothing less than a miracle. Just then, he noticed the severe bruising on Alex's neck.

"*Apa itu?*" as he pointed to the bruise.

"What is what?" he replied in confusion. A life without mirrors created a huge shift in Alex's life, he couldn't see what he looked like but he reached to feel his neck. *It must have left a bruise or welt or something,* he thought to himself.

"I don't think I know enough words to explain it," said Alex. "But here, sit down right here as if you were me." He motioned for Setiawan to follow his directions and used appropriate hand gestures to give a dramatization of what happened.

He acted out the part of Rival, "*Di mana* Setiawan?" and set Macchiato on the ground in front of him and pretended to kick the cuscus. He then showed him how he shoved Rival and then finished with putting Seti in a fake headlock, then pointed back to himself as he pretended to pass out on the ground.

He got up and asked Seti, "So what was that? *Apa itu?*"

"*Pencak silat,*" said Setiawan.

Alex had no idea that *pencak silat* was an ancient form of martial arts practiced throughout Indonesia with hundreds of various forms passed down from generation to generation in families and tribes. Both boys and girls are well trained on a regular basis throughout their lives. At several points in the nation's history, it was a vital skill to defend against enemies but now it was engrained in their culture not merely as defense but for the purpose of art and identity.

Setiawan stood across from Alex and motioned for him to try and attack.

Alex hesitated, "I don't want to accidentally hurt you, Seti. I know it's just pretend but you're an old man."

Seti kept motioning to him.

"Okay Seti." Alex half-heartedly pretended to try and hit Seti, but no sooner had he brought his arm back that he suddenly found himself being spun to the ground and held in a loose headlock. Seti was being mindful of his bruised and sore neck.

"That was it! Just like that," said Alex as he was allowed to get back on his feet. "Except I couldn't breathe and he had a knife."

This time, Seti handed him a stick and motioned for Alex to come at him again with this makeshift weapon. Alex seemed a little more confident that Seti could hold his own but he still wanted to be careful and not accidentally hurt his friend. There was no need for caution. He hardly moved his body with the stick when the island suddenly spun out from under his legs, the stick was transferred to Seti's hands, and Alex found himself in an immobile position once again on the ground with the stick pointed at his head. Once again, the moves were so fast and he was completely unprepared.

Little did Alex—a video game thumb warrior—know that this was the beginning of his own training in the island tradition of *silat*. It was so much a part of their culture that if Alex was going to integrate, he would need to learn the art. Alex considered his huge disadvantage. The untold hours of gaming provided no practical defensive or offensive skills in real or pretend combat. His self-inflated pride in hand-eye coordination did not transfer automatically in the tangible world.

Training would begin regularly once they moved into the village, but for now, they had some packing to do.

CHAPTER 61

Alex found it hard to believe, after the last three months in isolation that he and Setiawan were going to join society again. He grew more cognizant of the subtle changes happening in his own character since being away from others and everything once familiar to him. It forced him to contemplate life and he gained enough maturity to recognize that the countless hardships of this difficult summer also produced some positive effects.

Setiawan and Alex did not have many personal possessions to pack for their move to the village. Alex owned his little pocket Bible, a pet cuscus, a machete, and a few items of clothing. There were a variety of other small items including a collection of brightly colored bird feathers that he scavenged and attached to a braided twine that he wore around his neck.

Living in the same pair of shorts and the same T-shirt everyday didn't last long during the first couple weeks on the island. Alex realized that at least one change of clothes would be helpful. He rarely wore his shirt so that was easy enough to wash and hang out in the sun to dry from time to time, but the shorts were a different subject. Seti provided him with a simple cloth to wrap around his waist known as a sarong. Setiawan taught him how to tie it so that it was really more like a pair of shorts than a mini skirt. At first, he struggled with being self-conscious but now it no longer mattered. It was comfortable and easy to clean. He rotated between his one pair of shorts and his sarong. A few weeks after the addition of the sarong, Seti gifted him with another pair of handmade shorts, synched at the waist with a rope.

Today, Seti gave him a new sarong made of intricately woven fabric with beautiful patterns of maroon, black, and beige threads. He expected Alex to wear it for his introduction to the village. He also gave him a new loosely fitting white shirt with long sleeves, no buttons, and a decorative maroon colored sash to tie around his waist. Alex guessed that Seti wanted to make sure he made a good first impression but he wondered if he was overdoing it a little. Seti seemed delighted with how Alex looked in his new outfit and also approved of his multicolored feathers dangling from his necklace.

"You know, Seti, my mom would be all over this and think it was great. My dad on the other hand would definitely want me to go see a psychologist if he saw me in this costume."

This process of packing up, closing their remote camp, and getting washed and dressed did not take much time. Alex was anxious to get going but Setiawan seemed to find ways to stretch the day out unnecessarily. It was late afternoon before they took off down the trail for the hour-long journey.

As they neared the village, Seti followed a small trail leading to one of the first huts on the perimeter. Alex learned that it was Setiawan's own dwelling. He didn't get a chance to explore it since they were only there briefly to drop off their few belongings and continue towards the main village center. They noticed a couple of boys hiding among the nearby plants who ran off as soon as they were spotted. Seti ignored them.

They returned to the main trail and Alex noticed the distant sound of rhythmic drumming. They continued their walk and encountered a group of young girls coming towards them on the path, giggling and outwardly excited. As they came near, Alex noticed their elegant festive dresses, intricately woven like his new sarong and known by the islanders as *kemben* wraps. They were adorned with colorful wreaths of flowers on their heads.

With wide eyes and nervous giggling, they announced, *"Selamat datang tamu!"*

"Terima kasih banyak," said Setiawan.

Alex parroted him to the delight of these new acquaintances. Their new guest was a novelty to these girls. Even though Alex's skin had darkened a few shades since coming to the island, his skin was still lighter than the islanders and his blonde hair and bright blue eyes gave him a distinct foreign appearance.

They responded, *"Kembali!"*

This greeting and response sequence was about to become engrained in Alex who later confirmed it to be a formal welcome. In English it would be something like, "Welcome, guest," followed by the response, "Thank you very much," and completed with, "You're welcome."

The girls also presented Alex with a gift. A wreath of small white flowers which they placed on his head after some effort to get him to understand that they needed him to lower his head so they could reach him. The girls then turned to walk towards the village and sprinkled flower petals onto the path from baskets.

This deeply moved Alex who had never received such a welcome in his life, not even by close friends. Fist bumps, occasional handshakes, and half-hearted hugs didn't compare in the least. He felt sincerely honored but humbled, knowing there was no reason he deserved this attention. He had no idea that this was just the beginning of surprises. Not long after, they encountered two older girls also dressed in their festive outfits, waiting on each side of the trail, holding large trays on their heads piled with fresh fruits. Alex's attention was first drawn to the platters of fruit, but after they greeted each other, he noticed that they were very beautiful, though not as stunning as Indah. Setiawan redirected his young friend's distracted attention by motioning Alex to keep moving forward. The two young ladies began walking behind them.

Further down the trail, drawing closer to the village, women and children lined each side of the path, smiling and saying, *"Selamat datang tamu."* Younger children enjoyed throwing flower petals and getting their first look at a foreigner. Alex couldn't believe it, he felt euphoric inside. At the same time, he also had to suppress any negative thoughts that he might be in a procession to be thrown into a volcano to appease their gods or something similar. His consolation was Setiawan, his faithful friend, a man he had grown to trust, walking beside him. He determined to relax and not be afraid.

The sound of percussion became louder and more distinct. The people lining the trail fell in behind them. Alex wished he had candy to throw to the children like being in a parade, or at least a bag full of freshly toasted sago grubs to toss in appreciation.

He could now see the large clearing ahead for the main part of the village. Numerous huts lined the perimeter with the larger community hut standing prominently at the opposite end. The golden hour of the evening cast a warm glow on everything before him as the sun sat low on the horizon.

Alex guessed that there were hundreds of people gathered in the village center forming a large circle. He and Setiawan were led to the edge of the circle and given front row seats on a couple of mats reserved for them. The two large trays of fruit were placed in front of them.

Four dancers in elaborate oriental style dress glided into the center and began performing a beautifully choreographed dance to the sound of drums and music from a variety of unique instruments. Alex's attention focused on the dancers but his gaze wandered long enough to see the men sitting with drums across their laps with the drum heads being played on each end. A large hollowed log resonated a deep thumping sound as a couple of men drove large, heavy wooden poles up and down with both hands. The main music ensemble consisted of bamboo flutes and instruments that looked similar to xylophones with metal bars attached to vertical bamboo resonators and struck with mallets. There were also various sized gongs that looked like large empty kettles suspended from bamboo frames also being played with mallets. But the dancers drew his focused attention, especially when he recognized Indah.

The motions were gracefully oriental with intricate hand motions. The dress and accessories were more ornate than anything worn by the other women. The trademark woven material in a variety of colors was accompanied with beadwork and silky fabric scarves and streamers. Each dancer wore embellished headdresses and ornate earrings and bracelets. Alex noticed that they also wore facial makeup, though he didn't think any of them needed it. He assumed it must be part of the tradition and costume.

The dancers kept straight faces as they concentrated on their intricate synchronized performance, but Alex caught a few furtive glances from Indah who couldn't hold back a slight smile and her bright eyes when they momentarily met Alex's. The dance didn't last as long as Alex would have liked but the entertainment was not over.

The sun began setting in earnest but torches were already burning brightly throughout the encircled audience, illuminating the festive scene. Next came a series of martial arts demonstrations beginning with a group of very young children performing *jurus*, which are the choreographed movements that are taught in order to pass down the style and techniques of *pencak silat* and to train the body and mind for combat. This progressed into demonstration matches between two people at a time, often with weapons. Young women also demonstrated their skills of defense against other young women.

Alex recognized that the older men were more skilled than the younger men. Alex wasn't surprised to see Rival in the circle against another young man. He was not smiling at Alex when their eyes occasionally met.

The evening concluded with an official greeting by the village elders followed by a community feast. Alex didn't know it at the time but he had officially become a guest of the tribe and under their protection.

CHAPTER 62

The frightening dreams experienced by the village elders shook them to the core. It would be notable enough for just one of them to receive an omen in their sleep. The revelation that three of them experienced these dreams on the same night, and the surprise of having Setiawan arrive on his own the next morning, put them in a serious quandary.

They chose to revive their ancient custom of hospitality by honoring a welcomed guest. This proved to be an exciting change in the day-to-day existence of the community and they embraced the celebration wholeheartedly, not for Alex's sole benefit but for their own as well.

Setiawan understood how difficult this decision was for the elders. They were conflicted. He sensed that their decision was not from a true change of heart towards Alekus but a fear of the possible unknown consequences conveyed in their disturbing dreams. He wondered how this would affect Alekus in the future, but for now, he was glad they were both welcomed into the community. His own status changed overnight since he served as the direct guardian and host of the island's special guest.

He believed something significant was unfolding before his eyes after years of private struggle. The community faced needed change. He wondered if his prayers were being answered and if his quiet faithful service all these years was finally making a difference. Setiawan believed that God sent Alekus to him for the boy's sake and his own, but was it more than that? He believed the dreams, including his own, were sent by God. This was truly a new day, a new chapter in their history. He hoped it would be a good chapter, yet he felt the need for caution.

As the sun came up that morning, he could sense the coming rain. They were entering the season when regular bursts of rain and equal moments of clear skies would become part of the daily routine. Setiawan sat near the doorway of his hut, looking outside, pondering all these things.

Indah and her young cousin Aisyah approached the hut carrying baskets. Indah's mother didn't have the slightest clue about her daughter's personal interest in Alekus and therefore saw no problem with sending her on an errand.

"Hello Indah, hello Aisyah," greeted Setiawan. "Welcome."

"Thank you. My mother sent me with some food for you and Alekus. She says it is going to rain today and there will not be time for good hunting or gathering."

"She's right. Please tell her we are very grateful for the food."

It was obvious to Setiawan that she and Aisyah were disappointed to not see the young man.

"Alekus is still sleeping," he said.

"He is still sleeping?" said Aisyah, clearly disappointed.

"It was a big day for him yesterday and we were up late getting the hut ready for sleeping."

Just then, Macchiato lumbered to the doorway and peered out in curiosity of the new voices.

"Oh, a cuscus!" said Aisyah.

"Yes, I found it alone in the jungle and gave it to Alekus as a gift."

"Oh, does that mean I cannot bring him one of my puppies as a gift?" she asked.

"Well, if a puppy and cuscus are both young enough and spend time together, they can learn to be at peace. So we can try if you want to give him one from your litter."

"Yes, I do. That is why I asked to come along with my cousin." In her childlike frankness, she added, "I also wanted to see our guest and tell my friends about it later today. Can I peek at him sleeping?"

"You can, but be quiet and do not wake our guest, it is bad manners."

She slipped quietly in for a moment and came back exultant with a big smile.

"He's still sleeping!" she said.

"Good," said Indah. "Now you can go tell your friends, but be sure to let them know that Setiawan will not tolerate any other young visitors today."

"I will!" said Aisyah who skipped away content.

Indah had the opportunity now to speak with Setiawan privately. "You do not have any close family on the island, is it alright if I call you uncle?"

Setiawan was deeply touched by her thoughtfulness and respect. "Yes, you can call me uncle, I would like that."

"Please tell me, Uncle, how did you accomplish all this?"

"I was not alone in this new change of direction."

"Who helped you and how?"

"My God helped me by giving the elders dreams. Two of those dreams related to Alekus and to me."

"It is wonderful but what happens next?"

"Alekus needs to continue learning our language and our customs. I will begin training him in *silat*. He already knows a little about gathering food and hunting, though he is not good with a bow."

"Is he now safe from harm?"

"He is safe from harm for now, but not safe from the possibility of never being fully accepted into our tribe. He is a guest but that will fade away in time."

"You accept him, and I will accept him as long as he remains with us."

"That may be the rest of his life."

"I hope so."

Chapter 63

November

"We finally have a possible lead in the disappearance of your son," said Liam, his voice filled with optimism. The other end of the call was uncomfortably silent. "Mr. Brooks, are you there?"

"Yes, I'm here. I'm sorry, it just caught me by surprise. So many months without any progress and then this call out of the blue. It triggered something in me that I can't explain."

"You don't have to try and explain, Mr. Brooks. But let me get the point, it is someone claiming to have information—for a price of course. When do you want Super 8 to meet to make a plan for the next step? It needs to be soon."

"As soon as possible, but I want to see if Allison is available before I give you a definite time."

"Just give the word as soon as you're ready, I've informed Della and she's ready to get everyone together."

Mr. Brooks didn't wait a moment to call Allison.

"Hello Alex."

"Hi Allison, I just received a call from Liam and he has a possible lead on Alex." Nothing but silence on the other end mirrored his own response. "Allison? Are you still there?"

"Yes," she said with difficulty. "I'm so afraid, I'm holding on to hope but I'm afraid of another wild goose chase."

"I know. I was dumbstruck when I heard the news a few minutes ago. We can't give up hope, and if this amounts to nothing, we'll keep trying."

"But my heart is so fragile, as soon as I try and pull myself together for a day or two, it all breaks into pieces again. I feel like a child who has accidentally broken a family heirloom and is trying to glue it all back together to hide what I've done, but it keeps coming apart and pieces are missing. It's just a mess," said Allison.

"I know what you mean. I really do."

"So what is the nature of the lead?" she asked.

"All I know right now is that it is someone claiming to have information."

"At a price?"

"Yes, but we can't lose hope. We are going to have a team meeting as soon as possible to get the details and decide on an action step. Do you want to be there?"

"Yes, of course. What time?"

"Whenever we're ready. Can I come by and pick you up?"

"Can you give me a half hour to get ready?"

"It'll take at least that long to get there depending on traffic."

"Thank you, Alex."

The last several months were a roller coaster ride for both of them. The sudden and absolute silence of the abductors, the breaking story in the news, the subsequent media frenzy, the dicey relationship with the FBI, and the hesitation of Paradigm Technology Innovations to release project Mockingbird to the marketplace until there was some clear direction regarding their son. All these things were a like a hundred-ton weight pressing down on them every day.

The formerly estranged couple, involuntarily thrown together in this crisis, found themselves clinging to each other like desperate survivors of a sinking ship, adrift and alone in a tempest tossed sea.

Allison took an extended leave from her studio job and moved to San Francisco to be closer to PTI headquarters and to Alex. Their relationship remained rocky at times but a small spark had ignited a genuine interest in each other, not just the common bond of losing their son and the united effort to find him.

The man Allison once despised was clearly changing. His willingness to put everything on the table to ransom their son broke the ice in her soul. His relentless search and focused energy, once exclusive to business, now repurposed towards his missing son made a deep impression. Her growing admiration of him steadily morphed into something more.

It might have been a truly sweet time of rediscovering each other had it not been for the swirling eddy of painful realities facing them every day. A missing son who might be dead or alive, and if alive, seemingly hidden from all possible detection and without any explanation.

Anaconda never contacted them again. They made no further demands or gave any further proof of Alex being alive. The two pictures of his phone convinced them that the group demanding ransom were the real culprits and not opportunists intercepting someone else's nefarious plans, but what had they done with Alex? The fear of discovering the worst possible news of his death was slowly becoming less of a fear than not knowing anything for the rest of their lives.

Mr. Brooks found Allison waiting for him at the curb. Their practice of carpooling together gave them time to talk about their shared internal upheaval over the news of a possible lead. They had experienced so much grief over a lack of information and the overwhelming disappointments of false leads and misinformation. Which would this be? They both wondered. Holding on to hope became more elusive each day. Yet, if their son was alive, they would be betraying him if they didn't maintain a seed of hope no matter how small. Would this seed be watered today?

Allison broached a topic that was a touchy one for Mr. Brooks. "I attended Della's weekly Bible study and prayer time again last night." She and Della had become good friends since moving to San Francisco. The older woman took Allison under her wing with genuine concern.

"Della is the most wonderful secretary anyone could wish for but she's a bit of a religious fanatic. At least she keeps it to herself and I prefer it that way."

"I wouldn't call her a fanatic—just enthusiastic and demonstrative, but that might just be part of her African American heritage," said Allison.

"Maybe so, but I would be careful if I were you. I wouldn't want her religious ideas to add more trouble to your life right now."

"It's not adding any trouble. In fact, I really find a moment of peace with this small group of women. I don't pray with them but I like to hear them pray. And the reason I wanted to bring this up is because last night, during their prayer time, the ladies were getting all excited about their petitions to God for a breakthrough regarding Alex. They were praying as if they expected a breakthrough soon. Do you think there might be something to it?"

"I don't know. I personally don't think so, but if it gives you hope, I can't see how their little prayer meeting hurts anything. I just wouldn't put much stock in it. Let's see what comes up in the meeting today."

They arrived at the company headquarters and made their way to the tenth floor. This small dedicated team of assistants would likely receive enthusiastic job offers from the FBI if they ever wanted a career change. For now, they were more akin to Pinkertons, the private investigative agencies that existed before the founding of the FBI in 1908, except this group worked exclusively for Mr. Brooks.

Besides Mr. Brooks and Allison, the team consisted of Liam, a talented hacker for hire to help punch holes in security flaws; Greg, the faithful head of the company's security department; Nolan, one of the veteran engineers on project Mockingbird; Della, the dedicated secretary for the group; Parker, a savvy young attorney; Bailey, a private investigator and graduate of the Quantico FBI National Academy, specializing in profiling and criminal psychology; and last but not least, Miles, a quintessential super geek and devoted employee for many years at PTI, Inc.

These were not merely employees but a team who coalesced around a significant cause. They became more than coworkers and regarded each other as comrades and friends who referred to themselves as Super 8.

CHAPTER 64

The Super 8 settled around the conference table and Liam shared his laptop screen on the large wall monitor. "I can scrub through the recording of my interaction but it will be quicker to give you the cliff notes, then we can go back and discuss any details. I received a hit on one of my Darknet ads for a reward for any verifiable information on the abduction of Alexander Brooks with guaranteed anonymity, no Fed involvement, and a generous crypto currency payment.

"The person I've named Groundhog claims to have been directly involved but is presently on the run in an attempt to make a break from his former organization to join a 'smaller, less oppressive community' and is in need of funds. I promised him a token transfer of funds if he could first verify his involvement. You won't believe this—he gave me the serial number of Alex's phone."

"But is it possible he hacked the wireless carrier's data center?" asked Greg.

"That's possible," said Parker, "except the FBI has already acquisitioned and wiped that info from the carrier's database long ago."

"And as you see here, he provided this," Liam presented a picture of the SIM tray from Alex's phone.

"Did he tell you if Alex is alive?" asked Allison.

"This was only an initial meeting. I transferred some funds according to our predetermined plans but I promised him more if he could give us something significant. I offered an initial payment that would be hard to refuse. Groundhog explained his payment requirements, which would be a series of payments incrementally as he divulged what he knew. I'm familiar with this game and it can get pricey real fast, like feeding a downtown parking meter with Bitcoin. I told him I would need approval from Mr. Brooks and he said he could not wait long and was in personal danger for even attempting to give us any information."

The energized team believed this was a significant lead. It watered their seed of hope.

"Liam, I can't thank you enough for your unrelenting pursuit. Bailey, what is your assessment of the interaction? Could this be the FBI? Or someone else playing us?" said Mr. Brooks.

"I've poured over the transcript of the chat and also watched the video, checking response times, analyzing if the person is 'looking left' through their choice of words and behaviors. Of course, it's only a chat but my analysis is that Groundhog, as Liam is calling him, is shooting straight with us so far in essence, though the reasons for undermining the organizations brick wall of silence is questionable. His sentence structure and use of words make me believe he is a native of Taiwan with an English education."

Everyone else on the team gave their assessment and it was agreed they would make contact after a quick review of their plans. Liam made the connection as they all watched the conversation unfold in the chat window displayed on the large wall monitor.

Groundhog typed, "Please transfer your payment before proceeding."

This was the first risky step that might result in a cut and run contact after sending the money.

Liam typed, "Transfer complete. Now tell us what you've got. We're anxious to hear what you know. Dad and Mom are here with our small team, so fire away."

As Groundhog began to type, Mr. Brooks hung on every word like a drink of water from an oasis to a dying man in a desert. Reading them across the screen was a surreal moment. "The bottom line is that they lost your son and can't find him, leaving them with nothing to bring to the bargaining table. That is why you haven't heard from anyone."

The message stopped there.

"Ask him if he knows if Alex is alive," said Allison.

"Before I do that, you and Mr. Brooks need to know that every time he stops and every time we ask for more information, it is going to cost us. As long as you believe we are getting helpful information we can continue, but it's up to you."

Everyone believed they should proceed.

Liam typed, "That's a good start, but do you know if he's alive?"

They watched the expected response appear, "Payment due."

Turning to the team, Liam announced, "See, this is how it's going to go. He's savvy but let's make sure we get new information."

He turned again to his keyboard and once the payment transfer was initiated replied, "Payment transferred. Your turn."

The response appeared, "He was alive at last contact the night before his disappearance. None of us knows otherwise."

Nothing else followed.

"I can't believe this," said Mr. Brooks. "He's going to nickel and dime us."

"Mr. Brooks, I hope you know the equivalence in the currency we are sending him, it's hardly nickels or dimes but I get what you mean. This is going to be like an expensive game of twenty questions and we don't know how much he knows."

"Can you give him a little pushback?" said Parker. He looked to Mr. Brooks for approval and got a nod.

Liam typed, "That's not very helpful, can you elaborate a little more? We expected a little more love from you for that last payment."

The response was quick and terse, "Fine, we're done then. Find another mole."

"He's not ready to bolt yet," said Bailey. "He has more information and wants to make it as profitable as he can, but I don't think pushing back is going to work with him. He's holding the rare cards and he knows there are sufficient funds in our pocket to proceed. Better take another tact and pacify him."

Liam sent another transfer and replied, "No need to get testy with me, I've got some anxious parents who want to find their missing son. Have a little heart. You got your payment."

"Ask him what he can tell us about Alex's location," said Mr. Brooks.

Liam typed, "Where did they lose him? What do you know about his location?"

"He was being taken to a remote and uninhabited island to keep him unfindable until the ransom was paid."

Liam risked a quick follow up question to see if Groundhog would budge a little more after the last payment. "Our greater concern is to know the country and region if known. I'm sorry if I didn't make my question clearer."

A pause ensued. In moments like this, a few seconds seem like minutes but they did get a response.

"No one except the men assigned to take him knew where he was being taken. That is why they can't find him now."

"But did anyone know the region?"

"Payment due."

Liam transferred the next installment and wrote, "Better make it good because our patience and wallet is growing much thinner than anticipated." Liam was an intuitive master at this game and they all watched in amazement at his sense of things. He believed that Groundhog had limited cards in his hand but also must be trying to figure out how much they had in theirs. Liam didn't want to tip their hand to him, he wanted to make Groundhog nervous that they might end the conversation and refuse any more payments if he wasn't careful. His tact paid off.

"That information was known only by top leadership but I know they are looking for him and entrusting very few with that information. I was not someone they told."

"But do you have a guess or hunch and don't ask for another payment yet, the last bit didn't give us anything new."

Another pause before a reply "I'm not certain but probably Southeast Asia. Best guess is Indonesia, but I don't have direct knowledge."

Liam wrote, "Thanks and stand by."

Miles, sitting next to Liam, gave him a fist bump for that last risky maneuver as if they were buddies playing a video game and he just witnessed a clever move.

Mr. Brooks addressed the team, "What should we ask him next?"

"Ask him why they think he was lost and why they want to find him now," said Parker.

Everyone thought it was a good direction. They knew this guy was milking them but they believed he might have more information that could be helpful. He was clearly not going to give them any more than necessary to capitalize on.

Liam relayed the message, made another payment to Groundhog and awaited the response.

"At first, they thought they had been double crossed by the men in charge of the boy, possibly attempting to initiate their own negotiations with the Feds. But nothing came of it. The rest is only guesswork. Maybe they got lost, ran out of fuel, lost the satellite phone, sunk in a freak storm, no one knows. You tell me what happened and I'll be glad to sell that information to them. Your guess is as good as theirs."

There was an expected pause in correspondence at this point, so Bailey chimed in, "I think he's about out of profitable information."

"What about asking him if he'll tell us who the group is behind this. It's a long shot but if he's leaving the group, he may have nothing to lose by ratting them out," said Parker.

"What is the organization behind this?"

"Payment due."

Mr. Brooks authorized the payment and as soon as the transaction was complete, Groundhog signed off and was gone.

"I was afraid of that," said Bailey

"It was unavoidable, don't worry about it," said Mr. Brooks.

"It's your money not mine but that had to hurt," said Parker.

"Yeah, you're right. We just blew a wad of money but we have something real to work with now," said Mr. Brooks.

"No kidding, six payments at approximately twenty thousand each is a good day's work for Groundhog."

"I don't regret it. I don't feel my son is dead and they must not believe he's dead for certain or else they wouldn't bother searching for him."

"We will pore over the recording and transcript and see if there's anything else we can piece together from today's meeting," said Bailey.

Allison was beside herself with joy over this breakthrough, but at the same time, the elation was blended with sorrow over a lack of confirmation that Alex was definitely alive. She decided to hold on to hope. "I believe you're right, Alex. I feel he's alive, I always have, but I feel it more now. We've got to find him before they do."

CHAPTER 65

"Honestly, Mr. Brooks, the audacious claim that that these guys lost Alex and don't know where to find him sounds more like a tall tale than a serious lead," said Agent Hutchins.

"Then explain to me how he had a picture of the SIM tray from Alex's phone?"

"I'm not saying this anonymous person had nothing to do with the group that abducted your son, but for all we know, he likely made the story up to profit by it. How do you know it's not the actual abductors making the story up in response to your advertisements? So how much did you pay him, or them?"

Mr. Brooks hesitated to answer.

Hutchins looked incredulously at him, "Don't tell me you paid him more than fifty grand."

"It was a little more than that," said Mr. Brooks.

Agent Hutchins winced and shook his head in disbelief. "I take that back, I don't want to know how much you paid him. It will just make me think you're dangerously more gullible than I believe you to be already."

"Look, I don't give a rip what you think about my actions in connection with trying to find my son. You would change your attitude if it was your own child instead of just another assignment. I didn't come to meet you today in order to be held in derision and lectured about my tactics. I came to find out if you are willing to work together on this or not!"

Hutchins realized he was out of line in his response to this distraught father, regardless of his skepticism about the actions of Mr. Brooks. "Okay, I'm sorry I said what I said. I just don't understand why you've changed your tune all of a sudden from doing your own investigation without us to wanting now to work with us. Help me understand what's going on."

Mr. Brooks tried to cool his temper and show some self-control as he responded. "It's simple. Until we received this information, which I believe is true contrary to your apprehension and disparagement, I firmly believed that you were to blame for your faulty plan and botched negotiations. But with this new insight into the lack of any further communication from Anaconda, I realize that you are not to blame. And honestly, I realize that I'm not to blame either for attempting what I did or for what I'm doing now. I need your help to find my son. Would you please let me give you a copy of the transcript and our team's assessment along with the outline of our tentative plans to move forward?"

He handed Agent Hutchins a folder across the table. He had an uncanny power of persuasion that had served him well throughout his career. It had been the trait that propelled him to the status of a rising star among the tech giants of the twenty-first century. This barely perceptible influence was already taking affect with Hutchins after months of personal frustration towards Mr. Brooks for going out on his own and distrusting the Bureau.

"I'm going to level with you, regardless of your vigilante actions, we have continued our investigation for the last five months and I'm ashamed to say the case is cold. We have nothing. So yes, I have reasons to be suspicious of your wishful breakthrough. Nevertheless, it's more than what we have so I'm willing to give it consideration." Hutchins could see hope in the eyes of Mr. Brooks, eager to move forward. "Now don't jump the gun here. If our department agrees with you—and that's a big if—then we will get busy on this. Now what are your next steps?"

"This meeting is the first one. After this, we plan to try and track down every record of flights from South Korea to Indonesia on the day of Alex's abduction. Based on our timeline, he would have been on a boat heading to the undisclosed island the following day. That means it was necessary for them to transport him to one of the major islands by plane soon after his apprehension. Our estimate is a thirteen- to seventeen-hour window from South Korea to Indonesia."

"I'm impressed, you've got a decent investigative team but we've got better access to that information if it exists."

Hutchins said this with a gleam of genuine enthusiasm in his eyes for the revived case.

Alex read him like a book. He knew it was a done deal. Super 8 and the Bureau would team up to find his son. He was glad he wouldn't be around when Hutchins discovered in the transcript how much he had paid for the information.

CHAPTER 66

JANUARY

The Indonesian Maritime Security Patrol boat skirted the northern coast of Sulawesi. FBI Special Agents David Bennet and Drew Chambers leaned against the rail of the ninety-foot cutter moving at a cruising speed of twelve knots. The daily rainfall let up for a moment and the mountainous shoreline looked picturesque with its misty veil lifting from the ground to meet a low blanket of clouds resting atop the mountain peaks.

"What a view, I wish my family could witness this first hand," said Agent Bennet.

"Well, family man, as a content bachelor, I guess I'll just soak in the scenic view for my own personal enjoyment and be thankful I don't have to waste these moments fretting over a wife and kids who aren't here. Why did you sign up for a foreign assignment anyway?"

"You'll understand some day, but in the meantime, why don't you make yourself useful on this mission and snap a picture of me with this amazing backdrop so I can share this moment with my family later."

"You're right, at least about the need to be useful," said Chambers as he took a couple pictures on his partner's phone. "I feel like we've both been absolutely useless these last two months. It makes me question why I thought this was going to be a great assignment, besides getting real world experience to use my three years of training in the Indonesian language."

"Yeah, I know," said Bennet. "If you've never worked for a Legal Attaché overseas, it can be a bit jarring in comparison to field work back home."

"Don't get me wrong, I'm not complaining," said Chambers. "It's just hard not being able to conduct the investigation ourselves. The Indonesian authorities are great to work with but there is definitely a distinct difference in investigative skills and expectations."

"Well, we've got a little wiggle room since nobody really wants to pick through thousands of records, so they won't mind us doing some of the dirty work. We just can't operate without collaborating with them."

"I just think that we look bad after two months with nothing to report, like we're just on a vacation or something." Chambers said this while pointing to his partner's phone as Agent Bennet was cropping his photo and adding a color filter before sending it to his family.

Bennet put his phone away. "There's the possibility we're not in the right part of the world in the first place. It was a very thin lead that led the International Operations Division to send us to Jakarta in the first place. For all we know, the missing boy might be in Siberia."

"Remind me again, where are we stopping today?" asked Chambers.

"The Bay of Manado. It's a major port for this island of Sulawesi. There's an international airport and half a million people living in the city."

"And more boats!" said Chambers.

"You should be used to it by now. A nation composed of thousands of islands is going to have a lot of boats and a lot of ports," said Bennet.

"I realize we are the FBI, the illustrious G-men, but I'm beginning to wonder if our superpowers have met with kryptonite over here. This country can't keep track of its quarter of a million boats. Then there's the drug smugglers, the human trafficking, and the illegal fishing operations all using unregistered boats as well. It makes looking for a clue to a missing California teen like finding a needle in a haystack," said Chambers.

"Maybe so, but I think about my little boy at home and what it would mean to me as a dad if an FBI superman overcame the kryptonite and found some information in this case to give me a little hope, dead or alive."

"Not all of us have that sentimental weakness, but I agree that we need a break in this case if possible. By the way, how much farther?" asked Chambers.

"I can barely see the skyline of Manado now. Look over there," as he pointed in the direction of the city lying beyond the large bay they were approaching.

"Great," said Chambers. "Once we meet with the port officer, maybe I can get an action shot of you poring over dock records for your kids so they will know you're working and not just on a vacation."

"Believe me, I'd rather risk a shootout than wade through these piles of disorganized documents. It's certainly not the glamour job I imagined fifteen years ago when I graduated from Quantico."

CHAPTER 67

"So who has a specific pressing need for prayer tonight?" asked Della to a small group of six women. Lisa, a coworker; Latisha and Monique from Della's church; Chloe, a neighbor; and Allison Brooks.

"I hate to monopolize the prayer requests, especially since I don't contribute any prayers, at least not public ones yet, but I do have a specific need concerning the search for Alex."

"Don't apologize, missy, we bear these burdens together and until they find your son—alive—and bring him home, we are going to keep seeking, keep knocking, and keep asking!" said Latisha.

"Amen sister," said Monique. "That'll preach."

"Thank you! I'm so overwhelmed by your love and support. I'm truly inspired by your confident faith that Alex is alive."

"So tell us what's weighing on your mind," said Latisha

"As you know, the FBI sent a couple of agents to Indonesia to work with the Legal Attaché at the US Embassy in Jakarta. They've been working there for almost two months now and they have nothing to report. We need another breakthrough, the investigation has stalled."

"We've seen God answer prayers and give breakthroughs so let's pray through on this one. In fact, I feel led to just press in tonight with Allison's request. Everyone okay with that?" asked Della.

They all assented without hesitation. If Allison's tears could be interpreted as prayers that evening, then she truly was a contributor. She went home afterwards with a lightened heart and a sincere faith in the other women's faith.

Allison felt like she should talk to Alex that evening about it.

"Hi Alex, do you have a moment?"

"Of course, what's going on?"

"I just got home from our ladies get together."

"You mean your Bible study and prayer?"

"Yes, that. I know you are skeptical, but last time we had a real break-through was after one of these meetings that really seemed significant. But you thought it was just coincidence, and honestly, I sometimes wonder myself. But anyway, the reason I'm calling is for myself mostly and maybe for you, but really more for me."

"How so? What's shaken you tonight?" He could hear the excitement in her voice but misinterpreted it.

"Well, I always enjoy the prayer time but tonight, the women dedicated the whole time to pray for our situation. I can't explain it but the room… the atmosphere…I'm really not sure how to put it in words…as if God was near."

It was a good thing that Allison couldn't see Mr. Brooks roll his eyes over the phone. He had enough sense to just listen regardless of his oppos-ing thoughts. He tried to prepare himself to say something positive and not provoke an unnecessary backlash.

"Wow, I guess I can't say I've ever experienced what you're describing, but I'm glad if it is helping you cope."

"It's more than that, I really believe we will see another breakthrough in this investigation soon."

"I hope so too."

"No, you don't understand. I really believe a breakthrough will come soon because of these women's fervent prayer. I sensed it tonight."

"You said this was more for you than for me, why?"

"Because, like you, I have my doubts but the difference is I want to believe that God can hear their prayers and that He cares for them, for our son, and for me. Nobody knows where Alex is, but wherever he is, I want to believe that God knows. The reason I called is that I just wonder if it would make a difference if I made some effort to acknowledge Him."

"You mean God?"

"Yes. God," said Allison.

"Even if I believe God may not exist," said Mr. Brooks, "it's not going to hurt anyone if you want to say prayers. Except for the possibility of hurting yourself by suffering more disappointment from a false hope."

"It's just that. It seems like that is the tug of war I feel between believing and the fear of disappointment," said Allison.

"Know that I won't think the worse of you if you decide you want to exert faith in the unknown. I just hope you won't think the worse of me if I don't see it the same way as you."

"I understand. And no, I don't think worse of you, but I hope you won't mind me talking to you about it?"

"No, I don't mind. I just don't want to disappoint you if we don't see eye to eye on this."

"Sure. Well, thanks for listening," said Allison

"Sure, no problem. Anytime."

CHAPTER 68

A call from the studio production office took Allison by surprise. "Hello, this is Allison."

"Hi Allison, this is Rachel, Mr. Johansson's secretary."

"What can I do to help you?"

"Well, this is a little out of the ordinary but there's an old lady trying to get in touch with you. She called the main office and her message keeps getting passed along to various departments."

"With all due respect, Rachel, you know company policy plus the fact that I'm on leave. Why is this even an issue? I really can't be bothered with it," said Allison.

"Yes, I know. It wouldn't go anywhere except that it has something to do with your missing son."

Allison's heart jumped unexpectedly at those words. She changed her tone, "Oh, I see. What can you tell me?"

"She says she was on the same plane to Seoul and sat with your son for part of the trip."

"But that's not possible. At least not likely. Alex was booked in an executive seat. There's no place to sit together."

"I'm just repeating her message. She said she read the newspaper stories about the missing boy and recognized his picture. Then she saw you on TV and thought you might want to hear about her conversation with him. That's the gist of it."

"How do you know it's not some hoax or some aspiring actress trying to get a foot in the door?"

"Honestly, Allison, we don't know. That is why it keeps getting passed around. Nobody knows what to do. What if it's legitimate? We thought you would want to know."

"Yes, you're right. Did she leave her name and number?"

"Yes, would you like it?"

"Sure."

Rachel read the number and Allison brought the short conversation to a close. She sat stunned, staring at the name and number jotted quickly on the back of an unopened electric bill. Looking at her watch she thought, *It's late afternoon, there's no reason to delay calling. If she doesn't answer, I'll leave a message.*

The number rang. Then rang again. Then rang a third time. A deep sense of disappointment encroached on Allison as the phone rang a fourth time. The fifth ring and she began wondering if she would leave a voicemail. On the seventh ring the call connected.

"Hello?"

The sound of a frail old voice gave Allison an ounce of hope.

"Hello, is this Agnes?" said Allison.

"Yes, this is Agnes. May I ask who I'm speaking with?"

"I'm Allison Brooks, the mother of Alex Brooks, the missing boy in the news. I got a message from the studio office that you were trying to get hold of me."

"Oh yes. Oh, you poor mother who must be beside yourself with anxiety for your son. I couldn't help but go out of my comfort zone to find out how to reach you. It wasn't easy, I couldn't do it without the help of my granddaughter who goes on the internet."

"Thank you, but I was told that you talked with my son on the plane."

"Yes, and when I saw him on the television news while visiting my son and his family in Santa Clarita a few weeks ago, I thought the missing boy's parents might want to know about the time we had together on that long flight."

"Of course, we do, you're exactly right. It would mean a lot to me if you don't mind telling me. Do you have time now to talk or should I schedule a call later?"

"God bless you, there's no need to schedule anything. I'm by myself in an independent living home and though time in general is getting shorter for me, I have plenty of it today, and however many days the Lord gives me."

"You sound like a Christian."

"Yes, I am, and blessed beyond measure. Alexander told me you were a spiritual person but he didn't mention Christianity."

"No, he wouldn't have. I'm not technically a Christian, at least I don't think so. But my journey is leading me in that direction. But I would rather talk about Alex."

"Of course, but do you mind if I ask if there's any news of him yet?"

"No," she said. "The case is cold, but would you think I'm strange if I tell you that I've been attending a Bible study and prayer meeting with friends? And the other night, I really sensed the presence of God. It gave me hope. I believe my son is alive."

"I don't think that sounds strange at all. In fact, I believe Alex is alive and your hope is not in vain."

The confident and comforting words from this woman gave Allison moist eyes, a quivering lip, and a full heart. An hour later, she knew beyond doubt that she had just made a new friend and mentor for life.

"One last thing, Agnes, before we say goodbye. Just before Alex left, we had a little bit of turbulence between us. Did he say anything about that? I just can't get it out of my mind that our last conversation was an abnormally rocky one."

"Oh Allison, Alexander clearly loves you. He told me about the incident in his own unique way and he mentioned that he tried to get in touch with you but his phone was broken and he didn't have your number. I could read between the lines, he was certainly troubled about the way he spoke to you. Don't take it to heart, he's young and spoke rashly."

"Thank you, I can't tell you how much this call has meant to me."

"That was my hope," said Agnes. "I'd like to think that I still have opportunities in my old age to be used in missionary work."

The two agreed to talk once a week and make plans to meet each other in person in the near future.

CHAPTER 69

THREE DAYS LATER

"Hey Bennet, what do you think of this?" asked Agent Chambers, showing him a report from the port police records office. It was dated July 27th.

"I don't think anything about it unless you read it to me. You know I'm not as keen with this language in its written form as you are."

"Well, I won't read it, I'll just explain it. It's about a suspected murder of an owner of a fishing boat that was for lease. He was found in the bay, drowned. The report says he was drunk and most likely fell off a boat or the pier, but a couple locals gave anonymous tips saying otherwise. They claimed that the man had an ongoing dispute with a customer over the boat and they believed he was killed."

"Why should this have any bearing on our case? We're trying to help solve an abduction and ransom case not a suspected murder of a local businessman. How does it fit into the scope of what we're looking for?"

"That's just it," said Chambers. "We don't know what we're looking for. We have no description of the boat, where it was from, or where it went. And it's hard to know how we are supposed to hook something fishy other than narcotics or trafficking with all the missing boats involved in those cases. So to answer your question, I'm not sure what this has to do with price of tea in China. But...here's something else that caught my attention in the reports from the anonymous sources. One said the dispute was about a thirty-eight-foot Powercat commercial sport fishing boat that went missing."

This grabbed Bennet's attention. "That's a pretty nice boat for this harbor.

Did the owner report anything about it to the authorities before his death?"

"Yep, it's a nice boat, but no, he didn't file a report. His friends who knew him made these reports after his death. But there was no evidence of foul play at all so it was dismissed." Chambers, being the younger and less experienced agent, was glad to see the genuine enthusiasm of his partner. "And more than that, they claimed the dispute was about a cash sale for the boat, not a lease. They also claimed he was paid a decent price for the boat."

Bennet was puzzled, "That doesn't make any sense. So why would there be a dispute about a missing boat?"

"According to one of the accounts in the report, the owner had boasted to his friends over a few strong drinks that he had sold the boat for more than he had paid for it, but that the new owner would sell it back to him after a couple weeks of use for half the price and he could continue to lease it."

"This is an oddball story if true. Why would someone buy it and sell it back instead of leasing it? And why would the previous owner care if it wasn't returned?"

"At least one of those questions can be answered. The owner told his buddies that the buyer wanted to make a few small modifications to the boat. It seems that his buddies believed it would be used for smuggling and warned their friend not to get entangled. But they said the profit was too tempting, he looked the other way."

"But why would he be upset to not get the boat back?"

"There's nothing here about that but my guess is that he knew he would make more money through charters in the long haul and went along with this scheme with the thought that he would get the best of both worlds."

"I'm beginning to track with you, but is there anything else?"

"I've saved the best for last and maybe I should have started with this.

The man was found dead on July 19th but…the boat was last seen in this bay on June 23rd, two days after Alexander Brooks left Los Angeles and one day after, he went missing."

"Unbelievable! Why didn't you say that before?" said Bennet.

Chambers just grinned.

"I don't want to jump to conclusions," said Bennet excitedly, "but this looks like our needle in the haystack."

"That's my thinking. So what's next?" asked Chambers.

"Is there any registration information for this boat in the report?"

"Yes!"

"Then let's have the data center run the registration and see if this boat has shown up anywhere else on the planet. We need to convince the authorities to open this case back up and see if we can get a description, document, bank receipt, anything regarding the transaction with the person or group behind the purchase of that boat."

Chapter 70

February

"Liam did what?"

"He put the missing Norcat for sale on the black market," said Mr. Brooks.

"I wish you would consult me before launching out on hare-brained adventures like this," said Agent Hutchins.

"Look, this is how ingenuity and movement happens in the private sector. You have to cut the red tape and give people room to make decisions," said Mr. Brooks.

"Well, has anything turned up?"

"That's why I called, he's got an anxious inquirer."

"Give me as many details as you got."

"Okay, Liam had an idea and was so excited about it that he put it into action. I know it's impetuous but you've got to take the good with the bad. Honestly, he second-guessed himself and was conflicted about what to do. In this case, it seemed to work. The classified he posted sat idle for several days, then all of a sudden, he got a bite on the line. Someone wanted details about the boat and when he acquired it and where. The person wanted to know if it had the original identification number and registration, the make and model, the year, and any other description he could give. Finally, the inquirer wanted to know if the price was negotiable and where and when it could be delivered."

"What did he tell them?"

"Just the generic information for now, a 1996 thirty-eight-foot Powercat Norcat in good condition and a few other details that he learned from the report. Most importantly, he let them know that the boat was presently in Southeast Asia."

"What then?" asked Hutchins.

"They asked for pictures and offered a deposit to hold the sale until negotiations were finalized to everyone's satisfaction."

"What did he do for pictures?"

"He didn't. He said he would be glad to provide them but knew he needed to stall at that point since he was unprepared, so he offered to do better and give them a video tour of the boat in the next day or two if they wanted to reconnect tomorrow and make the arrangements. So can your team recreate some pictures?"

"Yes, but why did he say video? That's more complicated."

"I'm not sure. I think he panicked," said Mr. Brooks.

"Now it's my turn to panic," said Hutchins. "I'll need to locate that year and model and get a team on that right away. Then we need our Legal Attaché to convince Indonesian authorities to go along with this and see if they would be willing to help us. My thought is that this person or persons are really not interested in buying the boat but want the same information we are looking for—what happened to the boat, the men, the boy, and why?"

"But what if this person, if they are tied to Anaconda, smells a rat?"

"They already smell a rat if they had something to do with the abduction. This would at least confirm Groundhog's information about the boy being missing. It would mean they are truly in the dark and trying to solve this mystery themselves."

"Is there any way this may put Alex at greater risk if—"

"If he's alive, then they've either lost him or not. Either way, this is not going to affect his present situation, whatever and wherever it is," assured Hutchins. "On the other hand, this interested party may have nothing to do with the disappearance of your son and are simply trying to purchase a boat for some other illegal purpose."

Chapter 71

One Week Later

In Jakarta Bay, a 1996 Powercat Norcat commercial fishing boat lay still, anchored in the smooth water at the Ancol Marina. Two Indonesian undercover police waited on the rear deck for their contact, expected to arrive at any moment.

Agents Bennet and Chambers watched through high powered binoculars from a nearby hotel as three men approached the boat from the dock. Two of the men looked like native Indonesians in common indistinct clothes but the third man walking behind them looked foreign and was dressed in a tailored black suit and wearing dark glasses. They watched the men greet one another then disappeared into the cabin.

"This is really unnerving," said Chambers, "not being in the thick of it."

"We need to trust that these local guys can handle this without our help. After all, they've participated in our joint training program as part of the collaboration between countries."

"I'm not trying to be US-centric but I wish they would have allowed one of our SWAT teams to be at hand since there's no certainty how this is going to go down."

"I wish they would have allowed us to put a wire on one of their guys with an audio feed so we could hear what kind of negotiations are happening right now."

Just then four men reappeared on deck and were stepping off the boat onto the dock. The man in the dark suit apparently remained in the cabin.

"What's going on?" asked Chambers. "This wasn't part of the plan."

"I don't think they are leaving on their own accord. I hope they have a contingency plan."

Two more men could be seen walking towards the boat, acknowledging the others before stepping onto the Norcat's deck.

"What in the world is going on?" said Chambers, thinking out loud.

What they witnessed next took them somewhat by surprise. Seemingly out of nowhere, more than a dozen Indonesian special forces with full body armor and assault rifles emerged from cover and quickly surrounded the four men. The two undercover agents immediately dropped to the ground. The two suspects attempted to draw weapons and without delay, two shots rang out from hidden snipers and both men dropped involuntarily. At the same time the boat was covered by the tactical team on the dock and two police boats with men at mounted machine guns pulled alongside the fishing boat. In seconds, they thronged the boat with stealth and a tear gas canister was lobbed through the open hatch over the cabin. A moment later, the three remaining suspects emerged with hands raised above their heads.

Chambers looked at his partner with eyebrows raised, "Not bad!"

"Not bad at all. I think our joint tactical training has paid off," said Bennet. "Now it's a waiting game until they find out who these guys are. Let's keep our fingers crossed. We might have just stepped on the tail of Anaconda."

CHAPTER 72

"Mr. Brooks asked if I would meet with Super 8, as you call yourselves, to give my report on the search for Alexander Brooks Jr. This certainly breaks protocol, but under these unique circumstances and due to our ongoing collaboration, it seemed reasonable," said Agent Hutchins. "But please, Liam, don't go off half-cocked on some reckless adventure based on the insight I'm going to give."

Liam smirked, knowing his last "reckless adventure" was a successful one.

"I do welcome your team's input as we move forward," said Hutchins.

Super 8 was assembled once again on the tenth floor conference room. Agent Hutchins presented the first of a series of slides on the big screen.

"This is a picture of Cheng-han Lin, or Kuan-lin Chen, or Chia-hao Huang or several other aliases, but we will stick with Cheng-han for now. He was apprehended last week in Jakarta. He's the only serious player out of the three who lived through that operation. The other two are simply run-of-the-mill thugs, but Cheng-han has warrants for his arrest in at least four other countries for various crimes ranging from money laundering, possession of counterfeit documents, human trafficking, and cyber blackmail.

"I have good news and bad news. The good news is we believe Cheng-han is affiliated with an international crime syndicate which we have been calling Anaconda for lack of further information. The bad news is Cheng-han is a good catch but not the big fish. He's not a kingpin in the organization, he's not talking, and we don't have any new information yet regarding the disappearance of Alex other than what we can surmise."

"And what have you surmised?" asked Bailey.

"One thing is that we are now convinced that they are looking for a thirty-eight-foot Norcat because it has disappeared with a few of their men and their prize bargaining chip. We believe this confirms what you have learned already. Secondly, it nearly confirms the date and port which the abductors left from. Based on the average speed of that vessel and the time-line following the disappearance of Alex, we can now draw a search map and start from the furthest range of possibilities and work our way back towards the Manado Bay."

"How large of a search area is that?" asked Miles.

"Nearly all of the archipelago," he said with a tinge of sarcasm.

"But wouldn't this group do the same thing and be looking for him already?" asked Liam.

"Yes, that's almost certain," said Hutchins.

"So when will our search start?" asked Bailey.

"It has already. But you may not be able to imagine the daunting task ahead of us. The enemy might have skirted around Sulawesi and headed east or south or west or north. There's an estimated 17,000 islands in those surrounding seas."

"We know! But what can we do to help?" said Miles.

"Short of going door to door in a boat, so to speak, or helping with fly overs in search of a stray Norcat fishing boat, I'm really not sure," said Hutchins.

"What about contacting local authorities by phone or internet from smaller islands to help us by sending out search parties?" said Parker. "We can pay them for their time or offer a reward or both."

"That's a possible idea."

"What about hi-res satellite images? Can you hook us up with a spy satellite? I've heard you can read the time on someone's watch through those," said Bailey.

"Hmmm, that's a thought. I'm not sure if I can pull those strings but it's worth trying. It would be excruciatingly tedious to go looking for a thirty-eight-foot boat among all those islands. But if you want to burn your retinas trying, I don't mind trying to get you special access."

"If you have any other ideas, don't hesitate to run them past me. Just please don't start prowling around the Dark Web for connections to Cheng-han! We've got that one covered."

CHAPTER 73

MAY

A large outcropping of rock marked the end of a long sandy beach. Three older boys carrying net bags waded into the water until their heads barely rose about the surf. The incoming waves lifted them off their feet and back down again, and yet they were still thirty yards from the furthest edge of the jutting rock.

Gunadi looked to Alex and in his native language said, "Here we must swim."

"How far?" asked Alex.

"Not far, but keep away from the rock until we are beyond it."

Alex was getting better understanding the language having lived eight months in the village, but he struggled when under pressure to fully comprehend long sentences.

"I don't understand," said Alex, his voice raised a little to be heard over the noise of the surf.

"Follow us, Alekus,"

Alex nodded. Gunadi and Rimbo, a few years younger than him, took deep breaths and plunged underneath the waves. The boys were heading for a hidden cove on the other side of the rock that Alex had never seen but the others claimed was a great spot for finding clams and other seafood.

Alex delayed for a second before following. The islanders were expert swimmers and divers. Alex was only an average swimmer even though he grew up in Southern California with its beach and surfing culture. Consequently, he struggled to keep up. The water was generally pristine with amazing visibility, but the churning water against the rocks stirred up debris and limited Alex's view. He lost sight of the others.

Coming up for air, he realized the tide had moved him too close to the rock. The waves on this side of the island were not very large but big enough to create a downward pull into the cliff. This made it harder for Alex to swim; he worked twice as hard and made half the progress as normal against the current. His arms, legs, and lungs began to burn and he couldn't decide whether to try and head back to the beach or press on for the cove, still out of his sight. He tried fighting the temptation to panic, but his arms and legs gave out on him. In desperation and without premeditation, he cried out "Jesus, help me!"

He didn't have time to think about this unexpected reaction. A moment later, the two boys popped up out of the water in front of him, smiling. They had reached the cove before realizing Alex wasn't with them. They saw him struggling in the current and swam back to him. Working together, they helped him get to shore.

Alex flopped down on the pebble and shell strewn cove, exhausted and embarrassed. The two others never imagined he was actually in danger of drowning, so they reveled in some laughter over the ordeal and got to work looking for clams and other shellfish. Once Alex felt recovered, he got up and looked around in amazement of this hidden cove. A complete wall of rock surrounded the half-circle beach consisting mostly of shells, pebbles, bits of driftwood, and few patches of sand near the cliff.

Gunadi and Rimbo were excited to find several crabs scurrying around and a medium sized turtle. Their hunting expedition was already a success. As Alex scanned the area, he noticed what looked like a sea cave half submerged on the opposite side of the cove.

"What's that?" pointing to the cave.

"*Gua.*"

Alex didn't know that particular word yet but he knew he was looking at a cave. He just asked to make sure they knew it was there. Of course they did. He waded out in to the water to explore. The water splashed up to his chin and he was still out of reach. He swam out to the entrance and to his great disappointment, he found that the cave was shallow. Gunadi and Rimbo swam out to him and tried telling him something that he couldn't make sense of.

"Dive and back up."

They made motions with their hands as best as they could while treading water. Alex dropped below the surface to see if he understood them right. He could barely see the shallow cave sloping downward and opening up about five feet down. He thought, *It must be a tunnel to another cove or beach.* When Alex came back to the surface, the two other boys convinced him to follow them. He decided to watch them underwater as they dove one at a time and swam through the submerged opening and disappeared. *But how far does it go?* Alex wondered. A tinge of fear and a rush of adrenaline coursed through him. He went back up to the surface, took a deep breath, and joined the excursion. At five feet down, there was enough visibility to see the opening but not enough to see further. He hoped he would see light from the other side, but as he entered the tunnel, everything got darker.

The opening seemed to be about eight feet wide and about six feet high, but not high enough for Alex as his he felt the sharp sting of barnacles and shells scrape his back from miscalculating the space around him. Not too far into the tunnel, the area opened wide and he could see a faint glow not far above him. He cautiously rose, keeping an arm out in front of his face until he surfaced into a large cavity in the stone.

He misunderstood Gunadi and Rimbo's hand gestures and words. It wasn't a tunnel to the other side but an entrance to a cavern about twenty feet wide and thirty feet long with about four feet of headroom. The cavern would have been pitch black if it wasn't for a fissure in the stone above them that let in enough light to provide adequate visibility once a person's eyes adjusted from the outside.

The floor of the cavern sloped upward towards the back and Alex could see the other two sitting comfortably on a rock shelf with their upper bodies out of the water. Little did he know that this was a favorite spot for nearly all the young villagers at one time or another, but only when the tide was low enough. The water gently rose slightly and lowered in response to the waves outside. The excited chatter of the boys echoed with a muffled sound in the relatively small reverberating space.

After his eyes adjusted to the low light, Alex noticed pictures and shapes etched into the rock. He joined Gunadi and Rimbo on the rock shelf. They pointed out the bleeding scratches on his back and decided to take turns diving with a sharp stone to knock off the unwelcome barnacles and shells encroaching on their entrance. They indicated to Alex that is was a regular maintenance issue for them, though they knew the entrance well enough to swim through without touching the top, the bottom, or the sides of the opening.

The cave was cooler than outside and proved to be an unexpected treat to kick back and relax for a little while. No doubt, this must have been part of the appeal to others over the years.

The environment lent itself to personal reflections. The low light, the echoing sounds, the cool air all contributed to this restful place to contemplate. Alex thought about his first conscious prayer that came about during his swimming incident. *What made me call out like that? And what if it was coincidence that Gunadi and Rimbo showed up right afterward? If God did hear me, there wasn't enough time that passed between my prayer and their help unless somehow God anticipated me.*

As he thought about these things in the peaceful atmosphere, his eyes became heavy, his body relaxed, and without knowing it, he dozed off.

CHAPTER 74

Alex suddenly awoke with a strange sense that the indistinct amount of time that passed was longer than he imagined. Gunadi and Rimbo were gone. He realized that the steadily rising tide must have woken him up as it began to lap against his chin. He assumed the other two must have swam back to the cove to continue their search for clams. He took one last look of the cavern with the thought of coming back sometime soon, then took a deep breath and dove down to exit the cave. He misjudged the depth and violently knocked his head against the rock. Everything went black.

CHAPTER 75

When Alex regained consciousness he was perched back on the shelf, his head barely above the rising water line. His head ached and he could feel a warm trickle of blood down one side of his face. His eyesight was blurry and he felt dizzy and nauseous. He instinctively reached for his head and winced as he found a large knot on the top his head and a clot of blood matting his hair.

He wondered what he should do. He knew he was not in a state to swim and rightly afraid of repeating his mistake. Yelling for the others wouldn't help. *Where's Gunadi and Rimbo? Will they come look for me? How long before this cave fills with water? Should I try to swim for it? Oh, my head.*

The nausea overtook him and he threw up. "Ahhhh!" He splashed the nasty water away from him. The dizziness caused the small room to spin, he closed his eyes and tried to think. *They've got to come back soon and check on me, won't they? They wouldn't just leave me here, would they? How do I do it? Is my life cursed? I'll try to swim before I sit here and drown.*

But he truly doubted his ability to swim at all right now. He sat there feeling miserable, not able to gauge time at all. *How long have I been here?* His hands and feet were extremely puckered from being in the water so long but that didn't tell him anything specific. Thankfully, there were still places to shift in order to stay above water on top the rock shelf, but for how long?

Alex wondered if he should try another prayer. The first time was not premeditated and he surprised himself when he heard his own voice crying out. *What made me cry out? Is it from reading the Bible? Is something in me changing?*

But it might have been just a coincidence. Did the help come as a result? It had to be coincidence. He thought about Agnes and her confidence in God and the Bible. He memorized her little note to himself. *I wonder if she's praying for me. What if I pray and nothing happens? I don't know what I'm more afraid of—not getting an answer or getting one and doubting it if help comes. How can I know for certain if help really came from God?* If he prayed and help didn't come, he feared it would extinguish his hope that God did exist and knew his situation. *What do I do?*

The water slowly inched up. Alex kept shifting to find a higher point but noticed that the top of his head, though above water, was almost touching the roof of the cave. There were taller places in the ceiling but he would have to tread water and that was out of the question right now. He continued to struggle with thoughts about praying. *But if there is a god, maybe He knows that I doubt Him. But if there isn't a god, it wouldn't hurt to say a prayer even if it didn't help.* He reasoned all this out and decided to dive in, not the water but a deliberate prayer. He agonized over what he should say.

"God, I'm not sure you exist, but I think you do. If you do, I'm not sure you know who I am and where I am." He planned on composing more in his mind but something unexpected happened—he sensed a change around him, but it wasn't a change in the atmosphere happening in the cave. It felt closer, deeper. He couldn't explain it to himself. He thought it might be an awareness of God's presence, or at least a consciousness of God listening. *Is that what I feel? Is that what is happening?* he thought. He wanted to cry, his heart pounded, he felt a lump in his throat. He did begin to cry, not a bawl but almost a whimper. His head stopped spinning for a moment and everything else seemed to fade away in this surreal moment. He continued his prayer from his overwhelmed heart. "Agnes believes in you and Seti does also. I want to believe too, but I'm afraid—afraid of the unknown. But if you can hear me, I need help; please send someone to help get me out of here alive. I don't want to die. I'm not ready to die."

When he finished, he half expected the face of Gunadi or Rimbo to pop out of the water in front of him like last time. But instead, nothing tangible happened. Yet something did happen unexpectedly—his fear vanished. This surprised him more than if he had witnessed the two boys emerge from the water. More than that, he became distinctly aware of another dimension of life, a spiritual dimension beyond the tangible realities. Though he previously ignored this in his life, he, all of a sudden, acknowledged its existence that he somehow knew was there all the time. But he had suppressed it. First, suppressed by those around him in his developmental years and then unconsciously followed in his own outlook in life afterwards.

He now understood that what he was awakening to had always been present under the surface. The unmet elusive desire, the gnawing sense that there was something more to life, *Someone* more to life—God. He became entirely absorbed in these thoughts as if discovering all the border pieces of a puzzle and putting them together, giving definition to a bigger picture. He felt as if new thoughts were being downloaded into his previously limited experience. A mystery now manifested in his soul. But he not only experienced an absence of fear but something more—the presence of peace.

CHAPTER 76

The tide slowly continued rising. Alex continued shifting his position to keep his head above water. His headache and dizziness persisted but so did the peace he encountered. Then the surface of the water stirred and the concerned face of Setiawan appeared.

"Alekus, oh Alekus! You are alive," said Setiawan in his native tongue. "Rimbo told us you might be dead."

"Seti! I'm glad to see you. I'm not dead yet but I need help. I hit my head, I can't swim," said Alex, speaking in English.

Setiawan looked at the wound on his head with what little light there was. He made a clicking sound with his tongue and shook his head in dismay. "I will come back," and Setiawan dove out of sight. In a short time, he returned with a rope and a smooth stone the size of a football. He handed it to Alex, "Hold this," and Seti proceeded to tie the rope under his arms. Alex understood that the stone would help him sink in the water. Seti encouraged Alex to take a deep breath and promised he would get him out safely. "Follow me," said Setiawan just before disappearing.

Alex felt a tug on the rope. He took a deep breath, cradled the stone and slipped into the deep part of the cavern. Setiawan stayed close to Alex and precariously pulled him through the opening of the cave out into the cove. As they both came to the surface, Alex could see that the sun was beginning to set.

Gunadi and Rimbo were waiting anxiously on the shore with Indah. If not for his blurry vision, he would have seen relief come to their troubled faces as they gathered around him. He struggled to stand so they gently laid him down on the beach. Indah examined the wound on his head and gave instructions to the boys to take the canoe and fetch a list of supplies.

Setiawan also gave orders before they left. "Bring me some coals and food. I will stay here with Alekus tonight."

It was nearly high tide and very little beach was left in the cove. Indah and Setiawan helped Alex find a comfortable spot for him to lay down. She got on her hands and knees to move pebbles and shells off a small patch of sand and built up a small mound of sand to lay his head on. Setiawan brought him a bamboo container with fresh water.

Alex's aching head and dizziness did not let up and Setiawan and Indah could clearly see he was not well.

"How did you know to come for me?" He looked at their compassionate faces with drooping eyelids struggling to stay open from the throbbing pain in his head. He wasn't sure how much blood he lost, but he was nearly certain that he had received a concussion when he hit his head. He felt so exhausted and sleepy that he involuntarily nodded off while Setiawan and Indah watched in dismay.

CHAPTER 77

Alex awoke to the familiar sight and smell of a glowing fire nearby. At first, he couldn't remember where he was, but as soon as he shifted his sore body, he became conscious of his throbbing and dizzy head. He recalled the accident and the rescue. Alex carefully reached up to feel the spot on his head. He touched the perimeter of the wound which stung badly enough to stop his self-assessment. He felt a pasty substance, apparently some type of island salve for wounds. He also noticed that someone had put a shirt on him. He could feel it sticking to the scratches on his back from his dive into the cave. He shifted and saw Seti sleeping on the other side of the fire. He felt hungry and noticed a small stack of ripe bananas placed within reach. He helped himself, trying not to disturb Seti's sleep.

The stars were bright and the sound of the surf was soothing. His headache hadn't diminished but neither his new peace. His sense of wonder heightened as he looked at the endless sky and whispered, "Thank you for hearing my prayer. I'm sorry I've never paid any attention to you before. I'm beginning to think you have had some part in all this. I don't believe it is all coincidence. I'm not sure why you would think I'm worth the trouble, but you've got my attention. Show me what you want from me."

Suddenly, a warm sensation came over his head and the dizziness changed to tingling and the headache dissipated. All he could think of was the story he recently read in the Bible about a woman with a sickness who touched the robe of Jesus and felt His healing power. His voice rose in excitement, "It's gone. My headache is gone!"

Setiawan stirred from his sleep and groggily looked up at Alex who was now sitting and exclaiming with tears streaming down his face. "My headache went away, it's gone. I'm going to be okay, I know I will."

"Alekus, are you alright?"

"Seti, I'm alright. God has healed my head! I feel better."

"Ohhh Alekus, that is good. Praise God for His kindness."

"Seti, you won't believe it. I prayed three times and each time, I received a response. It's amazing! My head is better. I was just saying a prayer and I felt a warmth and my headache and dizziness went away!"

Setiawan got up to check on his wound. Alex winced, "Ouch, that still hurts, but I'm better, I know it. I've been healed, just like in the Bible. God is real, Seti, He's watching over me."

"Very good, Alekus, very good. Yes, God is watching over you."

"And He's used you, Seti. And Agnes. And my little Bible. I want to tell Indah. Where is she? She was here before."

"She has gone home but will come back tomorrow in the canoe with Rimbo."

"I can't wait to tell her. She's like me, she wants to believe what you have been teaching her but it's not been part of her growing up. I think she will believe now, Seti."

Tears of joy streamed down Seti's face. Alex couldn't understand how Setiawan's long life of toil and hope seemed to be paying off finally. He could see that the seeds he planted were beginning to grow. He felt that his life had finally reached a place he thought he would never see in his lonely lifetime. He believed that if he could help just one person to know God through his efforts, it was a life well lived.

The two continued to talk and feast through the night.

Chapter 78

I ndah woke at daybreak and slipped out of the family hut while everyone else continued to sleep. Other villagers were beginning to stir and start their day. News had spread of Alekus' accident and many were genuinely concerned. He had become a village pet of sorts among the older women and younger children. But many of the young men remained jealous since it was obvious to everyone that Indah paid special attention to him. The young women were jealous because Alekus paid special attention to Indah. Then there was Kadek, who intercepted Indah on her way to find Rimbo.

"Indah, you are making a fool of yourself worrying over that foreigner."

"When will you recognize that he is our guest?"

"If he is a guest then why is he still here? A guest doesn't stay forever. He is not a guest and he is not one of us. You should know better," said Kadek.

"No, it is you who should know better by now. Hating Alekus won't make me like you. If you want me to like you then stop your childish behavior!" She walked off.

Kadek seethed, *I hate him. I wish he would never have come to this island. If only we had killed him along with the others.*

Aisyah was up early and came walking alongside her cousin. "Indah, are you going to see Alekus this morning?"

"Yes, I'm going as soon as I gather some food and find Rimbo."

"Can I go with you, Indah? I can help."

"No, Aisyah, you cannot go."

"Oh, but you always say that!" said Aisyah, pouting.

"But you can help."

"I can? How?" asked Aisyah.

"Macchiato and Mocha are alone at Setiawan's hut. They need to be fed and cared for until Alekus gets back."

"Will he come back? Rimbo said he was almost dead."

"Can I tell you a secret, Aisyah?"

"You can tell me!"

"He will get better, I know."

"How do you know?"

"That's the secret. I know because I prayed to Setiawan's god to heal him. But it's a secret. You must not tell."

"Who is Setiawan's god? And how can he heal Alekus?"

"You are too young to understand but I will tell you someday if you promise to be responsible by looking after Macchiato and Mocha."

Aisyah thought about it for a moment, "Alright, I will."

"Good girl, Aisyah, I knew I could trust you."

Aisyah looked up and gave Indah a big smile and Indah stopped to lean over and give Aisyah a kiss on her forehead.

"What was that?" asked Aisyah.

"A kiss."

"What is a kiss?"

"It's a way for me to say that I care about you."

"Who taught you that?" she asked.

Indah smiled, "That's also a secret. But not one I am going to tell."

Aisyah skipped away towards Setiawan's hut and Indah continued through the village, encountering other women who asked about Alekus and gave her food for her basket along with advice and more herbs to help his recovery. She finally came to Rimbo's family hut. One of his little brothers sat quietly in the doorway.

"Where is your big brother?"

"Sleeping," said Ketut.

"Can you wake him for me?"

He shook his head no.

"Why not?"

He just shook his head no. Indah guessed that he had been corrected in the past for disturbing the family's sleep. She understood it was a problem that must be remedied in a home with little children but it frustrated her to not be able to get started early.

"Then tell him I am waiting for him when he wakes up."

Indah was anxious to get to Alex and Uncle Seti. She could handle a canoe alone but her father forbade her from going without someone. She continued walking through the village and found a small group of early risers of various ages practicing their *silat jurus*. She decided to join them to pass the time and expend some of her pent-up energy. The graceful and precise movements were fluid without sacrificing power and force. Not long afterwards, Rimbo came running up to Indah.

"I'm here, I'm ready to go."

Indah excused herself from the group with a bow and started walking briskly with Rimbo towards the beach.

"Do you think he is dead?" asked Rimbo.

"No, I don't think he died. He had a bad wound and is not himself but he will live. I just hope he gets better soon."

They got to the edge of the beach and pulled a small dugout canoe with an outrigger on one side attached by two long bamboo poles. As a general practice, the villagers kept the beach free from all signs of life unless they had some purpose otherwise. This side of the island was known as the "quiet side" but most villagers didn't know why. Setiawan and a few other older villagers knew it was because it faced the more remote region of small uninhabited islands. The other side of their island was equally remote but it faced the larger distant islands, some of which were inhabited.

The canoe was heavy enough to require both of them drag it out to the surf. Once off shore, they each worked an oar on the opposite side of the outrigger.

"Rimbo, why did you leave Alekus alone yesterday?"

"I didn't leave him. We were gathering food at the cove and Alekus saw the cave and wanted to see it. He was tired because he struggled getting around the rock. He got caught in the tide. So when he was in the cave, he fell asleep. We didn't want to wake him and we knew we needed to come back with food, so we left him to go back to gathering."

"Didn't you know to go back and wake him up?" she asked with a perturbed tone.

"Yes, but Gunadi filled his bag first and said he was going back so I should go get Alekus to help me finish filling my bag. When I went to the cave, I found Alekus lying on the rock, bleeding and not talking. I thought he was dead. I dove out to call Gunadi but he was already gone. I had to get help, that is why I left him. I didn't mean to do anything wrong. It is not my fault." Rimbo admired Indah like most boys and didn't want her to be angry with him.

"No, you didn't do anything wrong. But you should have been more careful."

They continued to row towards the cove.

"Indah, what is that sound?" asked Rimbo.

"What sound?"

"The sound like a flying beetle," said Rimbo.

"There are no beetles that fly over the sea, you should know that."

He took offense at her condescending remark. "I know that but listen and tell me what you think it is."

They stopped rowing and listened carefully.

"I do hear it but I don't know what it is," said Indah.

"It's getting louder."

They both stared in the general direction of the strange sound, it seemed to be coming from the far side of the island.

"Do you think it is a swarm of bees?" asked Rimbo.

"Maybe, but I've never heard a swarm that loud."

The noise grew louder and fear of the unknown came upon both of them. A low flying plane came into view. None of the younger generation on the island had ever witnessed one before. To Indah and Rimbo, it looked like a monstrous dark albatross. It flew directly over them. They covered their ears and ducked down in the canoe for fear of it alighting on them to snatch them out of the water like a seabird catching a fish. Indah screamed as it passed by. Their hearts pounded with terror, their eyes large and frightened.

"Indah, what was that?"

"I don't know. It's horrible."

They watched it get smaller but then it started turning around.

"Indah, it's coming back! What do we do?"

"Lie down! Hide your face!"

They both dropped to the floor of the canoe. The sound of the engine grew louder. The plane was now flying even lower. They felt the wind from it as it passed over them. After crossing over the island, it began to circle back again.

Indah got up and yelled, "Row, Rimbo, row! We must get to uncle Seti. He can protect us!"

And they rowed with all their might towards the cove. The sound grew louder again. "Row, Rimbo, row hard!"

CHAPTER 79

Setiawan and Alex were awakened by the sound. Setiawan knew it was an airplane but wasn't certain if this was good sign or not. Alex stood on the beach, watching and wondering if he should wave his arms as a signal or throw a bunch of green brush on the fire to make some billowing smoke. He thought out loud, "It may be my dad, maybe they have finally come for me."

Seti stood beside him watching the plane circle around. They both wondered if they could be seen.

"Don't you think they would drop a message if they are looking for me? Maybe they have," said Alex. He spoke in English and Seti couldn't follow his words, but he guessed that Alex was thinking about his family and his own country and if this might be his rescue off the island that he longed for.

"There's nowhere to land a plane but if they are looking for me, I think I should signal to them if they fly over."

It circled over several times but it never flew over the small cove. It eventually disappeared and left them to ponder.

"Seti, it only took a full day in a fishing boat for us to arrive from a bigger island somewhere out there. That means someone could be here for me in a short time."

They sat down again near their fire.

"Wow, that just came out of nowhere," said Alex. "It's been so long, there's a part of me that had given up hope of being found."

Once again, Alex rattled on in English, making it very hard if not impossible for Setiawan to understand him. Yet Setiawan still had a keen ability to interpret in his own mind what Alex meant. He could read the conflict in Alex's expressions. Just then, the canoe could be seen coming around the rock wall and in sight of the cove. Once Indah and Rimbo reached the shore, the two men helped them pull the boat onto the beach. Indah and Rimbo were dumbstruck and trembling with fright. Indah's eyes were swollen red from crying, but seeing Alex filled her with a sense of awe. He was walking, talking, and behaving completely normal.

"Alekus, are you better?"

Alex gave her a big smile, "Yes! But let's sit down first before I tell you."

They all sat around the coals as Setiawan assured them that they were not in any danger. He guessed that they were terrified by the airplane.

"They have never seen an airplane before," said Setiawan. "I must explain it to them."

It was hard for them to comprehend a flying canoe with people in it. Their island lay beyond established flight paths and if a plane or jet had ever flown over, they were high and easily mistaken for a migratory bird. Now that Indah had calmed down, she wanted to get back to the subject of Alex's recovery.

"Alekus, you are better?" she said.

"Yes, let me tell you all that has happened. Uncle Seti might need to help me with some words." Alex told her the whole story starting with his first prayer and ending with his miraculous healing.

In the meantime, the rest of the island was in an uproar.

CHAPTER 80

The rumble of the airplane caught the attention of more than just Indah and Rimbo. The elders recognized the sound while the plane was some distance away. They began ordering everyone, "Get to your huts! Stay in!"

Gusti sent his son, Kadek, and a couple other young men to run throughout the village with the urgent message. This unrehearsed drill effectively emptied the village of outside activity by the time the plane reached the island, and hid the people but it couldn't hide the village structures from an overhead gaze.

Birds and other animals displayed signs of dismay at the intrusion of the tranquil airspace. The sight and sound frightened many children but a few curious ones peeked through the bamboo walls in awe. Parents either chided the children or joined them in peering out through the gaps. A few of the oldest inhabitants among them knew exactly what the flying object was but they didn't know what it meant. Who was flying over their island and why? Was this a random event or was it somehow connected to Alekus?

After passing over the village several times, the mysterious overhead visitors vanished on the horizon. The elders listened keenly as the sound of the engine and prop grew faint. They sent the young men back through the village to give the equivalent of an all-clear signal.

The entire population poured out of their dwellings and instinctively gathered together in the center of the village. The buzz of chatter and questions might have been mistaken for another incoming plane. The leaders knew they would have to speak to their people right away before getting a chance to hold council with each other. Waniwan motioned for everyone to quiet down.

"Those among us who are older and were youth at the time of migration to this island have seen flying canoes like what everyone saw today."

The majority of the crowd gasped and looked at each other with disbelief. Waniwan used the description of a canoe for lack of any better comparison since their people were only familiar with boats for transporting people. The principles of aerodynamics to overcome the law of gravity never occurred to them as a possibility by anything other than birds. The plane appeared to many as some awful flying monster or evil spirit. Waniwan could tell the people needed more explanation but he didn't know where to begin. He chose to make light of it.

"There is no danger and we will probably never see it again in our lifetime. It must have lost its way and turned around to get back on its trail. Go back to what you were doing, and if the elders have anything more to say, we will tell you." Then he dismissed the crowd.

Suharto leaned over to Waniwan, "That will not satisfy their curiosity or calm their fears."

"What else could I tell them now?" said Waniwan.

"No, you are right. What else could be said right now?"

The people were slow to disperse. Their disturbed thoughts and unanswered questions kept their minds occupied and distracted from everything else on their daily agenda.

The four elders disappeared into the community house.

"What does this mean?" asked Gusti.

"It may be chance. Men will always explore," said Waniwan.

"But what if it is not chance? What if this has something to do with Alekus?" said Tomanti.

"Yes, I thought the same thing," said Waniwan. "His own people might be looking for him."

"Or the men we killed might have their own people looking for them," said Suharto.

"If it is his own people, then we should let them take him away and ask them to never return," said Gusti.

"But what if they are looking for the dead men?" asked Tomanti.

"When they find out we have killed them, they will want revenge on us. We must be ready to defend ourselves," said Gusti.

"But they cannot land an airplane on this island," said Waniwan.

"Yes, that is true unless new machines have a way," said Suharto. "They will most likely come by boat. We must keep men on lookout on each side of the island."

"What if they are satisfied to have Alekus and leave us alone?" asked Gusti.

"I have thought of that myself but we must not forget our dreams or that we have welcomed Alekus as a guest," said Waniwan.

"But how do you know that the dreams mean we must not let them take Alekus away and leave us in peace?" said Gusti.

"And if we kill more men, what will keep others from coming to look for them and taking revenge themselves?" asked Suharto.

"Don't forget, they have firearms and we do not," said Waniwan. "Three men, unaware, are easily killed by arrows, but if more men, if they come, will not be unaware."

"This is all guessing. We don't know who flew over. It may be explorers, or people looking for Alekus, or people looking for the dead men. We don't know," said Tomanti.

"One thing is for certain, we must have watchmen on every side of the island and a way to signal," said Suharto.

CHAPTER 81

An office phone rang and rang until someone finally picked up.
"Hello."

"We have found their location."

"Are you certain?"

"The water is clear. We could see a boat sunk not far off shore. The size and description are a close enough match. The island appears to be inhabited."

"Send a special team without delay."

CHAPTER 82

"It's time to dry your eyes, we must get back to the village soon," said Setiawan. He didn't say this coldly to Indah but from a practical matter-of-fact need to help the small group to transition to other matters at hand. He contemplated the tears of joy glistening down her cheeks after hearing Alex's story and especially about his healing. Her prayer for him had been a leap of faith. Setiawan rejoiced inside to see the spiritual seeds that he planted beginning to germinate in Indah.

"The village will be unsettled over this and the elders will determine a path for us in the days ahead. I want to be present in case Alekus is blamed," said Setiawan

"Why would they blame Alekus?" asked Rimbo.

"Because the people in the airplane are probably looking for him. They will attempt to come for him, which means more unwelcome visitors to our island. We will no longer be hidden from the rest of the world."

The thought of someone coming to take Alekus troubled Indah. It hadn't occurred to her that he would want to leave now that the village had welcomed him. She wished she could ask Setiawan to tell her what he thought about it but not with Alekus present. She decided to ask him privately at a later time.

They all loaded into the canoe and made their way out of the cove and back to the beach nearest the village. As they walked briskly towards the village, it didn't take long for them to encounter bewildered people who met them with surprised exclamations of Alex's well-being, then bombarded them with questions about the flying canoe.

"Oh Alekus," said a mother scurrying down the trail with two children. "You are well!"

"Yes, I am well," he said with a smile.

But her agitation over the plane could not be stifled very long after this brief moment of good news.

"Did you see the flying thing?" she asked Setiawan.

"Yes, it is an airplane and I have seen them before when I was young."

"That is what Waniwan said to us but it was frightening," she said.

"There is nothing to be frightened of," said Setiawan.

"Are they looking for Alekus? Will they come for him?"

"We don't know who was in the airplane, it might not be anyone who knows anything about Alekus, or this island, or us."

"You better get to the village soon, the elders are making plans and giving orders to everyone," said the mother.

"Yes, we are on our way now so let us be on our way," said Setiawan.

Similar encounters and conversations caused multiple delays on their way. Setiawan ordered Rimbo to run ahead of them and let the elders know they were coming. They slowly made their way to the village center and found Waniwan and the other chiefs giving instructions to a huddled group of men. They stopped momentarily upon seeing Setiawan and Alex.

"Alekus, I am glad you are well. We thought that you were severely injured," said Waniwan.

As usual, Alex could only pick out bits and pieces of Waniwan's words, but he made a good guess based on the man's countenance.

"I am well," said Alex.

Waniwan turned to Setiawan, "You know this is an unexpected intrusion to see an airplane searching our island."

"Yes, I do understand. But we don't know who is searching."

"No, we do not know, but that is why we are setting a watch around the island. Since Alekus appears to be uninjured, we will ask the two of you to return to your camp on the far side of the island to watch the coast carefully for boats or airplanes."

"What do you want us to do if we see something?"

"Take a young runner with you to send word."

"Rimbo is a good runner."

"Then take him but don't delay. We are sending others to do the same on other parts of the island."

"We will leave as soon as we find Rimbo and gather a few provisions."

Indah stood behind them the whole time trying to be inconspicuous but her father noticed her. He did not approve of her giving so much attention to Alekus but she was a stubborn child and being his oldest, a favorite. His disapproval was kept at bay by his own weakness of will due to the affection he had for his headstrong daughter. As soon as Waniwan finished speaking to the others, he called her.

"Indah, come here."

She obeyed and started walking towards her father but at the same time, Setiawan and Alex were leaving. She couldn't help looking back to Alex, hoping to catch his attention before he left. He was obviously thinking the same thing as he walked away. He looked back and caught her troubled gaze.

CHAPTER 83

Mr. Brooks and Allison stepped out of the Ronald Reagan Washington National Airport and were ushered to a black SUV waiting for them. Agent Davidson greeted them as he opened the back door for the couple to slide in. Their destination, 935 Pennsylvania Avenue, the Bureau's headquarters in Washington, DC.

Davidson climbed in the front passenger seat and shifted his body in order to turn his face to the back seat to talk as the driver took off. "We are glad you were able to respond to our request on such short notice."

"Can you tell us anything about this or do we have to wait longer?" asked Mr. Brooks.

"You have no idea how stressful this is," said Allison.

"Well, what have you been told so far?" said Davidson.

"Only that there is a new lead in our son's case and Agent Hutchins asked us to meet him here for further details," said Mr. Brooks.

"I'm afraid that's all that can be said for now, but I don't believe he will keep you waiting once we get to headquarters. Agent Hutchins is meeting right now with the director who just returned from his morning brief with the president."

"Can you tell us whether it is good news or bad?" asked Allison.

"If I knew that answer, I wouldn't want to be the person responsible to tell you unless it was certainly good news. But I'm not assigned to that task, I was simply asked to meet you at the airport."

"Can you at least turn on a flashing light or hit a secret button to make this slow traffic start moving?" she asked.

"No, I'm sorry to say. But some good news I can share is that we are less than five miles, and even in bad traffic, it shouldn't take more than fifteen minutes."

Allison leaned back against the headrest and closed her eyes in an attempt to shut out her anxiety and fears. Alex reached over and gently grabbed her hand. She didn't resist this thoughtful gesture. It comforted her. She looked over at him, he had his head back and his eyes closed.

They eventually reached the J. Edgar Hoover Building. A blocky monolithic Federal building. Allison wondered, *How can any good news emerge from such a cold, dismal, uninviting structure?* Her aesthetic and artsy side took offense at the lack of any beauty.

The SUV pulled into the underground parking lot. Mr. Brooks had never seen so many black vehicles with dark tinted windows in one place. "I don't know if I should feel secure or scared."

"This can certainly be an intimidating place for the public," said Davidson.

After the security check, they entered a special secured elevator. They had no idea yet if the floors going up should raise their hope or if they would raise their grief.

The sliding doors opened on the seventh floor and Allison wondered, *Is a door to finding my son opening or closing right now?* She decided to keep holding on to hope.

The three new arrivals joined Agent Hutchins who greeted them warmly in a meeting room. Mr. Brooks attempted a quick analysis of Hutchins' mood, but had a difficult time reading him. As they sat down, Hutchins began the meeting without further delay.

"I know you two are anxious to know why we have asked you to come here. First, I wish we could confidently tell you that we've found the location of your son and that he is alive, but I can't. But we believe Anaconda may have found the location and will be attempting to retrieve your son any day now. If he is alive, our goal is to intercept them or at least trail them if possible and call in one of our Hostage Recovery SWAT teams to rescue him. Since the arrest of Cheng-han nearly three months ago, we have not been able to get much information out of him. But the little we were able to get has given us several new leads including a couple low life associates who were quick to squeal. And I want to say that we are indebted to the successful efforts and ongoing collaboration with Super 8. Honestly, I'm glad to say we've finally had a little success ourselves to add to the mix.

"To explain the current situation in simple terms, word on the street, so to speak, is that they have made progress in their ongoing search for the location of the missing boat, its crew, and their collateral for ransom—your son. We believe that they are zeroed in on a location. Unfortunately, we don't presently know that location but we have some key operators of this ring in our sites, and as I said, we have some low level rats in the organization who are hungry for some cheese and are glad to exchange what little information they have for currency. Any questions before I move on?"

"Yes," said Mr. Brooks. "Why are we here?"

"The reason we want you here is because we believe this is all going to unfold in the next twenty-four to forty-eight hours. The best case scenario is that we recover your son alive and get you both to Southeast Asia ASAP to be with him for his return home.

"I don't want to imagine any other scenario, but what if it's not what we hope?" asked Allison.

"Then you will at least know. And we will apprehend whoever we can round up and bring them to justice. For now, we need to keep ourselves on their heels and see where it leads."

"Can you tell us how you plan to trail them?" asked Mr. Brooks.

"Sure, we recently tracked down a plane we believe has been used for a search operation by Anaconda. Unfortunately, small low-flying planes are too difficult to track by radar, especially with the limitations of working with a foreign government. So we don't know where the plane goes but we at least know where it comes from and where it lands. But a small plane is not able to land on most islands without a runway, so if they have located the island that we are all hoping to find, they will dispatch another boat. We have all the players we are aware of under surveillance, and if they make a move, we will do everything in our power to follow them."

"What if they discover you are following them?" asked Allison.

"That's a fair question. One of the strengths of the Bureau is our surveillance abilities."

"But you just said you were unable to track an airplane," said Mr. Brooks.

"Yes, but that's only due to the limitations we have to work with in Indonesia."

"But how will those limitations affect your ability to track a boat?" asked Mr. Brooks. "I'm not trying to say you can't accomplish your plan, but is there anything my team can do to help? Is there any need for a technology solution?"

"The plan is to follow the outgoing boat from a distance in order to stay out of direct sight, but keeping track of it using onboard radar. Once the island has been identified we will send in a tactical team, ready at a moment's notice."

"What if they have a faster boat that yours?" asked Allison. "And you can't keep up?"

"I know you mean well, Miss Brooks, but they are likely going to use another commercial fishing boat or something even more discreet. They are not fast boats, and though I'm not privy to what kind of boat our team will be using, I guarantee it will be able to keep up."

CHAPTER 84

"Suspects are boarding charter vessel. Stand by."

Agent Bennet kept his radio close and his voice low, "Copy."

A collaborative team consisted of US Federal Agents, Indonesian Security Forces, and a tactical Hostage Rescue Team ready to deploy from a nearby military airbase. For now, everything remained relatively old school with a cat and mouse strategy. Two undercover boats would stagger their departure and follow their target using onboard radar but keeping out of line of sight until the target boat led them to the island where they hoped to find and recover Alexander Brooks—if he was alive, or to confirm otherwise.

Agent Chambers and the team in boat number one idled in the bay. They maintained a coordinated surveillance with a ground team who kept their eyes on the suspect's movements on shore. The first objective was to track the suspect without tipping their hand.

"Charter vessel is departing," said Chambers, reporting via two-way radio from his vantage point.

"Remember, we must lay low and out of sight. Just keep the radar zeroed in on the target," said Bennet over the radio from the second surveillance boat.

It was hard for him to watch the fishing boat leave the bay, to keep the predetermined gap between boats. The second boat planned to fan out on a wider path and follow parallel, keeping their targeted radar fixed on the fishing vessel.

With so much nautical traffic close to the island, they decided on a two-mile distance which would extend to four miles once they got out to sea. The two surveillance boats worked in tandem, Bennet on one boat with a crew and Chambers on the other with his captain and crew. They kept in regular radio contact monitoring the speed of the suspects' boat, now cruising at a relatively slow pace. Being this close to the large island meant they had to contend with a variety of intruding blips that crossed the swath of the radar, but their target was not difficult to track. They had no idea how far they would have to follow before reaching the destination. A communications operator for the tactical team also stayed in contact with the boats in pursuit, ready to deploy as soon as they received the command. Another communications liaison also kept the FBI at the DC headquarters updated in real time. They anticipated that this part of the operation would be tedious and uneventful. The real action would begin once they discovered the destination and called in the Hostage Rescue Unit.

"What's happening now?" asked Bennet, speaking to the radar operator.

"All these other blips on the screen are random boats within range and crossing our path. We expect this to clear up the further we get from Sulawesi and out among the smaller islands," said the operator.

"Why are we slowing down?"

"Because our target has slowed down," said the operator. "They are probably being cautious with some of these other vessels in the area. As far as they know, other boats might be maritime security checking for smuggling."

"It looks like they've stopped."

"Yes, there is a larger boat coming towards them."

"It better not be the Indonesian Coast Guard. We have been assured by the authorities this area would stay clear during our operation to keep from scaring our mouse into a hole rather than getting caught in our trap."

Bennet gave orders to their communications operator, "Get our Coast Guard liaison on the line to confirm that this is not an ignorant patrol boat complicating matters right now."

"On it now."

"What is happening now?" asked Bennet as he looked at the radar screen.

"It looks as if the other boat has come alongside our target and they are both stopped. It could be a patrol boat search."

"What in the world?" said Bennet.

The target boat changed direction and began coming back towards them. The disappointment onboard the surveillance vessel was palpable.

"I can't believe this!" said Bennet.

Just then, another unexpected turn of events left the crews of both surveillance boats scrambling. The second boat on the radar began moving away from them at an extremely high speed.

"How many knots is that boat clocking?" asked Bennet.

"Sixty knots!" the operator replied.

"Unbelievable, what can go that fast out here?"

"A long hull cigarette boat, often used for drug smuggling. They can go even faster in calm waters."

"Oh no!" said Bennet.

He turned to the boat's pilot, "Get moving now! We've got to keep that boat in range of radar!"

He got Chambers on the radio, "Stay with the target boat and were going to try and follow the other one."

The motors of the commercial fishing boat they were using were almost at full throttle. "There is no possible way we can keep up with that boat. It will be beyond our range in about two minutes at this pace," said the radar operator.

Bennet gave orders to the communications operator, "Get Hutchins on the line."

Once they patched him through he explained the situation and asked for input. "I'm afraid if we deploy the tactical team now, the suspects will abandon their course. Can you get the Department of Defense to cooperate and get a military satellite on this ASAP?"

"Not likely, we tried earlier but I'll try again," said Hutchins, talking to Bennet from the operations room in Washington, DC.

"We've got one minute before the boat is out of range," said the radar operator to Bennet.

"I can't believe this!"

"But what about our target boat heading back to the bay?" asked Hutchins.

"We'll keep an eye on it but I will bet my last dollar that our suspect was just being shuttled to the fast boat. I'm afraid we've lost them."

CHAPTER 85

Setiawan and Alex's former camp remained surprisingly unchanged in Alex's view other than a few missing spots of thatch on the roof of their hut. The last eight months had flown by. They dropped off their food supply, water containers, and jar of coals but each kept his Bible with him. Their plan was to take shifts watching at the nearby beach. Alex asked Setiawan if they could stick together for now to give them a chance to talk. Rimbo didn't mind staying at the camp to get a fire going.

Setiawan didn't think it was likely that a boat would come today, if one was coming at all. Nevertheless, the two followed out their assignment and sat down on the top of a rock escarpment overlooking the coast at the edge of the jungle.

"Seti, you seem to have the amazing ability to understand what I'm saying, so I hope you don't mind if I use English?"

Setiawan gave him a nod.

"Because there's a lot going on inside me right now, I don't have a great vocabulary in my own language, but I certainly don't have enough words in yours to explain myself."

Setiawan just smiled with an understanding gaze. He interpreted in his mind more than he translated when listening to Alex talk as he often did. The island culture did not foster a lot of personal expression of thoughts, not that those internal thoughts didn't exist, they just hardly ever found ways to vent. Alex was a novelty in this aspect and it always amused Setiawan. He understood that Alex's need to talk today was not mere babbling, so he paid close attention.

"There's part of me that gave up hope that I would ever be rescued from this island. But then I learned that I could hitch a ride next year with the trading expedition and get dropped off on a more normal inhabited island. It was then that I realized that I really like being here and I would be a little sad to leave. A lot sad to leave. But there's part of me that knows that I don't fit in here and may never fit in. But you're here and Indah is here and Macchiato, Mocha, the best bananas on the planet, and the peaceful existence. And now it's also the place where I have met God and learned about Jesus. I know I could have read about Him back home but I never did and I probably never would have. Better yet, you are a good example. I think I learn as much or maybe more about Jesus from being around you.

"This may sound strange but I've been wondering if this all was planned by God. But the most difficult part is my doubts. Not doubts about God but doubts about me. I can't imagine why God would look down from heaven and say, 'I want to save Alexander Brooks.' I've never done anything to deserve it, and worse yet, I've done things to deserve not being saved. So why? Why save Alexander? Why did Agnes give me a Bible and how in the world did it end up with me on this island? Why did you save me when I was brought to the island? And why would God save me? It's beyond my ability to understand all this and yet…I still can't help but I think that it's been coordinated to get my attention but then I get stuck. Stuck with the question why? Why me? I don't deserve it. I don't want to leave this island but I don't think I'll be able to stay. And I know you may not understand this but I think I've really fallen in love with Indah, and I believe she loves me but you don't seem to have an equivalent word for love in your language. But if I can't stay and she can't leave, what then?

"And I miss my mom and I miss my dad even though we don't have a good relationship. I wish we did. You have been like a father figure to me. I just hope that if I ever get home, that me and my dad would get a second chance.

"So here's the last big thing in my heart, Seti, and it's what I mentioned before; I never knew anything about God or Jesus or the Bible or mission-aries before. And I still don't know very much. But I believe God exists. I believe God is looking out for me. And wants me to know about Him."

Setiawan's eyes were glistening with joy. He finally inserted himself into Alex's effusions from his heart. "Yes, Alekus, God cares for you."

"So what do I do now? I never intended or wanted to be a religious person. I don't know how. But you don't seem religious, you are just... you're good, you're kind, you care. You're so different than the others in your tribe."

"Let me teach you what I was taught when young like you," said Setiawan.

He had Alex open his Bible to the Book of Romans. In the previous months, they had developed a clever way to communicate by matching up Bible verses. They learned to identify the names of the New Testament books in both languages, and after that, it was simply a matter of locating the chapter and verse. One or the other would point out a verse that was meaningful to them and the other would read it in his own language.

Setiawan pointed to Romans 3:23 and asked Alex to read it out loud.

"For all have sinned and fall short of the glory of God."

"We have all sinned, Alekus, and must be sorry and tell God we are wrong and want to walk right."

"I understand that I need to be sorry," said Alex. "But you're different. Why would you be sorry? You didn't know any better. You weren't taught any different growing up, just like me."

"No, Alekus, we know. I knew inside," pointing to his heart.

"I think you're right about that. Somehow, I knew deep down inside and chose to ignore Him. But oh, I interrupted you."

This time Setiawan pointed to Romans 6:23.

Alex read it, "For the wages of sin is death, but the gift of God is eter-nal life in Christ Jesus our Lord."

"God wants you to have life forever as a gift, that is more important that being rescued from this island. But there is more, look at this verse," he pointed to Romans 5:8.

Alex enjoyed these Bible lessons and gladly read, "But God demon-strates His own love toward us, in that while we were still sinners, Christ died for us."

"When you and I did not know about God," said Setiawan, "He still loved us enough to give His Son to die for our sins. Do you understand this?"

"I think I understand it enough," said Alex. "But go on, did you have more on your mind?"

"Yes, look at this verse and the one after it," and he pointed at Romans 10:9.

Alex read, "That if you confess with your mouth the Lord Jesus and believe in your heart that God has raised Him from the dead, you will be saved. For with the heart one believes unto righteousness, and with the mouth confession is made unto salvation."

"Are you ready to follow Jesus and make this Scripture your own prayer?" said Setiawan. "If so, pray and ask God to save you, not from this island but from your sin and ignorance. If you are here or at home, follow Jesus with all your heart."

"I hope I can, Seti. I want to."

"Then pray and ask God."

"You mean now? Pray right here?"

"Yes."

"I guess I can. I've only prayed three times and they were all private. I don't have much practice but I guess you won't mind that."

Setiawan nodded in assent. And with childlike faith and sincerity of heart, Alex prayed.

"God, I do want to follow you. And I am sorry for ignoring you and all the things I've done wrong. I believe that you sent your Son to save us. I want to be saved. Please save me."

"Very good, Alekus, now one more Bible verse," he pointed to Romans 10:13.

Alex read, "Whoever calls on the name of the Lord shall be saved. "The rest of the night was uneventful besides what was stirring in Alex's soul. It felt to him like his life was previously a dry well which was now filling with water and ready to pour over. The exhilarating sense of a significant spiritual milestone filled him with wonder. He had never understood real peace until now and it was hard for him to believe that he could have ever been content without it.

In some mysterious, unexplainable way, he knew that his faith would be tested.

CHAPTER 86

The night passed and most of another day before Setiawan discerned the sound of a distant motor. He could hear it long before he could see it. He quickly got back to base camp to get Alex and send Rimbo to run to the village and alert the elders.

Alex experienced a confused excitement from the possibility of being rescued mixed with the threat of being apprehended. He didn't have much time to dwell on it since the distant boat came into view on the horizon and moved at a speed Setiawan had never witnessed before. It became apparent that the boat would reach the shore before the men of the village could reach this side of the island.

"Alekus, get your bow and come."

Setiawan already had his bow in one hand along with a fistful of arrows.

"We will hide where we can see them but they won't see us."

Setiawan knew the island as good as anyone, if not better. He chose the place where the rock escarpment stood about eight feet above the beach and stretched for a quarter of a mile. Palms, shrubs, and trees grew close to the edge, giving it plenty of shelter. This vantage point gave them an easy view of the largest stretch of beach on that side of the island and a likely place for a boat to land.

The sound of the twin high performance motors that propelled this long hulled racing boat gave these visitors no chance of showing up unannounced. But the boat didn't come to shore at first, it slowed down and made a couple passes parallel to the beach about a half mile away.

"What do you think they are doing?" asked Alex.

"They are looking for something."

"What would they be looking for out there?"

"The boat."

"You mean the boat that brought me here?"

"Yes, and it looks like they have already found it."

Unbeknownst to Setiawan or anyone else on the island, the sunk boat was not only visible from the sky in those clear waters, but easily picked up by basic underwater radar. They watched as a person in a diving suit and oxygen tank disappeared under the surface.

"That is where our men sunk the boat. The water is deep enough to bury it but not too deep," said Setiawan.

This took some time for the unknown visitors. Setiawan hoped that they would stall offshore long enough for the other village men to make it to this side, but that didn't happen. They watched the diver get back on the boat, and about fifteen minutes later, they were heading towards the shore. The boat was now close enough for them to count five men total in the small cockpit at the back of the monstrously long hull. The boat paused again about one hundred feet offshore. The sound of the motors at an idle still rumbled like distant thunder. Alex could see that someone was scanning the island with a pair of binoculars. He and Setiawan were lying down and most likely safe from view, but Alex instinctively dropped his head down low and moved back a couple feet. They heard the motors revving up, indicating they were moving again. Setiawan poked his head up to get a look. The boat was coming in hull first and coasted in with short bursts of the propellers in reverse, minimizing the speed as the nose slid up onto the beach.

To their disappointment, the boat came ashore further down the beach to their right and nearly out of view. They realized that if they were going to keep an eye on these strangers to determine whether they were friend or foe, they would need to reposition themselves carefully.

The rock escarpment they were presently on ran along the edge of the beach and gradually sloped downward until it became level with the beach at its furthest end. At its highest point, it stood about twelve feet above shore but ran about eight feet high on average. They quietly moved through the jungle, working their way closer to the place the boat landed. They didn't want to be too close, just close enough to keep them in sight, so they shifted to their right about fifty feet and quietly made their way back to the edge, keeping low on hands and knees then lying down on their stomachs. They kept their heads behind a patch of brush. They now had a better view and watched four men dropping down off the hull onto the beach. They could also see that the pilot remained on the boat.

Alex felt a moment of hope when he saw what looked like an organized SWAT team in black uniforms, modern body armor, and carrying assault rifles.

Alex's brief hopes were dashed when one of the men began calling out. "Hariyono! Come out if you are here! Hariyono!" Then the man called out another name and another, presumably the names of the other three men who were missing. Alex never knew their names but he knew it was unlikely that anyone coming to rescue him would have known them either.

In a panic, Alex looked at Setiawan and whispered, "These are the bad men that took me, not good men."

"I will not let them take you," said Setiawan. "Let us go further into the jungle until the others arrive." He carefully got up and quietly moved away from the edge of the steep bank.

As Alex got up from the ground his long bow slung across his back inadvertently got hooked on the limb of a nearby woody bush and stopped him in his retreat. The bush rustled loud enough to be noticed by Setiawan who suddenly looked back. They both glanced at each other, questioning in their expressions whether or not the intruders also heard it. Alex stood stock still for a moment and waited to see if the men on the beach had taken notice. Thankfully, they hadn't.

Alex carefully made a step back towards the ledge in order to gently lift his bow up and over the branch to dislodge it without making any noise. In the process he shifted his footing and lost his balance. He instinctively tried to recover and moved his other foot back to catch himself but some loose rocks on the sloping edge gave way underneath him. Setiawan watched in horror as Alex slipped over the edge.

CHAPTER 87

Alex's fall off an eight-foot ledge could only be bad news, with just one exception—he landed flat on his back in sand and did not break anything. He was momentarily stunned when the impact knocked the wind out of him. He wasn't the only one stunned, the four men—calling out for the missing fugitives heard the loud thud and looked in Alex's direction—were surprised to see a body lying in the sand about a hundred yards from them.

They began advancing towards Alex cautiously, anticipating a possible trap. Each man worked together as a team to cover every direction of the beach as the leading man called out in Indonesian, "Don't move!"

Alex leaned his head over and saw them coming, then looked up at the ledge to see Setiawan laying down on the edge, reaching down, ready to give him a hand, and motioning for him to get up and climb the bank. Presently, Setiawan remained out of view of the approaching men but not for long.

Alex knew that if he was going to try and scramble up the bank he would need to get up off the ground and do it quickly. The lead man aimed his rifle at him and continued to shout, "Don't move!" The other three men continued to scan in all other directions with military like discipline.

Alex attempted to stall them by yelling out in English, "Stop! I don't understand you! What do you want?"

One of the men told his partner out front, "Don't shoot if you value your life, it's the boy! Look at the color of his skin and hair."

As they slowly started advancing again, the man shouted back in English this time. "Where is Hariyono?"

Alex pointed beyond them, "He's right behind you, over there!"

All four men quickly looked behind them and in that split second moment Alex made a couple quick steps and jumped up to grab Setiawan's down stretched arm. He missed and came tumbling back down. The gap was closing fast between Alex and the four men. To Alex's astonishment, Setiawan jumped down and helped give him a boost up the steep ledge. He didn't have time to question his friend's action, the men were getting closer.

As soon as Alex was at the top Setiawan yelled, "Run, Alekus, they have come for you not me! I will find you! Go!"

Alex turned and ran, looking behind him a couple times hoping to see Seti ascend to the top of the rim. Instead he heard two gunshots echo through the jungle in rapid succession. His heart sank and he stopped in his tracks, horrified with the unknown fate of his friend. *No! This can't be happening*, he agonized internally. He turned and ran back towards the beach with no thought of what he would do when he reached it.

As he got nearer, he stopped and crouched behind a palm because he could see one of the men with his back to him helping a second man up the ledge. Alex dropped to his hands and knees and kept behind the ground cover of thick vegetation. He started working his way quietly towards the beach at an angle that veered away from the men. As soon as he felt he was at a safe distance he carefully peered above the cover and guessed that the men had passed him and continued searching deeper into the jungle. He wondered where the other two men were. Making his way to the ridge overlooking the beach, the two other men were nowhere to be seen but Alex spotted Seti, lying on his back in the sand, deathly still.

"No, oh God, no!" he cried as he quickly found a place to scramble down and ran to his friend. Dropping down next to him, his eyes opened slowly as Alex called his name.

"Setiawan, you're alive, I thought you were dead." Alex surveyed the bullet wound in his right shoulder and a deadlier one just right of his sternum.

"Alekus, you should be hiding, this is not safe."

"I couldn't leave you. I heard the gunshots," Alex cried. "I don't know first aid. I don't know how to help you. Can you move at all?" He said all of this while taking his own shirt off and tearing several pieces from it, folded them and gently placed them on the wounds. "I know this won't do any good but I've got to try something."

"Alekus, I can't move and I will die here, but I will live." He lifted his eyes upward towards the sky.

"Don't die, Seti, don't leave me here alone."

"You are not alone, Jesus is with you and now I am going to Him," whispered Setiawan.

"I'm not ready for you to go, Seti." Alex's voice cracked in a high pitch as he stroked the old man's head.

"I am ready to go…it is my time. I wish you would go hide but I'm happy you are with me. I'll see you again someday. Trust God, Alekus. He has a reason for this. Thank you for being my friend."

Alex couldn't help recognizing the peace on his face, a complete lack of fear on the threshold of death and a confidence of entering the presence of his Lord.

Setiawan closed his eyes and seemed to be resting. He was still breathing. Alex held his hand which gave no response, yet it was not cold. He wondered if the bullet had paralyzed his friend and hoped that he was free from any pain.

Setiawan suddenly opened his eyes again. They were filled with joyful tears on his serene face. "I'm going home. I see Him, Alekus, I see Him." And he shut his eyes for the last time and gave his last breath.

Alex fell over the dead body, buried his head against Setiawan's wounded chest, and wept, temporarily oblivious to the events beginning to unfold around him.

CHAPTER 88

The distinct and unmistakable sound of a helicopter grew louder. Though the sound reached Alex's ears, it did not immediately reach his comprehension. Lost in a sacred moment, everything else disappeared around him and the only thing he could hear was his own heart-wrenching groans from the depths of his soul.

Yet the sound grew deafening and the turbulent wash of the blades began pelting him with sand mixed with ocean mist, and would have knocked him over if he had not already been on the ground. He emerged from his grief stricken shock and looked up to see a military style helicopter descending less than a hundred feet from him. Apparently the beach was not wide enough to land and Alex watched in amazement as two ropes dropped from the open cabin and an FBI Hostage Rescue Team began fast-roping into the shallow water then rushed to the beach.

Alex just sat there on his knees next to his dead friend with Setiawan's blood smeared across his own body. Several armed men in camouflage and body armor came rushing towards him with their assault rifles trained on him. As they drew near, he heard one of them shouting orders as several others on the team began surveying the beach. The helicopter took off in pursuit of the fast boat that departed as soon as they had arrived.

"We've found him, it's the missing boy. Get the medic over here!"

"Don't hurt the islanders, please don't hurt them," said Alex.

One of the men quickly checked Setiawan's vitals and then began checking Alex.

The commander of the unit calmly said, "You're safe now. We're here to bring you home. Can you tell us quickly what's going on?"

"There are four men dressed similar to you but in black and have guns. They're looking for me inland. They shot my friend. Don't hurt the natives, they've helped me but they won't understand why you're here. They may try to defend themselves."

"Do they have weapons?" asked the commander.

"Arrows, spears, and machetes. But they won't know the difference between you and the others. You are all intruders to them."

The commander left Alex with the medic and gathered the others to relay some orders. There were nine total including the medic. Even as they huddled, the men organized themselves to cover each direction for a possible confrontation.

"Men, we are in a unique situation. We have the hostage but not the perpetrators. They are presumably looking for the hostage and armed. I just received word that the chopper has the speed boat at bay and our own boat is on its way now that they have the coordinates. The boy tells me there are natives on the island and should be considered friends not foes, but they won't discern between us and the enemy. Our main objective is to get the boy out safely if we found him alive and we are going to stick to that as priority one and remain on this beach with all vigilance. We will await any further orders from headquarters. In the meantime, keep a careful watch since we are in the open and the enemy has the advantage of cover."

CHAPTER 89

The four men intent on taking Alex captive split up in two to hunt down the missing hostage. They were not concerned about native islanders with bows and machetes against their assault weapons, but being armed is not the same thing as being quiet. Little did they know they were being watched by the first group of men who ran across the island in response to Rimbo's alert. They also heard the two gunshots ring out through the jungle.

The two pairs of men looking for Alex kept about fifty yards apart and moved forward in unison. A bird call rang out, followed by rustling noises to the left of the intruders and then to the right. All four stopped and aimed their guns in opposite directions. All at once, each man lost sight from a sarong being quickly wrapped around each head and pulled back with a snapping force. At the same time, quick and heavy blows came down on their arms, causing a few random shots to fire just before the rifles were dislodged.

Each stranger had two men on top of him and found it hard to breathe as the sarongs had strategically been twisted on their fall backward to the ground. The art of *silat* included specific training to disarm an assailant with a weapon. This technique anticipated a sword or a knife, but worked equally well with a rifle. The unwelcome aggressors were stripped of all their weapons and their hands and feet bound with cords. Several village men were dispatched to the beach to check on Setiawan and Alex. Rimbo insisted on going with the men.

Peering through the dense foliage, their hearts sank as they saw Setiawan laying in the bloodstained sand and Alex sitting a little way off, surrounded by a half dozen armed men. They were not sure what to do. Without warning, Rimbo made a loud piercing bird call. The man closest to him smacked him on the back of his head for carelessly putting them all at risk.

But Alex recognized Rimbo's unique call and shouted to his friend hiding somewhere close in the jungle. "Rimbo! Listen carefully! I'm okay! These men are here to help me and capture the bad men. Come here and I will tell you more."

Rimbo turned with a questioning look to the group of men standing beside him. They all heard Alex's words and the leader among them asked Rimbo, "Are you afraid to go to Alekus?"

"I'm not afraid," said Rimbo.

"Then go to Alekus and we will wait to see what becomes of it."

"Rimbo, you are safe, come here," said Alex.

Rimbo took a few cautious steps forward out from under the cover of the jungle and stood in view.

"Don't scare him off," he said to the men around him. "I need to talk with him." He waved to the boy, "Rimbo, come here, you are safe."

Rimbo stood still, hesitating to venture any farther.

"Can I go to him?" asked Alex.

"Not in your life. You wouldn't believe how hard it has been to find you. Your dad would never forgive us if we lost you now. We can't put our weapons down but I'll give him a friendly wave. How do you say 'friend' in their language?"

"*Teman,*" said Alex.

The commander waived and repeated, "*Teman.*"

Rimbo looked back at the others and they nodded for him to go. He took slow steps across the beach, staring at the intimidating men with camouflage, body armor, helmets, and weapons. They didn't react and Rimbo continued walking until he reached his friend.

Alex motioned him to sit down, "Rimbo, you see, Setiawan is dead."

Rimbo's eyes were big and he nodded his head in acknowledgment.

His own eyes became misty after looking at Alex's watering eyes and tearstained face.

"These men did not kill him. They are here to help me. They are looking for the men who killed Setiawan and disappeared into the forest to look for me."

"We have captured them," said Rimbo. "They are tied up and without their weapons."

"Rimbo, that's good! It's over then! Let me tell these men."

Alex relayed the information to the commander. Then told Rimbo, "Go get Waniwan and have him come here. Tell him these men on the beach are good and have come to take me home and capture the bad men. It is safe for him to come. Go quickly."

While they awaited the chief's arrival, an agent walked over and handed Alex a satellite phone, "You have a phone call."

"Hello Alex? This is your dad."

"Dad!" was all Alex could get out of his mouth at that moment.

"Alex, you're alive! I'm sure you've been through a lot, are you alright?"

"I'm not hurt, I'm just...just a little overwhelmed right now."

"Of course, of course. I've missed you and I can't wait to see you soon. I want to say more but your mom's here and she won't last much longer if I don't put her on."

"Alex? This is Mom."

"Mom!" Alex's voice gave way to convulsive sobs when he heard her voice.

"Oh Alex, praise God you're alive." And now she was sobbing. She tried to eke out a few more words but her voice was barely discernable. "I love you, Alex. You would never believe all that your dad has done to find you." She couldn't say anymore for now.

His dad got back on the line, "Alex, we're getting on a flight soon to come get you and will meet you in Jakarta. Hang in there, your mom and I can't wait to see you. You're in good hands, they'll make sure you get to Jakarta safely."

"Thank you, Dad. I love you."

"I love you too, Alex.

"Can I tell Mom I love her before you hang up?"

"Of course, you can. Let me put her back on. She's a little overwhelmed so don't feel bad if she's having a hard time talking. Here she is."

"Hi Mom, I just want to say I'm sorry I didn't treat you very well when I left on the trip. I love you and I miss you."

His dad was right, she couldn't talk. She experienced a fit of hysteria over hearing the voice of her son speaking those humble words. A voice she thought she might never hear again.

Alex could tell his mom couldn't talk just then but he didn't need a response, he just needed to get that off his chest. "I can't wait to see you, Mom. Bye." He handed the phone back to the agent and then laid down in the sand and closed his eyes tight.

The medic sat next to him and put a compassionate hand on Alex's shoulder. "You've been though a lot. Is that your friend lying over there?"

A feeble "yes" was barely audible. "He saved my life when I was brought here."

The medic tapped Alex's shoulder, "Hey son, there are a bunch of men standing at the edge of the jungle."

The commander came over to Alex. "I think you may need to talk with them. Tell them they can come here. I'll have my guys keep their weapons down." He shouted the order.

Alex sat up and told the commander, "If you want this to go well, let me walk over to them. They aren't going to harm me, they've been protecting me long before you showed up."

He hesitated but said, "Go ahead."

The rescue team watched closely as Alex walked over to the islanders and sat down. They watched four older men who also sat down while a large number of men stood, keeping watch at the edge of the jungle armed with their own weapons. The meeting lasted for nearly a half hour before the five got up and Alex made his way back to the rescue team while the villagers disappeared into the forest.

"I'm sorry that took so long, I'm still learning the language and I don't always understand certain phrases or know how so say the right words that I need. Anyways, the village leaders are asking if you all can move down the beach a ways so they can come and get the body of Setiawan to get it ready for burial. Then they are going to bring the four men they captured to the edge of the jungle and tie them to a tree, and after they leave, you can come and get them. They don't want any more intrusion and they hope we will all leave the island as soon as possible."

"A boat is on its way and will be here late tonight," said the commander.

"Once you have those other men under guard, can I go and get my things and say goodbye to my village? Plus, I've got to make arrangements for my two pets and have an important talk with…well, never mind for now, I really need to go."

Once again, the commander was hesitant with an answer before saying, "How about I send someone with you?"

"That won't work, you don't understand. These people just want to be left alone. Sending one of your guys into the village uninvited is not going to go over well, trust me. Besides, I've been safe on this island for a long time without your guys or your guns. By the way, how long have I been gone?"

"Almost a year."

"Really? It felt longer than that."

"No, today is May 23rd," said the commander. "Alright kid, I'm going to give you an hour and you're going to take a radio with you so we can reach you. If you're not back in time, I guarantee we will come for you."

"Can you give me a watch and a flashlight? I don't know what an hour is anymore and it's going to be getting dark soon." The commander had one of his team lend Alex his watch and tactical flashlight.

They all moved their base further down the beach from where Setiawan lay, covered with an emergency blanket. The setting sun reflected off the thin metallic sheet with spectacular effect noticed by everyone. The radiant array filled Alex with awe and a sense of deserved dignity and honor for his fallen friend. He watched as four men walked out to the body to carry it back to the village. A sudden fresh breeze came wafting over the beach and the solar blanket took flight and with surreal precision dropped back to the beach at Alex's feet. Not a single person who observed this could ever doubt some mysterious significance to the sacred moment they just witnessed. Alex picked up the blanket and held it tight.

Chapter 90

As promised, the islanders brought the captives, lashed them to trees, and piled their weapons on the beach before leaving. The sun was setting and Alex was anxious to get back to the village one last time before he had to leave. The reluctant commander let Alex go.

As much as Alex wanted to catch up with the men carrying Setiawan's body, he knew he needed to stop at his nearby camp to grab his Bible and a few other items before making the trek to the other side. Visiting the site put Alex in a severely melancholic mood. He remembered the time when all he could think about was getting off the island and back to civilization, but now the island and this spot in particular was special to him. He couldn't linger since time was short and he sensed a fit of grief beginning to swell the longer he remained. He knew a brisk walk would do him some good and give him time to think.

He was glad to have the radio since he knew it would take a good part of the hour just getting to the village and another hour to get back in the dark, plus he needed time to say goodbye. He didn't want to risk the chance of being denied the three hours he needed so he made a call on the radio. The commander had a few choice words for Alex in frustration but now that Alex had someone he could speak to in his own native language of English, he revived his dormant skill of smooth talking when getting in trouble. It worked. All the better since his next talk would not be smooth. He stopped just outside the village and stashed the radio and flashlight under a bush.

A somber mood overshadowed the community as night settled in and a central fire and many torches illuminated the heart of the village. They seemed to be aware that Alex would be coming to say goodbye and most gathered for the occasion. There were no festivities, only downcast looks on most faces. The events of the last few days had shaken them and even though they had held Setiawan at arm's length during his life, everyone felt the loss at his death. They were also disturbed by their sanctity and anonymity being violated. This gloom outweighed their justifiable sense of pride in overcoming the intruders so quickly and without further loss of life. The generations of training in *silat* did not fail them in a time of need. But the strange heaviness that seemed to weigh them down was the pending departure of their historic guest.

The elders gathered the people so that Alex could speak to them all at once.

"I want to thank the elders for protecting me and showing hospitality. I did not choose to come to your island but I'm sad to leave. I'm going home now to my family and my village. I will never forget your kindness." Alex practiced this short speech on his trek that evening hoping to impress them with his progress in their language. Everyone seemed pleased.

A few people came forward to give Alex parting gifts: several necklaces with beads and carvings, some rare fruits, a knife, and a new basket. Aisyah came up to him with some flowers she had picked, her eyes red with tears. Alex knelt down to her height.

"Aisyah, you are just who I wanted to see."

"I brought you these," she said.

"Thank you. Will you take care of Macchiato and Mocha for me?"

"But I gave Mocha to you as a gift."

"I know but they won't be able to come with me. I need someone to take care of them."

"I will. But do you have to leave? I want you to stay."

"I have to leave."

"But Indah doesn't want you to leave either and she is crying more than me."

"Where is Indah? I need to see her before I go."

"She's at your hut."

"I have to say goodbye to you now," and he leaned over and gave her a kiss on the forehead. The gesture produced a smile. He excused himself from the others to go find Indah. It was his last stop before heading back to the beach to begin his journey home.

CHAPTER 91

Alex found Indah sitting in the doorway of Setiawan's hut, leaning against the support with her head down. Alex's dog, Mocha, lay next to her with his head in her lap as she ran her fingers through the short fur.

"Indah," he said.

She looked up with her face glistening with tears in the dim light of the moon. He sat down in the entryway next to her and his dog, Mocha.

She looked over at him, "Setiawan is dead and you are going away. This is the worst day of my life."

"Indah, I want you to know that I plan to come back for you if you'll wait for me. I have to go home now because I was stolen from my village and family and they miss me and I miss them. But I will miss you and come back and see if I can arrange for you to come to be a guest in my village."

Her heart seemed to lighten a little. She leaned her head onto his shoulder as he placed an arm around her. Macchiato unsuccessfully tried nosing his way between them from behind but had to take an alternate route before finding a way to settle onto Alex's lap. They sat for some time without saying a word.

Alex finally broke the silence, "I have to go back to the beach soon before the men come looking for me."

She knew he had to leave but it was painful and she wished they had more time together.

"I brought something for you." He reached over and grabbed a basket he had set down earlier. "It's not *tombulu*," he said with a smile to try and lighten things up. She gave a reluctant smile in return. "It's Setiawan's Bible."

"But I cannot read very well and my teacher is dead."

"Setiawan told me that Waniwan, Gusti, and Suharto also know how to read so you should ask them to teach you. He thought your father might also know how to read."

"My father?"

"Yes, ask him sometime."

"I will."

"I also have this for you." He took off his own necklace he made with his special collection of rare bird of paradise feathers and placed it around her neck.

"My heart is like the sea during a storm," she said with a choked voice. She couldn't hold back the suppressed sobs.

Alex was beside himself to know what to do. He didn't want to leave like this. He could see her heart was breaking while his own heart suffered the same turmoil.

"Please don't cry, Indah, remember, I'm going to come back for you. I promise. I want to remember you smiling, not crying as I leave."

She seemed to realize that he was right and it would be better if she could pull herself together and face the inevitable goodbye bravely with a smile. It was hard for her but she made an effort.

He could tell that she was trying. "Promise me you won't become Kadek's wife," he said with a sly look. This made her laugh as he hoped it would.

"If you don't come back I may have to become Kadek's wife."

Alex knew this lighthearted moment was the ideal time for both of them to part. He leaned over and gently kissed her forehead. He set Macchiato down next to her, gave him a couple scratches behind the ear and took a moment to pet jealous Mocha, now pawing at his legs for attention. Alex picked up his basket and started to slip away.

Indah remained sitting and watched as Alex took a few steps and looked back. He recalled the first time they met.

She must have been thinking the same and said, *"Kembali."*[9]

Alex replied, *"Selamat tinggal,"*[10] and whispered under his breath, *"Aku akan datang kembali."*[11]

---

[9] "Come back."

[10] "Goodbye"

[11] "I will come back."

CHAPTER 92

Alex knew he needed to make haste back to the beach before the SWAT team stormed the community in search of him. He didn't go back through the village; he couldn't bear to see anyone else after saying goodbye to Indah. He felt it would ruin the special moment he wanted to cherish in his heart. So he skirted the village until he got to the place where he left the radio and flashlight.

He turned the radio back on and announced himself, "This is Alexander Brooks, I'm on my way back to base camp. I'll be there in about an hour."

"Hey rascal, I'm glad you're on your way back. You better get your butt here soon because they decided to send a chopper for you and everyone at headquarters is ready to have my head for letting you out of our sight. Promise me there will be no more antics!"

"Roger."

"And leave the radio on!"

"Wilco." And off he went, basket in one hand and flashlight in the other.

CHAPTER 93

The hotel room phone rang several times before Alex could orient himself after being wakened from a deep sleep. The thick, soft mattress and pillows were a luxury to him now.

"Hello?" he asked in a mental fog.

"Hello Alex. This is Agent Bennett. It sounds like I woke you up."

"Yep."

"Well, I definitely want you to get rest but it's almost four in the afternoon and your parents will be arriving soon."

There was silence on the other end, "Alex? Are you there?"

He had fallen back asleep. Bennet hung up and tried to call his room again but the line was busy.

"We'll just have to go to his room," said Agent Chambers.

The two agents had to fight past crowds of journalists who somehow caught wind of the rescue and knew the lost survivor was being housed at this particular hotel. Local police kept them out of the lobby and helped legitimate patrons in and out.

"Where did all these journalists come from?" asked Chambers.

"They're usually spread out a little more among the islands, but this is international news and every network around the globe wants a piece of it. This is going to be a challenge," said Bennet.

They got inside and a hotel bellman helped direct them to his room on the fifth floor. They knocked but no answer. They pounded on the door and still no answer. They were about to send for the manager when Alex finally cracked the door.

"Hello?" he said in an extremely groggy voice.

"It's Agent Bennett and Chambers."

"Oh okay. Come in." He opened the door for them and lumbered back to the bed and laid down again.

"Maybe you should order up some coffee," said Bennet to his partner. "Did the doc give him sedative?"

"Not that I know of, but he did give him a clean bill of health. In fact, he said he was in excellent condition but said the shock of being rescued after being gone this long could take a toll. Plus, the emotional rollercoaster he's been through might be affecting him."

They were standing just inside the door. Alex looked asleep but was listening.

"I'm fine, I'm just really tired. Give me a minute or two to wake up."

The two men sat down, "Alex, do you remember we called a few minutes ago?" said Bennet.

"Hmmm, oh yeah, I guess I remember. What did you say?"

"It's after four and your parents will be arriving soon. We wanted to make sure you were up and dressed before they get here."

This news helped Alex to start snapping out of his exhausted stupor.

"My parents? They're here?"

"Not yet, but they will be here soon," said Chambers.

"Oh wow, I better get dressed. Excuse me for a moment." He rustled through a couple packages of clothes and disappeared in the bathroom to change.

Bennett noticed the room phone still off the hook and got up to put it back on the cradle.

Alex popped his head out through the bathroom door. "Do either of you have a comb or brush? I haven't seen myself for a year other than my reflection in water and I'm just now realizing that the method of cutting hair on the island was a bit rustic."

"You should find a comb and brush in that bag over there with your toothbrush and a few other items," said Chambers.

"Oh, a toothbrush! I forgot, I haven't brushed my teeth in a year. Thanks for the reminder." He disappeared again with his bathroom items.

When he came out Bennet began to prep him. "After you reunite with your parents, we will be shuttling all of you to the US Embassy to take care of some necessary paperwork before you can leave this country, especially since you will need a new passport issued and there are some other details that need to be arranged before your trip back to the US."

"We need to forewarn you that you'll need to stay close to us once we leave this room. There's a media frenzy going on over your rescue. You're famous," said Chambers.

Alex looked stunned and upset. "I don't want to be famous, I just want to see my mom and dad and go home. Can you make everyone go away?"

"We can't, they've practically got the hotel under siege, waiting to get a glimpse of you through their cameras for the evening news."

"Is there a back door we can slip out?"

"They've got that covered also."

"Can you have a helicopter land on the roof to give us a ride?"

"No, I'm afraid not. The hostage rescue team played that card already," said Bennet.

"Oh, I almost forgot," said Chambers. "There's a package that was delivered early this morning from South Korea. It was shipped overnight express and I had to sign for it."

"What is it?" asked Alex.

"Well, we did open it already for security purposes. It's a phone, charged and ready to go." Chambers walked over to the desk and picked the package up to give to Alex.

"That's okay, just leave it there for now, I'm not ready for it yet." In his mind he thought, *I'm not sure I'll ever be ready for it.*

"That's fine," said Chambers, a little confused. "There's no law that says you've got to have one but we thought you might not survive long without it."

All Alex could say to that was a cynical, "Sure."

The room phone rang and Bennet answered it. Alex's parents were in the hotel lobby and would be on their way to his room soon.

"Do you guys mind waiting for us in the lobby?" asked Alex.

"For sure. That's not a problem. Take your time, we are not in a hurry," said agent Bennet, "But Alex—"

"Yes?"

"Don't fall asleep when we leave the room and be sure to answer the phone if it rings," he said.

They left the room and Alex paced impatiently back and forth. Not only had it been a year since seeing either of them, it had been much longer since all three of them had been together, and longer still since there was ever a happy time. He wondered if they were getting along.

A knock at the door made his heart jump. He opened it cautiously. The room filled immediately with pure joy.

Alex's mom was first to wrap her arms around him. She squeezed until he could hardly breathe.

"Alex," she cried. "I can't believe it. You're here! We're here! Together. Thank God we've got you back."

His dad stood close with tear-filled eyes as he watched this precious reunion of a mother and her boy. Alex finally peeked past his mom's constricting embrace to look at his dad. Their eyes met and Alex saw something that rocked his world. He saw a look of unconditional love from a father to his son. It could be seen in his father's eyes, the expression of his face, and in something deeper emanating from his soul, only perceivable through some mysterious bond between them. Alex could read him as if he were holding up a large sign with bold letters which said, "I love you. I'm sorry. Please forgive me and let's start a new chapter."

When his mom finally released him to make room for his dad, the two embraced and wept on each other's shoulders. Another cavernous void in Alex's life filled with meaning and purpose. The first page in a new chapter, for all of them, turned.

CHAPTER 94

It took two days for the US Embassy and the Indonesian officials to get all of the necessary paperwork filed for Alex's release from the country. That gave his dad enough time to charter a private flight back home and gave this previously estranged family some much needed time to share each other's stories. Now they were on their way back to California with only one stop for refueling.

Alex opened a leather bound journal and read the few words living on the empty pages. This gift and the note inside were from Agnes.

Dear Alexander,

You may not be familiar with the word "providence," but it refers to circumstances in our lives that are not by chance but orchestrated by God. I believe providence brought our paths together for a brief but critical time in your life. I also believe that God's providence has brought me into friendship with your mom. The Lord prompted me to purchase this gift for you and I'm passing it on to your mom even though your whereabouts are not presently known at the time that I'm writing this. God knows where you are and I believe He will help others to find you soon. I'm certain that whatever you have experienced in this last year of your life should be written down and reflected on. I look forward to meeting you again.

Love,
Agnes

Alex reread this note several times before taking up the pen conveniently clipped to the cover. He stared at the first empty page, unsure where to begin.

I'm not used to writing but here goes nothing. I guess this is like the hours I spent sharing my thoughts with M...

He paused and turned to his mom next to him. "How do you spell Macchiato?"

"Macchiato? Like the coffee drink?"

"Yes, I'm not sure how it's spelled but it's the name I gave to my pet."

"I think it is m-a-c-c-h-i-a-t-o, but you can always double check on the phone your dad sent you."

"Oh yeah, I forgot about that. It's in airplane mode anyway."

"You didn't mention you had a pet."

"Yeah, it was something they called a cuscus. Sorta like a cat but maybe closer to a raccoon without the mask. I wish I could have brought him."

"Well, maybe we can get you one when we get home."

"Probably not, but anyway, I should get back to writing in my journal from Agnes."

"Of course, we'll have plenty of time later to learn about your pet."

...Macchiato. I talked and he listened. I think I'll name this journal Macchiato. There's so much going through my head right now but I'm on my way home except I feel like I'm leaving home at the same time. Mom tells me that I need to brace myself for the media frenzy that has already begun. I have somehow become famous by doing nothing other than getting lost for the last year. It wasn't too long ago that I really wanted to be famous. To be famous for playing video games better than most others. But it doesn't matter to me now. I'm not the same person I was a year ago. I guess the studio is hoping to secure the book and movie rights of my story, crazy. What do they think the story would be about? A lazy idiot who nearly gets killed because of his stupidity and lack of skills? Nobody would want to read about that. They don't even know what I've gone through. Dad reminded me that I missed a year of school but the school

administration has agreed to give me all my credits for cross cultural studies, that's helpful. I think I learned more this last year on the island than I did my previous three years of high school. I really miss Setiawan. I know he's in a better place but I still wish he was here. I don't know how I'm going to adjust. I miss Indah, of course, that goes without saying. I promised her I would come back and I will. But I definitely need to get some things in order in my life first. I want to know my dad better and try to be a better son. I can't believe he was willing to give up his dream in order to find me. It's beyond me to imagine my dad taking the risks he took and having his own adventures to rescue me. I really don't know him that well but I want to start. I secretly hope Dad and Mom will get back together. They seem comfortable around each other. I also want to get baptized. I hope it can be at the beach. I'm not sure how or where, but from what I've read in the Bible, it seems to be the next step for me to take. Where will I find someone like Setiawan to help me? There's Agnes, I'm sure she can tell me how to get baptized. Mom hasn't said anything about our show. I'm guessing it's been cancelled. I don't think I care. What are my friends going to think about my faith in Jesus? I know them, anything else would be acceptable but that. They're probably going to think I have some rare jungle fever affecting my brain, or maybe they'll excuse it as symptom of PTSD. I know what I know and this is for real. I know I have a lot to learn but I want to learn. I'm just a little nervous about not finding anyone my age who can relate. I know how cynical I was before this adventure so I don't blame them if they think I've gone off the deep end. Who knows, maybe I can help them understand why they feel as empty as I felt and how they are searching for purpose and meaning in the wrong places like I did. Wow, I haven't even started writing my story yet! Well, Macchiato, this is how it started. We were in LAX waiting for our flight and I threw a childish tantrum and broke my phone in the process...

About The Author

Phillip Telfer began his journey as a creative communicator through singing and songwriting. He also started teaching and mentoring teens as a youth pastor and camp speaker. He currently serves as a teaching pastor and is the director of the non-profit ministry Media Talk 101. Phillip is author of the book *Media Choices: Convictions or Compromise?* He wrote, produced, and co-directed the award-winning documentary *Captivated: Finding Freedom in a Media Captive Culture*, and founded the annual Christian Worldview Film Festival and Filmmakers Guild. Phillip loves Jesus, his family, and his local church. He's finicky about coffee so he took up the hobby of home roasting and when he needs to unplug he can be found in his workshop crafting things from wood. He and his wife Mary have been happily married for twenty-eight years and are blessed with four amazing children, one fantastic son-in-law, and two precious grandchildren. When all is said and done, Phillip's core identity is defined as a child of God and a disciple of Jesus Christ. He believes that what you do is not as important as who you are.

Find out more by visiting
www.philliptelfer.com